Penguin Books
Inside Mr Enderby

D0242794

Anthony Burgess was born in Manchester in 1917
and is a graduate of the University there.
After six years in the Army he worked as an
instructor for the Central Advisory Council for
Forces Education, as a lecturer in Phonetics and
as a grammar-school master. From 1954 till 1960
he was an education officer in the Colonial
Service, stationed in Malaya and Brunei.

He became a full-time writer in 1960, though his
first novel had been published four years earlier.
A late starter in the art of fiction, he had spent
his creative energy previously on music, and
he has composed many full-scale works for
orchestra and other media.

Anthony Burgess maintains his old interest in
music and in linguistics, and these have
conditioned the style and content of the novels he
writes. Though he and his wife no longer live
abroad, foreign travel remains a great source of
inspiration. He has, to date, published many
novels, a book on linguistics, and various critical
works.

His other books in Penguin's are
Enderby Outside, *Tremor of Intent*, *The Doctor
is Sick*, *The Malayan Trilogy*, *Nothing Like the
Sun*, a story of Shakespeare's love-life,
Shakespeare, a biography, and *A Clockwork Orange*.

Anthony Burgess

Inside Mr Enderby

Penguin Books

Penguin Books Ltd, Harmondsworth,
Middlesex, England
Penguin Books Australia Ltd, Ringwood,
Victoria, Australia

First published by William Heinemann Ltd 1963
Published in Penguin Books 1966
Reprinted 1973
Copyright © Anthony Burgess, 1963

Made and printed in Great Britain by
Hazell Watson & Viney Ltd,
Aylesbury, Bucks
Set in Linotype Baskerville

To D'Arcy Conyers

– Allons, dernier des poètes,
Toujours enfermé tu te rendras malade!
Vois, il fait beau temps, tout le monde est dehors,
Va donc acheter deux sous d'ellébore,
Ça te fera une petite promenade.

Jules Laforgue, Dimanches

Part One

Chapter One

1

PFFFRRRUMMMP.

And a very happy New Year to you too, Mr Enderby!

The wish is, however, wasted on both sides, for this, to your night visitors, is a very old year. We, whispering, fingering, rustling, creaking about your bedroom, are that posterity to which you hopefully addressed yourself. Congratulations, Mr Enderby: you have already hit your ball smack over the pavilion clock. If you awaken now with one of the duodenal or pyloric twinges which are, to us, as gruesome a literature-lesson spicer as Johnson's scrofula, Swift's scatophobia, or Keats's gallop of death-warrant blood, do not fancy it is ghosts you hear sibilant and crepitant about the bed. To be a ghost one has first to die or, at least, be born.

Perrrrrp.

A posterior riposte from Mr Enderby. Do not touch, Priscilla. Mr Enderby is not a *thing* to be prodded; he is a great poet sleeping. Your grubby finger out of his mouth, please, Alberta. His mouth is open for no amateur dental inspection but to the end that he may breathe. That nose is, at forty-five, past its best as an organ, the black twitching caverns – each with its miniature armpit – stuffed and obtuse. The world of smell is visited by his early poems, remember (pages 1 to 17 of the Harvard University Press selection which is your set book). There we have washed hair, pickles, gorse, bath-salts, skin, pencil-shavings, tinned peaches, post offices, Mrs Lazenby at the corner-shop in his native slum, cloves, diabetes. But it has no existence in his maturer work; the twin ports are closed for ever. That gentle noise, Harold, is snoring. That is so, Christine; his teeth, both upper and lower, are removable: they have been removed to that plastic night-jar there. Child,

9

child, you have spilt denture-fluid on to Mr Enderby's landlady's carpet. No, Robin, the carpet is neither beautiful nor rare, but it is Mrs Meldrum's property. Yes, Mr Enderby himself is our property, the world's property, but his carpet is his landlady's. Mrs Meldrum's.

Now. His hair goes a daily journey from head to brush, squad by tiny squad on a one-way ticket. Here on the dressing-table are the imitation-silver-backed brushes bequeathed by his father, the tobacconist. The bristles are indeed dirty, Mavis, but great poets have other things to do than attend to the calls of hygiene. See how the bristles have trapped their day's quota of Mr Enderby's few remaining hairs. Holy relics, children. Do not rush. One each for everybody. There. Keep it safe, each of you, in your little diary of posterity's present year. Shed hairs, Henry, become the property of the picker. They are of no use to Mr Enderby, but they are already fetching, at classical auction-rooms, a pound or so each if nicely mounted. It is not proper, Audrey, that you should try to pick your hair *alive*. Such a rough tug at the scalp is enough to wake Mr Enderby.

Querpkprrmp.

You see? He's disturbed. Let him settle as one lets churned water settle. Right. A better view of Mr Enderby, you will agree, children, as he flops on his back cruciform and sends the bedclothes sliding and plopping to the floor. His belly bulges in two gentle hills, one on either side of the cutting pyjama-cord. There is a wealth of hair, see. It is one of the abominable ironies of middle age that hair should march down from the noble summit, the eagle's lodge, to leave that bare as an eagle, in order that the camps and barracks and garrisons of the warm vulgar body be crammed with a growth that is neither useful nor pretty. The flabby chest too, see. Rich in hair, aflame with whorls and tendrils of it. And for good measure, chin and jowls bristling. Horrent, Milton might say.

Yes, Janice, I am constrained to agree that Mr Enderby does not make a pretty sight when sleeping, even in total darkness. Yes, we all remark the scant hair, the toothless jaws, the ample folds of flesh rising and falling. But what has prettiness to do with greatness, eh? There is something for you all to ponder on. You would not like to have been married to him, Alberta? Might not the reverse also have applied, even more so, you stupid giggling silly thing? Who are you to think that you would ever be meet to mate with a great poet?

The extremities. The feet that trod Parnassus. Callosities on the intricate map of the sole, see. Torn toenails, though that of the great toe too rocky to be tearable. They could both do with a long sudsy soaking, agreed. The outstretched right hand, like a beggar's, really a king's. Gaze with reverence on those fingers that rest now from writing. Tomorrow they will write again, continuing the poem that he considers to be his masterpiece. Ah, what these fingers have produced! Each of you kiss the hand, more gently, though, than a fly crawling. I realize that the act of kissing needs an effort of will to overcome a certain natural revulsion. Here, however, is a little lesson for you in scholastic philosophy. The grubby knuckles, the nails with black borders, the deep stains of tobacco-tar (the cigarette was held interdigitally, forgotten, while the poet's mind soared above the smell of burning), the coarse skin – these are the accidents, the outer aspects of the hand, their concession to the ordinary world of eating and dying. But the essence of the hand – what is that? A divine machine that has made our lives more blessed. Kiss it, come on, kiss it. Althea, stop making that vomiting noise. Your face, Charles, is ugly enough without contorting it to a rictus of nausea. That's right, kiss it.

It has hardly disturbed him at all. He scratches it gently in his sleep, the tickle of a questing alighting moth. Listen. In his sleep he is going to say something. Your kiss has prodded a sleeping inspiration. Listen.

My bedmate deep
In the heavy labour of unrequited sleep.

11

No more? No more. There, children, what a thrill! You have heard his voice, a mumbly sleepy voice, true, but still his voice. And now let us pass on to Mr Enderby's bedside table.

Books, children, Mr Enderby's bed-reading. *Blondes Like Bullets*, whatever that means; *Who Was Who in the Ancient World*, useful, no doubt; *Raffity's Deal*, with a brutish cover; *How I Succeeded*, by a tycoon who died of arteriosclerosis; *Little Stories of the Marian Martyrs*, sensational. And here, dears, is one of Mr Enderby's own: *Fish and Heroes*, his early poems. What a genius he had then! Yes, Denis, you may handle it but, please, with care. Oh, you stupid boy, you have sent a shower of things to the floor. What are these, that were hidden between the well-thumbed pages? Photographs? Don't touch, leave them, they are not for you! Merciful heavens, the weaknesses of the great. What shame we have unintentionally uncovered. Do not giggle, Brenda and Maureen, and hand that photograph back to me this instant. You will wake Mr Enderby with those obscene girlish noises. What, Charles, are they doing? The man and woman in the picture? They are minding their own business, that's what they're doing.

Bopperlop.

Rest, rest, perturbed spirit. That picture, please, Robin. I can see it in your blazer pocket. Thank you. Fellation, if you must know, is the technical term. And now, no more of that. Shall we tiptoe into Mr Enderby's bathroom? Here we are. This is where Mr Enderby writes most of his verse. Remarkable, isn't it? Here, he knows, he can be truly private. The bath is full of manuscripts and dictionaries and ink-milked ballpoint pens. In front of the W.C. is a low desk, just the right height. There is an electric heater to glow on to his bared legs. Why does he choose this meagre chamber? Poetry, he has already said in an interview, is appropriate to it; the poet is time's cleanser and cathartizer. But, one may be sure, there is much more to it than that. Some childhood agony not yet to be uncovered by us. But Educational Time Trips are already talking of pushing further back into the past. Who knows? Before you leave school you may yet visit Shakespeare struggling, in the parish of St Olave, with verse quantities and a quill. Nigel, leave those rusty razor-blades alone, stupid boy. Softly, softly, now. To the room where he eats and, when not writing, lives is but a step. No, Stephanie, Mr Enderby lives alone through choice. Love, love, love. That's all that some of you girls can think about. Mr Enderby's love-life up to this point is obscure and shrouded. His attitude to women? You have his poems, though they, admittedly, mention the sex but little.

Porripipoop.

The horns of Elfland. We have left him to his poet's peace. There is one thing, though. The poems of this year – which, of course, he has not yet written – show a shy stirring of a more than photographic interest in woman. But we have no biographical evidence of an affair, a change of ménage. We have little biographical evidence of anything. He was essentially a man who lived inside himself. And this sandy seaside address is the only one we have. Can you hear the sea, children? It is the same sea that we know, cruel, green, corrupt.

And what of Mr Enderby do we find in this room? It is Mrs Meldrum, his landlady, who speaks out clear in all this ranged bric-à-brac. Yes, survey it with wonder: a geometrical series of baby ebony elephants, the sweetest of china shepherds flute-blowing to unseen lambs, a plaster toy toast-rack with ancient Blackpool gilding, a tea-caddy replica of tarnished Brighton Pavilion, an enmarbled papier-mâché candlestick, a china bitch and her china litter, a filigree sheet-iron button-box. Do you like the picture above the electric-fire mantelpiece? It shows men in rusty red preparing for the hunting morning, all men identical because, we presume, the pseudo-artist could afford only one model. And, on the opposite wall, British admirals of the eighteenth century unrolling maps of *terra incognita*, wine being poured for them in tankards that catch the fire's glow. Here, jolly monks fish on Thursday; there, they lap up their Friday feast. A pot head of a twentyish flapper, hatted and lipsticked, on that strip of wall past the kitchen door. Emily, leave your nostrils alone. To blow spittle-bubbles on your nether lip is, need I say, Charles, childish. The kitchen is hardly worth examining. Very well, if you insist.

What a strong stench of stale bread! See that fish glow in the dark. Pans on the high shelf. Do not touch, Denis, do not. Oh you damnable young idiot. The whole blasted flaming lot clanking and clashing and ringing down. You bloody young fool. You will all laugh on the other sides of your faces when I get you back to civilization. Oh God, a frying-pan has knocked the kettle over. The gas-stove is full of water. What a filthy, damnable, metal noise! Who has spilt the pepper? Stop sneezing, blast the lot of you. Aaaaaarch! Howrashyouare! Out of here, quickly.

You can't be trusted, any of you. This is the last time I arrange such an expedition. Look down on all those Victorian roofs, fishscaled under the New-Year moon. You will never see them again. Nor any of this town, in whose flats and lodgings the retired and dying wheeze away till dawn. It is all very much like a great hair-comb, isn't it? – the winking jewelled handle, the avenues of teeth combing the hinterland of downs, the hair-ball of smoke which is the railway station. Above us, the January sky: Scutum, Ophiuchus, Sagittarius, the planets of age and war and love westering. And that man down below, whom that clatter of cheap metal has aroused from dyspeptic and flatulent sleep, he gives it all meaning.

2

Enderby awoke, aware of both noise and heartburn. Clamped to his bedhead was a lamp in a plastic shade. He switched this on, realized he was shivering and saw why. He picked up the tangle of bedclothes from the floor, covered himself roughly, and lay back again to savour the pain. It had an inexplicable note of raw turnip about it. The noise? The kitchen-gods fighting. Rats. He needed bicarbonate of soda. He must, he reminded himself for at least the seven-thousandth time, remember to keep it ready-mixed and handy by his bed. The stab of sharpened raw turnip shattered his breastbone. He had to get up.

He saw himself in the wardrobe mirror as he slapped stiffly out of the room into the tiny hallway of his flat, a rheumatic robot in pyjamas. He entered the dining-room, switching on, sniffing like a dog as for a craftily hidden presence. Ghosts had been whimpering around, he was sure, ghosts of the dead year. Or perhaps, he smiled wryly at the conceit, posterity had been shyly looking in. He was astonished at the mess in the kitchen. Such things happened, though: a delicate balance upset by a micrometric subsidence of the old house, an earth tremor, self-willed monads in the utensils themselves. He took a cloudy glass from the draining-board, snowed in some sodium bicarbonate, stirred with two fingers, then drank. He waited thirty seconds, squinting at the glazed pane of the back door. A tiny hand hidden beneath his epiglottis gave a come-up signal. And then.

Delightful. Oh, doctor, the relief! I feel I must write to say thank you for the benefits I have obtained from your product. Aaaaaaarp. Almost immediately after the second spasm of release came a fierce and shameless hunger. He moved the three steps necessary from sink to food-cupboard and found himself freezingly sploshing in spilt water by the stove. He dried his feet in the dropped tea-towel, rearranged the fallen pans on their shelf, wincing with old man's bent pain as he picked them up. He then remembered that he needed his teeth, so he padded back to the bedroom for them, switching the living-room fire on on the way. He clacked a false gleam at the mirror when he returned to the living-room, then did a brief lumbering dance of rage at his reflection. In the food-cupboard were pellets of rocky cheddar, greasily wrapped. A lone midget cauliflower swam like a doll's brain in dense pickle. There was half a tin of sardines, soft plump knives in golden oil. He ate with fingers that he then wiped dry on his pyjamas.

Almost at once his bowels reacted. He ran like a man in a comic film, sat down with a sigh and clicked on the bathroom heater. He scratched his bare legs and read, thoughtfully, the confused draft he was working on. Pfffrumpfff. It was an attempt at allegory, a narrative poem in which two myths were fused – the Cretan and the Christian. A winged bull swooped from heaven in a howling wind. Wheeeeeee. The law-giver's queen was ravished. Big with child, called whore by her husband, she went incognita to a tiny village of the kingdom, there, in a cheap hotel, to give birth to the Minotaur. But the old gummy trot who tended her would keep no secret; she blazoned it about the village (and this spread beyond to the towns, to the capital) that a god-man-beast had come down to rule the world. Prrfrrr. In hope, the anarchic party of the state was now ready to rise against the law-maker: tradition had spoken of the coming of a divine leader. Civil war broke out, propaganda flashed in jagged lightnings from both sides. The beast was evil, said King Minos: capture it, kill it. The beast was God, cried the rebels. But nobody, except the queen-mother and the toothless midwife, had ever seen the beast. Brrrrbfrrr. The baby Minotaur was growing fast, bellowing lustily, hidden away safely with its dam in a lonely cottage. But, by treachery, the forces of Minos were given knowledge of its whereabouts. Manifestly, thought Minos, when it was brought to his palace, though technically a monster it was no horror: its gentle eyes were twin worlds of love. With the talisman and mascot of the rebels in his power, Minos was able to call for surrender. He had a labyrinth built, vast and marbly splendid, with the Minotaur hidden in its heart. It was a horror, unspeakable, reputedly fed on human flesh; it was the state's bogey, the state's guilt. But Minos was economical: the peripheral corridors of the labyrinth became a home of Cretan culture – university, museum, library, art gallery; a treasury of human achievement; beauty and knowledge built round a core of sin, the human condition. Prrrrf. (Enderby's toilet-roll span.) But one day, from the west, there flew in the Pelagian liberator, the man who had never known sin, the guilt-killer. Minos by now was long dead, along with his shameless queen and, long, long before, the midwife. Nobody living had seen the monster and survived, so it was said. Greeted with cheers, flowers and wine, the liberator went to his heroic work. Blond, bronzed, muscular, sinless, he entered the labyrinth and, a day later, emerged leading the monster on a string. Gentle as a pet, with hurt and forgiving eyes, it looked on humanity. Humanity seized it and reviled it and buffeted it. Finally it was nailed to a cross, where it died slowly. At the moment of giving up the ghost there was a sound of rending and crashing. The labyrinth collapsed; books were buried, statues ground to chalk-dust: civilization was at an end. Brrrrp.

The poem was to be called, tentatively, *The Pet Beast*. Enderby realized that a great deal of work had to be done on it, symbols clarified, technical knots unravelled. There was the disinterested craftsman, Daedalus, to be brought into it, the anti-social genius with the final answer of flight. There was Pasiphae's pantomime cow. He tried out, in his deep woollily inept voice, a line or two on a hushed audience of hanging dirty towels:

> He, the cold king, judged cases in his dreams.
> Awake, lithe at his task,
> The other whistled, sawing pliant beams.
> Law is what seems;
> The Craftsman's place to act and not to ask.

The words, resounding in that tiny cell, acted at once like a conjuration. Just outside the flimsy door of Mr Enderby's ground-floor flat was the entrance-hall of the house itself. He heard the massive front door creak open and the hall seemed to fill with New Year revellers. He recognized the silly unresonant voice of the salesman who lived in the flat above, the stout-fed laugh of the woman who lived with him. There were other voices, not assignable to known persons but generic, voices of *Daily Mirror*-readers, ITV-viewers, HP-buyers, Babycham-drinkers. There were loud and cheerful greetings:

'Happy New Year, Enderby!'

'Prrrrrrrrp!'

The stout-fed woman's voice said, 'I don't feel well. I'm going to be sick.' She at once, by the sound of it, was. Someone called:

'Give us a poem, Enderby. "Eskimo Nell" or "The Good Ship Venus".'

'Sing us a song, Enderby.'

'Jack,' said the sick woman weakly, 'I'm going straight up. I've had it.'

'You go up, love,' said the salesman's voice. 'I'll be after you in a minute. Got to serenade old Enderby first.' There was the noise of a staggering fall against the door of Enderby's flat, a choirmaster's 'One two three', and then the vigorous ragged strains of '*Ach Du Lieber Augustin*', but with rude English words:

Balls to Mister Enderby, Enderby, Enderby;
Balls to Mister Enderby, ballocks to you.
For he keeps us waiting while he's masturbating, so —

Enderby stuffed moistened pellets of toilet-paper in his ears. Locked safely enough in his flat, he now locked himself safelier in his bathroom. Scratching a warmed bare leg, he tried to concentrate on his poem. The revellers soon desisted and dispersed. He thought he heard the salesman call out, 'That's the enderby, Enderby.'

3

Cosily muffled against the sharp marine morning, Enderby walked down Fitzherbert Avenue towards the sea. It was ten-thirty by the Town Hall clock and the pubs were just opening. He passed Gradeleigh ('for Gradely Folk'), Kia-Ora (retired Kiwis), Ty-Gwyn (couple from Tredegar),

Channel View, White Posts, Dulce Domus, The Laurels, Ithaca (former classics master and convicted pederast). Converted to flats, humbled as guest-houses, all were owned by foreigners from north and west of the downs, bemused by an image of the glamour of the south coast: France winked at night across the water; here the air had a fancied mildness. Not today, thought Enderby, smacking his woolly bear-paw palms together. He wore a scarf coloured like a Neapolitan ice; his overcoat was a tightly-belted Melton; he was shielded from heaven by a Basque beret. The house wherein he had a flat was, he thanked that same heaven, nameless. Number 81, Fitzherbert Avenue. Would there ever, some day, be a plaque to mark that he had lived there? He was quite sure not. He was one of a dying race, unregarded by the world. Hurray.

Enderby turned on to the Esplanade, joined a queue of old women in a cake-shop, and came out with a seven-penny loaf. He crossed over to the sea-rail and leaned on it, tearing the loaf. The gulls wheeled screaming for the thrown bread, beady-eyed greedy creatures, while the sea whooped in, the green-grey winter Channel, then grumbled back, as at the lion-tamer's whip, grudgingly rattling many tambourines. Enderby tossed the last crumbs to the bitter air and its grey planing birds, then turned from the sea. He looked back on it before he entered the Neptune, seeing in it, as so often from a distance, the clever naughty green child which had learned to draw a straight line free-hand.

The saloon-bar of the Neptune was already half-filled with old people, mainly widows. 'Morning,' said a dying major-general, 'and a happy New Year to you.' Two male ancients compared arthritis over baby stouts. A bearded lady drank off her port and slowly, toothlessly, chewed the mouthful. 'And to you too,' said Enderby. 'If I can live to see the spring,' said the general, 'that's all. That's as much as I can hope for.' Enderby sat down with his whisky. He was at home with the aged, accepted as one of them, despite his ridiculous youth. Still, his recorded age was a mere actuarial cipher; his gullet burning as the whisky descended, his aches and pains, his lack of interest in action – these made him as old as the crocks among whom he sat.

'How,' asked a gentle tremulous man made of parchment, 'how,' his hand shaking his drink like a dicebox, 'how is the stomach?'

'Some quite remarkable twinges,' said Enderby. 'Almost visible, you know. And flatulence.'

'Flatulence,' said the major-general, 'ah, yes, flatulence.' He spoke of it as though it were a rare old vintage. 'Many years since I've had that. Now, of course, I eat nothing. A little bread soaked in warm milk, morning and evening. I swear it's this rum that's keeping me alive. I told you, did I, about that contretemps over the rum ration at Bruderstroom?'

'Several times,' said Enderby. 'A very good story.'

'Isn't it?' said the general, painfully animated. 'Isn't it a good story? And true. Incredible, but true.'

A plebeian crone in dirty black spoke from a bar-stool. 'I,' she said, 'have had part of my stomach removed.' There was a silence. The aged males ruminated this gratuitous revelation, wondering whether, coming from a female and a comparative stranger, it was really in the best of taste. Enderby said kindly: 'That must have been quite an experience.' The old woman looked crafty, gripped the counter's edge with papery hands that grew chalky at the knuckles, canted her stool towards Enderby and said, very loudly, 'Pardon?'

'An experience,' said Enderby, 'never to be forgotten.'

'Six hours on the table,' said the woman. 'Nobody here can't beat that.'

'Crump,' called the major-general in an etiolated martinet's voice. 'Crump. Crump.' He was not reminiscing about the first World War; he wanted the barman to replenish his rum-glass. Crump came from behind the bar, seventyish, in a waiter's white jacket, with a false smile both imbecilic and ingratiating, his grey head cocked permanently to one side like that of a listening parrot. 'Yes, General,' he said. 'Similar, sir? Very good, sir.'

'I'm always telling him,' said an ancient with the humpty-dumpty head of Sibelius, 'about that use of the word. It's common among barmen and landlords. They say you can't have the *same* again. But it is, in fact, precisely the same again that one wants. One doesn't want anything *similar*. You deal in words, Enderby. You're a writer. What's your view of the matter?'

'It *is* the same,' agreed Enderby. 'It's from the same bottle. Something similar is something different.'

'Professor Taylor used to argue that out very persuasively,' said an old man mottled like salami, a dewdrop on the hook of his nose.

'What's happened to Taylor?' asked the major-general. 'We haven't seen him for quite some time.'

'He died,' said the mottled man. 'Last week. While drawing a cork. Cardiac failure.'

'He'd just turned eighty,' said a man just turned eighty. 'Not all that old.'

'Taylor gone,' said the general. 'I didn't know.' He accepted rum from obsequious Crump. Crump accepted silver with an obsequious inclination of a broken and mended torso. 'I thought I'd go before him,' said the general, 'but I'm still here.'

'You're not all that old yourself,' said the tremulous parchment man.

'I'm eighty-five,' said the general in puffy indignation. 'I call that *very* old.'

Higher bids came from the corners. One woman confessed coyly to ninety. As if somehow to prove this, she performed a few waltz-twirls, humming from *The Merry Widow*. She sat down again to genteel shocked applause, her lips blue, her heart almost audibly thumping. 'And,' asked the Sibelius-man, 'how old might you be, Enderby?'

'Forty-five.'

There were snorts of both contempt and amusement.

One man in a corner piped, 'If that's meant to be funny, I don't think it's in very good taste.'

The major-general turned sternly and deliberately towards Enderby, both hands resting on the ivory bulldog-head of his malacca. 'And what is it you do for a living?' he asked.

'You know that,' said Enderby. 'I'm a poet.'

'Yes, yes, but what do you do for a living? Only Sir Walter made a living out of poetry. And perhaps that Anglo-Indian man who lived at Burwash.'

'A few investments,' said Enderby.

'What investments precisely?'

'I.C.I. and B.M.C. and Butlin's. And local government loans.'

The major-general grunted, as though none of Enderby's replies was above suspicion. 'What was your rank in the last war?' he asked, a last throw.

Before Enderby could give a lying answer, a widow in antique tweeds, a long thin woman with black-rimmed spectacles, fell from a low stool by a wicker table. Old men reached trembling for their sticks, that they might lever themselves up and help. But Enderby was there first. 'Sho kind,' said the woman genteelly. 'Sho shorry to cauzhe all thish trouble.' She had evidently been tanking up at home before opening-time. Enderby lifted her from the floor, as light and as stiff as a bundle of celery. 'Thezhe thingzh,' she said, 'happen in the besht of familiezh.'

His hands still hooked in her armpits, Enderby was shocked to see the image of his stepmother in the big Gilbey's Port mirror on the wall opposite. Shaken, he nearly dropped his burden to the floor again. The image nodded to him, as out of some animated painting in a TV commercial, raised its glass in New Year salutation, then seemed to hobble out of the picture, into the wings, thus disappearing.

'Get on with it, Enderby,' said the peevish major-general. 'Put her back on her seat.'

'Sho very kind,' said the woman, trying hard to focus on

her gin-glass. Enderby looked in the room for a source of that mirror-image, but saw only a bent back hobbling to the Gents. That might be it, a trick of the light or the New Year. It was his stepmother, strangely enough, who had told him as a child that, on New Year's Day, a man walked the streets with as many noses on his face as there were days in the year. He had gone looking for this man, thinking of him fearfully as of the family of the Antichrist that walked the world before the day of judgement. Long after he had seen through the trick, New Year's Day still possessed for him an irritating macabre flavour, as a day of possible prodigies. His stepmother was, he was pretty sure, dead and buried. She'd done her work, as far as he was concerned. There was no point in her staying alive or coming back from the grave.

'Now,' said the major-general, as Enderby sat down again with a new whisky, 'what did you say your rank was?'

'Lieutenant-general,' said Enderby. In speech a comma is as good as a hyphen.

'I don't believe you.'

'Look it up.' Enderby was almost sure he saw his stepmother leave the jug-and-bottle department, a quarterbottle of Booth's in her bag. The Neptune was the sort of pub in which any of the three parts – saloon, public, outdoor – is visible from any other. Enderby spilt whisky on his tie. An old man who had not previously spoken pointed at Enderby with shaky care and said, 'You've spilt whisky on your tie.' Enderby felt that fear would possibly make worse happen. The outer world was not safe. He must go back home and closet himself, work at his poem. He finished the driblet in his glass, buttoned himself up and donned his Basque beret. The major-general said, 'I don't believe you, sir.'

'You must please yourself, General,' said Ex-lieutenant Enderby. And, with a general salute, he left.

'He's a liar,' said the major-general. 'I always knew he wasn't to be trusted. I don't believe he's a poet, either. A very shifty look about him this morning.'

'I read about him in the public library,' said the salami-mottled man. 'There was a photograph, too. It was an article, and it seemed to think quite a lot of him.'

'What is he? Where does he come from?' asked another.

'He keeps himself very much to himself,' said the mottled man and, just in time, he snuffed up a perilous dewdrop.

'He's a liar, anyway,' said the major-general. 'I shall look up the Army List this afternoon.'

He never did. A motorist, irritable and jumpy with a seasonal hangover, knocked him down as he was crossing Nollekens Avenue. Long before spring, the major-general was promoted to glory.

4

Out in the gull-clawed air, New-Year blue, the tide crawling creamily in, Enderby felt better. In this sharp light there was no room for ghosts. But the imagined visitation had acted as an injunction to honour the past before looking, as at every year's beginning, to the future.

Enderby first thought of his mother, dead at his birth, of whom there had seemed to be no record. He liked to imagine a young woman of gentle blondeness, sweetly refined and slenderly pliant. He liked to think of her swathed in gold, in a beeswax-breathing drawing-room, singing 'Passing By' to her own accompaniment. The dying heat of a July day sang in sadness through the wide-open french windows from a garden that glowed with Crimson Glory, Mme L. Dieudonne, Ena Harkness and Golden Spectre. He saw his father, become bookish, wearing bookman's slippers, O-ing out smoke from an ðval-bored Passing Cloud, nodding his head in quiet pleasure as he listened. But his father had never been quite like that. A wholesale tobacconist, ruling linès in the ledger with an ebony sceptre of a ledger-ruler, sitting in the office behind the shop in waistcoat and black bowler, always glad of opening-time. Why? To escape from that bitch of a second wife. Why in God's name had he married her? 'Money, son. Her first one left her a packet. Her stepson will, we hope, reap the benefit.' And, to some extent, it had turned out that way. Hence the few hundred a year from I.C.I., British Motors, and the rest. But had it been worth it?

Oh, she had been graceless and coarse, that one. A hundredweight of ringed and brooched blubber, smelling to high heaven of female smells, rank as long-hung hare or blown beef, her bedroom strewn with soiled bloomers, crumby combinations, malodorous bust-bodices. She had swollen finger-joints, puffy palms, wrists girdled with fat, slug-white upper arms that, when naked, showed indecent as thighs. She was corned, bunioned, calloused, varicose-veined. Healthy as a sow, she moaned of pains in all her joints, a perpetual migraine, a bad back, toothache. 'The pains in me legs,' she would say, 'is killin' me.' Her wind was loud, even in public places. 'The doctor says to let it come up. You can always say excuse me.' Her habits were loathsome. She picked her teeth with old tram-tickets, cleaned out her ears with hairclips in whose U-bend ear-wax was trapped to darken and harden, scratched her private parts through her clothes with a matchbox-rasping noise audible two rooms away, made gross sandwiches of all her meals or cut her meat with scissors, spat chewed bacon-rind or pork-crackling back on her plate, excavated beef-fibres from her cavernous molars and held them up for all the world to see, hooked out larger chunks with a soiled sausage-finger, belched like a ship in the fog, was sick on stout on Saturday nights, tromboned vigorously in the lavatory, ranted without aitches or grammar, scoffed at all books except *Old Moore's Almanac*, whose apocalyptic pictures she could follow. Literally illiterate all her life, she would sign cheques by copying her name from a proto-type on a greasy piece of paper, drawing it carefully as a Chinese draws an ideogram. She provided fried meals mostly, ensuring first that the fat was tepid. But she brewed good tea, potent with tannin, and taught young Enderby the technique, that he might bring her a cup in the morning: three for each person and two for the pot, condensed milk rather than fresh, be lavish with the sugar. Enderby, sixth-form boy, would stand over her while she drank it in bed – tousled, wrinkled, puffed, ill-smelling, a wreck – though she did not really drink it: the tea seemed to soak into her as into parched earth. One day he would put rat-poison in her cup. But he never did, even though he bought the rat-poison. Hate? You've just no idea.

When Enderby was seventeen, his father went off to Nottingham to be shown over a tobacco factory, was away for the night. July heat (she showed up badly in that) broke in monsoon weather, with terrifying lightning. But it was only the thunder that scared her. Enderby awoke at five in the morning to find her in his bed, in dirty winceyette, clutching him in fear. He got up, was sick in the lavatory, then locked himself in, reading till dawn the scraps of newspaper on the floor.

Her death was reported to him when he was in the Army, L. of C. troops in Catania. She had died after drinking a morning cup of tea, brought by his father. Heart failure. The night of hearing the news, Enderby went with a woman of Catania (one tin of corned beef and a packet of biscuits) and, to her almost concealed laughter, could do nothing. Also, on arriving back at his billet, he was sick.

Well, there it was. His stepmother had killed women for him, emerging in a ladylike belch or a matchstick picking of teeth from behind the most cool and delectable façade. He had got on quite nicely on his own, locked in the bathroom, cooking his own meals (ensuring first that the fat was tepid), living on his dividends and the pound or two a year his poems earned. But, as middle-age advanced, his stepmother seemed to be entering slyly into him more and more. His back ached, his feet hurt, he had a tidy paunch, all his teeth out, he belched. He had tried to be careful about laundry and cleaning the saucepans, but poetry got in the way, raising him above worry about squalor. Yet dyspepsia would cut disconcertingly in, more and more, blasting like a tuba through the solo string traceries of his little creations.

The act of creation. Sex. That was the trouble with art. Urgent sexual desire aroused with the excitement of a new image or rhythm. But adolescence had prolonged its techniques of easy detumescence, normal activities of the bathroom. Walking towards the Freemason's Arms he felt wind rising from his stomach. Damn. Brerrrrp. Blast. He was, however, on the whole, taking all things into consideration, by and large, not to put too fine a point on it, reasonably well self-sufficient. Brrrrrp. Blast and damn.

5

Arry, head cook at the Conway, was standing by the bar of the Freemason's with a pint tankard of brown ale and bitter mixed. He said to Enderby, ' 'Ere yar.' He handed over a long bloody parcel, blood congealed on a newspaper headline about some woman's blood. 'A said ad get it an a got it.' Enderby said, 'Thanks, and a happy New Year. What will you have?' He eased away some of the newspaper at one end, 'Missing Persons', covered with blood, and the head of a mature hare stared at him with glass eyes. 'Yer can joog it today,' said Arry. He was in a brown sports-coat that reeked of old fat, a tout's cap on his head. His upper jaw had only two canines. These were gateposts between which his tongue, car-like, occasionally eased itself out and in. He came from Oldham. 'Red coorant jelly,' said Arry. 'What a generally do is serve red coorant jelly on a art-shaped croutong. Coot out a art-shaped bitter bread with a art-cooter. Fry it in 'ot fat, quick. Boot, livin' on yer own, a don't suppose yer'll wanter go to that trooble.' He drank down his brown ale and bitter and, on Enderby, had another pint. 'Good job yer coom in when yer did,' he said. ' 'Ave to go now. Special loonch for South Coast Association of Car Salesmen.' He swigged the pint in one lift of the tankard, had another, yet another, all in two minutes flat. Like most cooks he could eat little. He had ferocious gastric pains which endeared him to Enderby. 'Seein' yer,' he said, leaving. Enderby nursed his hare.

This bar was the haunt of all local lesbians over fifty. Most of them fulfilled the paradigms of marriage, a few were divorced, widowed or estranged. On a stool in the corner was a woman called Gladys, a peroxided Jewess of sixty with tortoise-shell spectacle-rims and leopard-skin jeans. She was kissing, more often and more passionately than seemed necessary, another woman in New-Year greeting. This woman wore a bristling old fur coat and was delicately cross-eyed. A fierce-looking thin woman in a dress as hairy and simple as a monk's habit, a nutria coat swinging open over it, crashed into the bar and greeted her too, long and gluily. 'Prudence, my duck,' she said. Prudence seemed to be a popular girl. The peculiar charm of strabismus. And then the fragments of a new poem came swimming with a familiar confidence into Enderby's head. He saw the shape, he heard the words, he felt the rhythm. Three stanzas, each beginning with birds. *Prudence, prudence, the pigeons call.* And, of course, that's what they did call, that's what they'd always called. *Act, act, the ducks give voice.* And that was true, too. What were the other birds? They weren't sea-gulls. The dyed-blonde Jewess, Gladys, suddenly, raucously, laughed. It was a bird like that. *Caution, caution.* Rooks, that was it. But why were they calling, giving voice, proclaiming?

He had a ball-point pen, but no paper. Only the wrapping of the hare. There was a long empty stop-press column, two forlorn football results at the head. He wrote the lines he had heard. Also other fragments that he could hear dimly. The meaning? Meaning was no concern of the poet. *The widow in the shadow. The widow in the meadow.* A voice, very clear and thin, spoke as though pressed to his ear: *Drain the sacrament of choice.* Gladys began to sing, pop garbage composed by some teenager, much heard on radio disc-programmes. She sang loudly. Excited, Enderby cried, 'Oh, for Christ's sake shut up!' Gladys was indignant. 'Who the bloody hell do you think you're telling to shut up?' she called across, with menace. 'I'm trying to write a poem,' said Enderby. 'This,' said someone, 'is supposed to be a respectable pub.' Enderby downed his whisky and left.

Walking home quickly he tried to call back the rhythm, but it had gone. The fragments ceased to be live limbs of some mystical body that promised to reveal itself wholly. Dead as the hare, meaningless onomatopoeia; a silly jingle: *widow, shadow, meadow*. The big rhythms of the nearing tide, the winter sea-wind, the melancholy gulls. A gust shattered and dispersed the emerging form of the poem. Oh, well. Of the million poems that beckoned, like coquettish girls, from the bushes, how very few could be caught!

Enderby stripped the hare of its bloody paper as he approached 81 Fitzherbert Avenue. There was a public litter basket attached to a lamp-post almost in front of the front-steps. He threw the crumpled mess of news, blood, inchoate poetry in, and got out his key. A tidy town, this. Must not let our standards relax even though there are no holiday visitors. He entered the kitchen and began to skin the hare. It would give him, he thought, stewed with carrots, potatoes and onions, seasoned with pepper and celery salt, the remains of the Christmas red wine poured in before serving, enough meals for nearly a week. He slapped the viscera on to a saucer, cut up the carcass, and then turned on the kitchen tap. Hangman's hands, he thought, looking at them. Soaked in blood up to the elbows. He tried out a murderer's leer, holding the sacrificial knife, imagining a mirror above the kitchen sink.

The water flowing from the faucet cast a faint shadow, a still shadow, on the splashboard. The line came, a refrain: *The running tap casts a static shadow*. That was it, he recognized, his excitement mounting again. The widow, the meadow. A whole stanza blurted itself out:

'Act! Act!' The ducks give voice.
    'Enjoy the widow in the meadow.
Drain the sacrament of choice.
    The running tap casts a static shadow.'

To hell with the meaning. Where the hell were those other
birds? What were they? The cuckoo? The sea-gull? What
was the name of that cross-eyed lesbian bitch in the Freemason's? Knife in hand, steeped in blood to the elbows,
he dashed out of his flat, out of the house, to the rubbish-
basket clamped to the lamp-post. Others had been there
while he had been gutting and skinning and quartering. A
Black Magic box, a Senior Service packet, banana-peel. He
threw it all out madly into the gutter. He found the defiled
paper which had wrapped the beast. Frantically he
searched page after crumpled page. THIS MAN MAY KILL,
POLICE WARN. NOW THIS BOY IS LOVED. *Most people stop
Acid Stomach with Rennies.* Compulsive reading. He
read: "The pain-causing acid is neutralized and you get
that wonderful sensation that tells you the pain is beginning to go. The antacid ingredients reach your stomach
gradually and gently – drip by drip. . . .'

'What's this? What's going on?' asked an official voice.
'Eh?' It was the law, inevitably. 'I'm looking for these
blasted birds,' said Enderby, rummaging again. 'Ah, thank
God. Here they are. Prudence, pigeons. Rooks, caution. It's
as good as written. Here.' He thrust the extended sheets
into the policeman's arms.

'Not so fast,' said the policeman. He was a young man,
apple-ruddy from the rural hinterland, very tall. 'What's
this knife for, where did all that blood come from?'

'I've been murdering my stepmother,' said Enderby,
absorbed in composition. *Prudence, prudence, the pigeons
call.* He ran into the house. The woman from upstairs was
just coming down. She saw a knife and blood and screamed.
Enderby entered his flat, ran into the bathroom, kicked on
the heater, sat on the low seat. Automatically he stood up
again to lower his trousers. Then, all bloody, he began to
write. Somebody knocked – imperious, imperative – at his

front door. He locked the bathroom door and got on with his writing. The knocks soon ceased. After half an hour he had the whole poem on paper.

> 'Prudence! Prudence!' the pigeons call.
>   'Scorpions lurk in the gilded meadow.
> An eye is embossed on the island wall.
>   The running tap casts a static shadow.'

> 'Caution! Caution!' the rooks proclaim.
>   'The dear departed, the weeping widow
> Will meet in you in the core of flame.
>   The running tap casts a static shadow.'

The injunction of the last stanza seemed clear enough, privy enough. Was it really possible, he wondered, for him to follow it, making this year different from all others?

> 'Act! Act!' The ducks give voice.
>   'Enjoy the widow in the meadow.
> Drain the sacrament of choice. . .'

In the kitchen, he could now hear, the water was still flooding away. He had forgotten to turn it off. Casting a static shadow all the time. He got up from his seat, automatically pulling the chain. Who was this blasted widow that the poem referred to?

Chapter Two

1

While Enderby was breakfasting off reheated hare stew with pickled walnuts and stepmother's tea, the postman came with a fateful letter. The envelope was thick, rich, creamy; richly black the typed address, as though a new ribbon had been put in just for that holy name. The notepaper was embossed with the arms of a famous firm of chain booksellers. The letter congratulated Enderby on his last year's volume – *Revolutionary Sonnets* – and was over-joyed to announce that he had been awarded the firm's annual Poetry Prize of a gold medal and fifty guineas. Enderby was cordially invited to a special luncheon to be held in the banqueting-room of an intimidating London hotel, there to receive his prizes amid the plaudits of the literary world. Enderby let his hare stew go cold. The third Tuesday in January. Please reply. He was dazed. And, again, congratulations. London. The very name evoked the same responses as *lung cancer, overdrawn, stepmother.*

He wouldn't go, he couldn't go, he hadn't a suit. At the moment he was wearing glasses, a day's beard, pyjamas, polo-neck sweater, sports-jacket and very old corduroys. In his wardrobe were a pair of flannel trousers and a watered-silk waistcoat. These, he had thought when sett-ling down after demobilization, were enough for a poet, the watered-silk waistcoat being, perhaps, even, an un-seemly luxury of stockbroker-like extravagance. He had had it, by mistake, knocked down to him for five shillings at an auction.

London. He was flooded with horrid images, some derived from direct experience, others from books. At the end of the war, searching for William Hazlitt's tomb in its Soho graveyard, he had been abused by a constable and had up in Bow Street on a charge of loitering with intent. He had once slipped on the greasy pavement outside Foyle's and the man who had helped him up – stocky, elderly, with stiff grey hair – had begged five bob to 'elp aht a bit cos they was on strike that week, guv. That was just after he had bought the watered-silk waistcoat: ten bob down the drain. In the urinal of a very foggy pub he had, unbelievably, been invited to a fellation party by a handsome stranger in smart city wear. This man had become nasty at Enderby's polite refusal and threatened to scream that Enderby was assaulting him. Very unpleas-ant. Along with other memories that made him wince (including one excruciating one of a ten-shilling note in the Café Royal) came gobbets from *Oliver Twist, The Waste Land,* and *Nineteen Eighty-Four.* London was unnecessarily big, gratuitously hostile, a place for losing money and contracting diseases. Enderby shuddered, thinking of Defoe's *Journal of the Plague Year.* And there he was – as he emptied his cold plateful back into the saucepan – with his stepmother again. At the age of fifteen he had bought off a twopenny stall in the market a duo-decimo book of recipes, gossip, and homilies, printed in 1605. His stepmother, able to read figures, had screamed at the sight of it when he had proudly brought it home. 1605 was 'the olden days', meaning Henry VIII, the executioner's axe, and the Great Plague. She thrust the book into the kitchen fire with the tongs, yelling that it must be seething with lethal germs. A limited, though live, sense of history.

And history was the reason why she would never go to London. She saw it as dominated by the Bloody Tower, Fleet Street full of demon barbers, as well as dangerous escalators everywhere. As Enderby now turned on the hot-water tap he saw that the Ascot heater did not, as it should, flare up like a bed of pain. The meter needed a shilling and he was too lazy to go and look for one. He washed his soup-plate and mug in cold water, reflecting that his step-mother had been a great one for that (knives and forks wrapped in grease as if they were guns). She had been very lazy, very stupid, very superstitious. He decided, wiping the dishes, that he would, after all, go to London. After all, it wasn't very far – only an hour by electric train – and there would be no need to spend the night in a hotel. It was an honour really, he supposed. He would have to borrow a suit from somebody. Arry, he was sure, had one. They were much of a size.

Enderby, sighing, went to the bathroom to start work. He gazed doubtfully at the bathtub, which was full of notes, drafts, fair copies not yet filed for their eventual volume, books, ink-bottles, cigarette-packets, the remains of odd snacks taken while writing. There were also a few mice that lived beneath the detritus, encouraged in their busy scavenging by Enderby. Occasionally one would surface and perch on the bath's edge to watch the poet watching the ceiling, pen in hand. With him they were neither cowering nor timorous (he had forgotten the meaning of 'sleekit'). Enderby recognized that the coming occasion called for a bath. Lustration before the sacramental meal. He had once read in some women's magazine a grim apothegm he had never forgotten: 'Bath twice a day to be really clean, once a day to be passably clean, once a week to avoid being a public menace.' On the other hand, Frederick the Great had never bathed in his life; his corpse had been a rich mahogany colour. Enderby's view of bathing was neither obsessive nor insouciant. ('Sans Souci', Frederick's palace, was it not?) He was an empiricist in such matters. Though he recognized that a bath would, in a week or two, seem necessary, he recoiled from the prospect of preparing the bathtub and evicting the mice. He would compromise. He would wash very nearly all over in the basin. More, he would shave with exceptional care and trim his hair with nail-scissors.

Gloomily, Enderby reflected that most modern poets were not merely sufficiently clean but positively natty. T. S. Eliot, with his Lloyd's Bank nonsense, had started all that, a real treason of clerks. Before him, Enderby liked to believe, cleanliness and neatness had been only for writers of journalistic ballades and triolets. Still, he would show them when he went for his gold medal; he would beat them at their own game. Enderby sighed again as, with bare legs, he took his poetic seat. His first job was to compose a letter of gratitude and acceptance. Prose was not his *métier*.

After several pompous drafts which he crumpled into the waste-basket on which he sat, Enderby dashed off a letter in *In Memoriam* quatrains, disguised as prose. 'The gratitude for this award, though sent in all humility, should not, however, come from me, but from my Muse, and from the Lord . . .' He paused as a bizarre analogue swam up from memory. In a London restaurant during the days of fierce post-war food shortage he had ordered rabbit pie. The pie, when it had arrived, had contained nothing but breast of chicken. A mystery never to be solved. He shrugged it away and went on disguising the chicken-breast of verse as rabbit-prose. A mouse, forepaws retracted like those of a kangaroo, came up to watch.

2

Enderby found Arry in white in his underground kitchen, brown ale frothing beside him, slicing pork into blade-thin shives. An imbecilic-looking scullion in khaki threw fistfuls of cabbage on to plates. When he missed he picked up the scattered helping carefully from the floor and tried again. Massive sides of beef were jocularly being unloaded from Smithfield – the fat a golden fleece, the flesh the hue of diluted Empire burgundy. Enderby said:

'I've got to go up to London to be given a gold medal and fifty guineas. But I haven't got a suit.'

'Yer'll be able to buy a good un,' said Arry, 'with that amount of mooney.' He didn't look too happy; he frowned down at his precise task like a surgeon saving the life of a bitter foe. 'There,' he said, forking up a translucent slice to the light, 'that's about as thin as yer can bloody get.'

'But,' said Enderby, 'I don't see the point of buying a suit just for this occasion. I probably shan't want to wear a suit again. Or not for a long time. That's why I'd like to borrow one of yours.'

Arry said nothing. He quizzed the forked slice and nodded at it, as though he had met its challenge and won. Then he returned to his carving. He said, 'Yer quite right when yer suppose av got more than wan. Am always doin' things for people, aren't a? Boot what dooz any bogger do for me?' He looked up at Enderby an instant, his tongue flicking out between its gateposts as if to lick up a tear.

'Well,' said Enderby, embarrassed, 'you know you can

rely on me. For anything I *can* do, that is. But I've only one talent, and that's not much good to you. Nor, it seems,' the mood of self-pity catching, 'to anyone else. Except a hundred or so people here and in America. And one mad female admirer in Cape Town. She writes once a year, you know, offering marriage.'

'Female admirers,' said carving Arry, pluralizing easily. 'Female admirers, eh? That's wan thing a 'aven't got. It's *me* oo admires *er*, that's the bloody trooble. It's got real bad, that as.' He became violently dialectal. 'Av getten eed-warch wi' it,' he said. Then, as an underling sniffed towards him with a cold, 'Vol-au-vent de dindon's in that bloody coopboard,' he said.

'Who?' said Enderby. 'When?'

''Er oopstairs,' said Arry. 'Thelma as serves int cocktail bar. A knew it definite ender the moonth. Bloody loovely oo is boot bloody cruel,' he said, carving steadily. 'Oo's bloody smashin',' he said.

'I don't know,' said Enderby.

'Don't know what?'

'Who's bloody smashing.'

'Oo is,' said Arry, gesturing to the ceiling with his knife. 'Oo oop thur. That Thelma.'

Enderby then remembered that two Anglo-Saxon feminine pronouns co-existed in Lancashire. He said 'Well, why don't you go in and win? Just put a few teeth in your mouth first, though. The popular prejudice goes in favour of teeth.'

'What's pegs to do with it?' said Arry. 'A don't eat. Pegs is for eatin'. Am in loove, that's bloody trooble, and what's pegs to do with that?'

'Women like to see them,' said Enderby. 'It's more of an aesthetic than a functional thing. Love, eh? Well, well. Love. It's a long time since I've heard of anybody being in love.'

'Every boogger's in loove nowadays,' said Arry, ending his carving. He drank some brown ale. 'There's songs about it ont wireless. A used to laff at 'em. And now it's me oo's copped it. Loove. Bloody nuisance it is an' all, what with bein' busy at this timer year. Firms givin' loonches an' dinners till near the end of February. Couldn't 'ave coom at a worse time.'

'About this suit,' said Enderby. He faced a vast carboy of pickled onions and his bowels melted within him. He wanted to be gone.

'Yer can do summat for me,' said Arry, 'if am to do summat for you.' He tasted this last pronoun and then decided that his revelation, his coming request, called for *tutoyer* intimacy. 'Summat for thee,' he amended. 'Al lend thee that suit if tha'll write to 'er for me, that bein' thy line, writin' poetry an' all that mook. A keep sendin 'er oop special things as av cooked special, boot that's not romantic, like. A nice dish of tripe doon in milk, which were always my favourite when a were eatin'. Sent it down, oontooched, oo did. A reet boogger. What would go down best would be a nice loove-letter or a bitter poetry. That's where *you'd* coom in,' said Arry, and his snake-tongue darted. ' 'Av a grey un, a blue un, a brown un, a fawn un an a 'errin-bone tweed. Tha's welcome to any wan on 'em. Thee write summat an' sign it Arry and send it to me an' a'll send it oop to 'er.'

'How shall I spell Arry?' asked Enderby.

'With a haitch,' said Arry. 'Two a week should do the bloody trick. Shouldn't take yer not more than a coupler minutes to write the sort of thing that goes down all reet with women. You and yer bloody female hadmirers,' he said.

Before going back to his flat, Enderby used – long, lavishly and painfully – the gentlemen's lavatory on the ground floor of the hotel. Then, shaken, he went to the cocktail bar for a whisky and to have a look at Thelma. It would not do if he dug up old poems, or wrote new ones, celebrating the glory of fair hair or pegs like margarite if she should chance to be black, grey, near-edentate. The bar seemed full, today, of car salesmen, and these chaffed and mock-courted, with ha-ha-ha and obso-

lete pilot's slang, a quite personable barmaid in her late
thirties. She had all her front teeth, black hair, naughty
eyes, ear-rings that jangled tinily – clusters of minute coins
– a snub nose and a comfortable round chin. She was
superbly bosomed and efficiently uplifted. She seemed to
be a repository of old bar-wisdom, epigrams, radio-show
catch-phrases. A car salesman bought her a Guinness and
she toasted him with 'May you live for ever and me live to
bury you.' Then, before drinking, she said, 'Past the teeth
and round the gums, look out, stomach, here it comes.'
She had a fair swallow. She had decorated her little bar
with poker-work maxims: 'Laugh and the world laughs
with you; snore and you sleep alone.' 'Water is a good
drink when taken with the right spirit.' 'When you're up
to your neck in hot water be like the kettle and sing.'
There was also a Browningesque couplet (content if not
technique) above the gin bottles:

> For when the last great Scorer comes to write
> against your name,
> He writes not that you won or lost, but how you
> played the game.

Enderby doubted whether he could achieve the same
gnomic tautness in anything he wrote for her. Still, that
wouldn't be called for, love being essentially imprecise and
diffuse. He drank his whisky and left.

3

Enderby's attitude to love-poetry was dispassionate,
impersonal, professional. The worst love-poems, he had
always contended, were the most sincere: the lover's
palpitating emotions – all too personal, with an all too
particular object – all too often got in the way of the ideal,
the universal. A love-poem should address itself to an idea
of a loved one. Platonism could take in ideal breasts, an
ideal underarm odour, an ideal unsatisfactory coitus, as

well as the smooth-browed intellectual wraith of the old sonneteers. Back in his bathroom, Enderby rummaged for fragments and drafts that would serve to start off the *Arry to Thelma* cycle. He found, mouse-nibbled:

> I sought scent and found it in your hair;
>   Looked for light, and it lodged in your eyes.
> So for speech: it held your breath dear;
>   And I met movement in your ways.

That felt like the first quatrain of a Shakespearian sonnet. It wouldn't do, of course; the sprung rhythm and muffled rhymes would strike Thelma's world as technical incompetence. He found:

> You were there, and nothing was said,
> For words toppled over the edge or hovered in air.
> But I was suddenly aware, in the split instant,
> Of the constant, in a sort of passionless frenzy:
> The mad wings of motion a textbook law,
> Trees, tables, the war, in a fixed relation,
> Moulded by you, their primum mobile,
> But that you were there really was all I knew.

He couldn't remember writing that. The reference to the war dated it within six years. The place? Probably some town with avenues, outdoor tables for drinking. Addressed to? Don't be so bloody stupid; addressed to nobody, of course; pure ideal emotion. He continued rooting, his arms deep in the bathtub. The mice scuffled to their primary home, a hole. He found half of a priceless piece of juvenilia:

> You are all
> Brittle crystal,
> Your hands
> Silver silk over steel.
>
> Your hair harvested
> Sheaves shed by summer,
> Your repose the flash
> Of the flesh of a river-swimmer ...

Then a jagged tear. He must have been, sometime, taken short. There was nothing in the bath that would do for Thelma, even an ideal Thelma. He would have to compose something new. Stripping his lower half for poetic action, he took his seat and got down to work. Here was a real problem, that of bridging the gap, of making something that should not seem eccentric to the recipient and at the same time not completely embarrass the author. After an hour he produced the following:

> Your presence shines above the fumes of fat,
>   Glows from the oven-door.
> Lithe with the litheness of the kitchen cat,
>   Your image treads the floor
> Ennobling the potato-peel, the lumps
> Of fallen bread, the vulgar cabbage-stumps.
> 'Love!' cry the eggs a-whisk, and 'Love!' the beef
>   Calls from the roasting-tin.
> The beetroot blushes love. Each lettuce-leaf
>   That hides the heart within
> Is a green spring of love. Pudding and pie
> Are richly crammed with love, and so am I.

But, after those first two painful stanzas, he found it hard to stop. He was led on ruthlessly, horrified by a growing facility, a veritable logorrhoea. At the end of the ode he had emptied Arry's kitchen and filled ten closely written sheets. One point, he thought, he had very clearly established, and that was that Arry was in love.

4

It was the day of the London luncheon. Tremulous Enderby fell out of bed early to see snow staring through the morning dark. Shivering, he snapped every electric heater in the flat on, then made tea. Snow gawped blankly at him through all the windows, so he drew the curtains, turning raw morning into cosy muffiny toast-toe evening. Then he shaved. He had washed, fairly thoroughly, the night before the night before last. He had almost forgotten what it was like to shave with a new blade, having – for nearly a year now – used the old ones stacked up by the previous tenant on top of the bathroom cupboard. This morning he slashed cheeks, underlip, and Adam's apple: shaving-soap froth became childhood ice-cream sprinkled with raspberry vinegar. Enderby found an old poem beginning *And if he did then what he'd said he'd do*, and with bits of this he stanched the flow. He started to dress, putting on a new pair of socks bought at a January sale and tucking the ends of his pyjama-trousers well inside them. He had a white shirt specially laundered, he had found a striped tie – lime and mustard – in a suitcase with the name PADMORE in marking-ink on white rag attached to its lining (who was, or had been, or might be in the unrealized future, Padmore?) and had cleaned with care his one pair of brown shoes. He had also, for show and blow respectively, saved two clean handkerchiefs. He would beat these city-slickers at their own game. The suit from Arry was sober grey, the most Eliotian one in his whole wardrobe.

He was pleasantly surprised by the decent gravity of the figure that bowed from the wardrobe mirror. Urban, respectable, scholarly – a poet-banker, a poet-publisher, teeth a flashing two double octaves in the electric firelight, spectacles drinking of the bedlamp's glow. Satisfied, he went to get his breakfast – a special breakfast today, for God knew what ghastly sauced muck he might be coldly given in the great hotel. He had bought a Cornish pasty but had, coming out of the shop, slipped on an ice-patch. This had hurt him and flattened the pasty, but its edibility was hardly impaired. It was to be eaten with Branston pickle and, as an extra-special treat, washed down with Blue Mountain coffee. He felt an unwonted exultation as he prepared this viaticum, as if – after years of struggle – he had at last arrived. What should he buy with the prize-money? He couldn't think what. Books? He had done reading. Clothes? Ha ha. There was nothing he really needed except more talent. Nothing in the world.

The coffee was disappointingly cool and weak. Perhaps he had not made it properly. Could he take lessons in that? Were there teachers of such things? Arry. Of course, he would ask Arry. At nine-fifteen (train at nine-fifty, ten minutes walk to station) he sat with a cigarette, hypnotized by the gash-gold-vermilion of the electric fire, waiting. He suddenly caught another memory like a flea. Far childhood. Christmas Day, 1924. Snow came down in the afternoon, transfiguring the slum street where the shop was. He had been given a magic lantern and, after dinner, he was to project slides of wild animals on to the sitting-room wall. Powered by a candle, the lantern had been fitted with a candle – a new one, its flame much too high for the lens. His Uncle Jimmy the plumber had said, 'We'll have to wait till it burns down. Give us a tune, Fred.' And Fred, Enderby's father, had sat at the piano and played. The rest of that dim gathering – only the stepmother bright in memory, belching away – had waited for the candle to burn down to lens-level, the coloured animals suddenly to appear on the wall.

Why, wondered Enderby now, why had nobody thought to cut the candle? Why had they all, every single one of them, agreed to wait on the candle's convenience? It was another mystery, but he wondered if it was really a mystery of a different order from this other waiting – waiting on Shakespeare's time's candle to burn down to time to dress warmly, time to leave for the station. Enderby suddenly passionately wished he could cut the whole long candle to its end – have written his poetry and have done. Then he grinned as his stomach, having slyly engineered this melancholy, plaintively subscribed to it.

Pfffrrrp. And then Brrrrrrr. But that, he realized, after surprise at his stomach's achievement of such metallic ectophony, that, he heard with annoyance, was the door-bell. So early, whoever it was, and coming so inconveniently. Enderby went to his flat-door and saw, waddling down the hallway of the house itself, his landlady, Mrs Meldrum. Well. He paid her by post. The less he saw of her the better. 'If I can trouble you for a moment, Mr E,' she said. She was a woman of sixty, with pinched East Midland vowels. Her face was modelled on that of a tired but cheerful crescent moon in a bedtime-malted-milk-drink advertisement that even Enderby had seen often: Punch-nose meeting cusp-chin, but no jolly Punch plumpness. She had a full set of Tenniel-teeth of the colour of small chips of dirty ice, and these she showed to Enderby now as to a mirror. Enderby said:

'I've got to go up to town.' He thrilled gently, saying that, a busy man of affairs.

'I shan't keep you not more than one minute,' said Mrs Meldrum, 'Mr E.' She waddled in past Enderby as if she owned the place, which she did. 'It's really to empty the shillings out of the electric meter,' she said, 'which is, in one way of speaking, why I called. In another way of speaking, it's about the complaints.' She went ahead of Enderby into the living-room. At the table she examined minutely the remains of Enderby's breakfast, shook her head comically at them and then, picking up the pickle-jar, read from the label like a priest muttering the Mass: 'Sugar cauliflower onions malt vinegar tomatoes carrots spirit vinegar gherkins dates salt marrow . . .'

'What complaints?' asked Enderby, as he was expected to.

'New Year's Eve,' said Mrs Meldrum, 'being a special occasion as calls for jollifications, nevertheless Mrs Bates down in the basement has complained about loud singing when she couldn't go off to sleep with the backache. Your name came into it a lot, she says, especially in the very rude singing. On New Year's Day you was seen running up and down the street with a carving-knife and all covered with blood. Well, Mr Enderby, fun's fun as the saying goes, though I must confess I'm surprised at a man of your age. But the police had a quiet word with Mr Meldrum, unbeknownst to me, and I could only get it out of him last night, him being shy and retiring and not wanting to cause trouble. Anyway, we've had a talk about it and it can't go on, Mr E.'

'I can explain,' said Enderby, looking at his watch. 'It's all really quite simple.'

'And while we're on the subject,' said Mrs Meldrum, 'that nice young couple upstairs. They say they can hear you in the night sometimes.'

'I can hear *them*,' said Enderby, 'and they're *not* a nice young couple.'

'Well,' said Mrs Meldrum, 'that's all according as which way one looks at it, isn't it? To the pure all things are pure, as you might say.'

'What, Mrs Meldrum, is this leading to?' Enderby looked again at his watch. In the last thirty seconds five minutes had gone by. Mrs Meldrum said:

'There's plenty as would like this nice little flat, Mr E. This is a respectable neighbourhood, this is. There's retired schoolmasters and captains of industry retired along here. And I wouldn't say as how you kept this flat all that clean and tidy.'

'That's my business, Mrs Meldrum.'

'Well, it may be your business, Mr E, but then again it might not. And everybody's putting the rents up this year, as you may as well know. What with the rates going up as well and all of us having to watch us own interests.'

'Oh, I see,' said Enderby. 'That's it, is it? How much?'

'You've had this very reasonable,' said Mrs Meldrum, 'as nobody can deny. You've had this at four guineas a week all through the season. There's one gentleman as works in London as is very anxious to find respectable accommodation. Six guineas to him would be a very reasonable rent.'

'Well, it's not a very reasonable rent to me, Mrs Meldrum,' said Enderby angrily. His watch-hand leapt gaily forward. 'I have to go now,' he said. 'I've a train to catch.

Really,' he said, shocked, 'do you realize that that would be eight guineas more a month? Where would I get the money?'

'A gentleman of independent means,' said Mrs Meldrum smugly. 'If you don't want to stay, Mr E, you could always give a week's notice.'

Enderby saw with horror the prospect of sorting out the bathful of manuscripts. 'I'll have to go now,' he said. 'I'll let you know. But I think it's an imposition.'

Mrs Meldrum made no move. 'You go off then and catch your train,' she said, 'and think about it in your first-class carriage. And I'll empty the shillings out of the meter, as has to be done now and again. And if I was you I should stack those plates in the sink before you leave.'

'Don't touch my papers,' warned Enderby. 'There are private and confidential papers in that bathroom. Touch them at your peril.'

'Peril, indeed,' scoffed Mrs Meldrum. 'And I don't like the sound of that at all, continental papers in *my* bathroom.' Meanwhile Enderby wrapped his muffler on and fought his way – as if towards the light – into his overcoat. 'I never heard of such a thing, and that's a fact,' said Mrs Meldrum, 'and I've been in the business a fair amount of time. I've heard of coals in the bath with some of them slummy people, though I thank the Almighty God I've never harboured any of them in *my* bosom. You're going out like that, Mr Enderby, with bits of paper stuck all over your face. I can read a word there, just by your nose: *epileptical*, or something. You're not doing yourself or me or any of the other tenants any good at all, Mr E, going out in that state. Peril, indeed.'

Enderby dithered out, doubtful. He had not reckoned on having to search for new lodgings, not in the middle of *The Pet Beast*. And this town was becoming more and more a dormitory for bald young men from London. In one pub he had met the head of a news-reel company, a lavish gin-man with a light, fast voice. And there had been a processed-cheese executive heard, loud and unabashed, somewhere else. London was crawling southward to the Channel.

Enderby crawled northward to the station, picking off odd words from his razor-cuts. The snow had been trodden already, by people rushing earlier with insincere eagerness to get to work in London. Enderby teetered in tiny gavotte-steps, afraid of slipping, his rump still aching from last night's fall. Work-trains, stenographer-trains, executive-trains. Big deals over the telephone, fifty guineas nothing to them. Golfball-money. But, thought Enderby, that would provide for half a year's rent increase.

Looking up at the zinc sky he saw a gull or two flapping inland. He had neglected to feed the gulls for two days now; he was becoming careless. Perhaps, he thought vaguely, he could make it up to them by buying some special treat at the Army and Navy Stores. He passed a block of bright posters. One of them extolled domestic gas: a smiling toy paraclete called Mr Therm presided over a sort of warm Holy Family. Pentecostal therm; pentecostal sperm. Two men in dyed army overcoats marched, as in retreat, from the station, with demoralized thug faces. One said to the other, 'Can't make up its bleeding mind. Rain one day, snow the next. Be pissing down again tomorrow.' Enderby had to stop, short of breath, his heart martelling away as though he had just downed a half-bottle of brandy, his left hand clutching a snowcapped privet-hedge for support. *The pentecostal sperm came pissing down.* No, no, no. *Hissing down.* The line was dealt to him, like a card from a weighing-machine. He had a sudden image of the whole poem like a squat evil engine, weighing, waiting. The Holy Family, the Virgin Mary, the pentecostal sperm. He heard a train-whistle and had to rush.

Panting, he entered the little booking-hall and dug out his wallet from his right breast. There was still a Christmas tree by the bookstall. That was wrong: Twelfth Night was over, St Distaff's Day had set the working year spinning again. Enderby approached the stern shirt-sleeves behind the *guichet*. 'A day return to London, please,' he begged. He picked up his change with his ticket and sent a shilling over the floor. 'Don't lose that, mister,' said a lively old woman in black. 'Need that for the gas.' She cackled as Enderby chased the shining monocycle to the barrier. The ticket-collector flapped a heavy boot on to it, trapped. 'Thank you,' said Enderby. Rising from picking it up his eyes misted, and he saw a very clear and blue picture of the Virgin Mary at a spinning-wheel, a silver queen set in baby blue. This had nothing to do with *The Pet Beast* and its Mary-Pasiphae. This had something to do with his stepmother.

> In this spinning womb, reduced to a common noun,
> The pentecostal sperm came hissing down . . .

That was not it, the rhythm was wrong, it was not couplets. The couplets came from the doves in the Queen's speech in *Hamlet*. Doves, loves, leaves. Enderby clomped down the steps and up the steps to the up-train platform. The train was just arriving. There was an *-eave* rhyme somewhere. Enderby boarded the train. There were few passengers at this hour – women going up to fight in the January sales, a scholarly-looking police-inspector with a briefcase, two men looking much, Enderby thought distractedly, like himself – smart, normal, citified. Doves came from dove, dove meant paraclete. A dove in the leaves of life. Eve, leave, thieve, achieve, conceive.

'I beg your pardon?' said a woman sitting diagonally opposite to Enderby. They were the only two in the compartment. She was thin, blonde, washed-out, fortyish, smart with a mink cape-stole and a hat like a nest. 'Peeve,' said Enderby the city-man. 'Believe. Weave.' The train began to pant north-east with urgent love of London, a sperm to be swallowed by that giant womb. 'Swallowed,' announced Enderby, with loud excitement, 'by the giant stomach of Eve. I knew Eve came somewhere into it.' The woman picked up her folio-sized handbag and silver-grey couplet of gloves and left the compartment. 'Eve leaves,' said Enderby. Where was paper? None. He had not expected this to be a working day. Inkpencil he had. He rose and followed the woman out to the corridor. She scampered, with a kitten-scream, to the next compartment, which held a trio of talking and nodding wives drably dressed for sales-battle. Enderby, a homing dove, went straight to the lavatory.

5

> In this spinning room, reduced to a common noun,
>   Swallowed by the giant stomach of Eve,
> The pentecostal sperm came hissing down.

Enderby sat, fully dressed, on the seat of the W.C., swaying as on a father's rocking knee, a cock-horse to Charing Cross. No, London Bridge. No, Victoria. An electric sperm plunging towards Our Lady of Victories, Enderby astride. He had removed the toilet-roll from its holder and scratched away on panel after panel of paper with his inkpencil. The poem was definitely a song for the Blessed Virgin.

Whence this Marianism? Enderby knew. He remembered his bedroom with its devotional pictures by Italian commercial artists: Pius XI with triple tiara and benedictory gesture; Jesus Christ with radioactive heart exposed and – for good measure – indicated by a divine delicate index-finger; saints (Anthony, John the Baptist, Bernadette); the Virgin Mary with tender smile and winsome wimple:

> I was nowhere, for I was anyone –
>   The grace and music easy to receive:
> The patient engine of a stranger son.

Outside the bedroom door had been a holy-water stoup, dried up with the drought of Enderby's boyish disbelief. All over the house, as far as the frontier of the shop's neutral or Protestant territory, there had been other stoups, also crucifixes, plaster statuettes, withered Holy-Land palm-leaves, rosaries blessed in Rome, an Agnus Dei or two, decorative pious ejaculations (done in Dublin in pseudo-Celtic script) as brief as snarls. That was his step-mother's Catholicism, imported from Liverpool – relics and emblems and hagiographs used as lightning-conductors; her religion a mere fear of thunder.

The Catholicism of the Enderbys had come from a small Catholic pocket not far from Shrewsbury, a village which the Reformation had robbed only of its church. Weak in the tobacconist-father (his pan scraped on Holy Saturday, a drunken midnight Mass at Christmas – no more), it had died in the poet-son, thanks to that stepmother. It had been too late now for more than twenty years to look at it afresh – its intellectual dignity, its cold coherent theology. He had struggled out of it with bitter tears in adolescence, helped by Nietzsche, Tolstoy, and Rousseau, and the struggle to create his own myths had made him a poet. He couldn't go back to it now, even if he wanted to. If he did, he would be seeking the converts who wrote thrillers out of a sense of damnation or who, forming an exclusive club out of the converts of Oxford and pretending that that was the Church, would not let Enderby join. Publicly known as an apostate, Enderby would have to be bracketed along with various wild Irish. It was best, therefore, to be quiet about his faith or loss of it (asked for his religion when joining the army, he had said 'Hedonist' and been made to attend parades of the United Board); the only trouble seemed to be that his art refused to be quiet.

> His laughter was fermenting in the cell,
>   The fish, the worm were chuckling to achieve
> The rose of the disguise he wears so well.

Ultimately religious belief didn't matter; it was a question of what myths still carried enough emotional weight to be used. So the Virgin Mary now spoke her final triplet, smiling faintly in elegant blue at the distaff:

And though, by dispensation of the dove,
    My flesh is pardoned of its flesh, they leave
The rankling of a wrong and useless love.

There was too much love in the air, worried Enderby, as he read over this poem with displeasure. He saw that, apart from the obvious surface myth, there was something there about the genesis of the poet. He wrote on a final panel of toilet-paper: *Every woman is a stepmother*, then committed it to the lavatory-pan. That, he thought, has general validity. And now, judging from the loud darkness outside the cell where his poem had been an hour fermenting, they had arrived. Roars of seals in a circus, collapse of crates, high heels on the platform, a hiss, shudder and recoil as the train, in Elizabethan locution, died.

Chapter Three

1

Some hours later Enderby sat under a magnificent ceiling, bemused by food and drink and insincere laudations. A not very choice cigar shook between fingers which, he now saw, he had neglected to pumice. In a winter afternoon's dream he failed to register many of the words of orating Sir George Goodby. Across the table and at either side twenty-odd fellow-writers were suspended from the ceiling by cigarette-smoke, their faces flapping before Enderby's eyes like two lines of drying smalls. Very solid in his stomach there pawed and pranced a sort of equestrian statue that symbolized both Time and London. He desired to pick his nose. A Hangman's Blood cocktail of all the liquids he had so far taken that day was swiftly mixed in a deep visceral shaker and then shot up to his mouth for tasting. There had been an oily mock turtle with very fresh rolls and rose-shaped butter-pats. Roast duck, of which Enderby had been served with one of the greasier segments, peas and *sauté* potatoes, acid orange sauce and a thick warmish gravy. Cranberry pie, the pastry soggy, with rich whipped cream-substitute. Cheese.

Cheese. Enderby smiled across back at some woman who had smiled at him. I have always admired your poetry but to see you in the flesh is a revelation. I bet it bloody well is. Perrrrrp.

'A revelation,' said Sir George, 'of the purest beauty. The magical power of poetry to transmute the dross of the everyday workaday world into the sheerest gold.' Sir George Goodby was an ancient man whose visible parts were made mostly of sewn bits of well-tanned skin. He had founded the firm which bore his name. This firm had become rich mainly by selling rude books which other firms had been too squeamish to handle. Knighted by Ramsay MacDonald for services to the cause of mass-literacy, Sir George had always desired to serve literature otherwise than by selling it: he had aspired from youth to be a starving poet recognized only after death. Starved poetry he had continued to write long after fate had condemned him to the making of money, and this he had blackmailed one small miserable firm into publishing, brandishing the threat of a chain-boycott of all its publications. He had paid all costs of printing, publicizing, and distributing, but the firm's reputation had been ruined. The volumes of Sir George's doggerel most memorable for badness were *Metrical Yarns of a Pipeman, A Dream of Merrie England, Roseleaves of Memory* and *An Optimist Sings*. He could not, of course, force people into buying or even reading these atrocious collections, but once a year, presenting a cheque and medal to, as he coyly termed him, a brother-singer, he would lard his speech richly with gobbets of his own work and render his auditors sick with embarrassment.

'The giants of my youthful days,' Sir George was saying, 'Dobson, Watson, Sir Edward Arnold the mystic, Bridges the revolutionary, Calverley for laughter, Barry Pain for the profounder sigh.' Enderby took a shallow draught of his cigar and felt it bite rawly. A childhood image again: the woman teacher in the elementary school explaining the soul and sin's carious effect upon it. She had chalked on the blackboard a big whitish shape like a cheese (the soul) and then, using a spit-wet finger, had spotted it like a Dalmatian (sins). For some reason, Enderby had always been able to taste that chalk-soul – a sharp vinegary raw potato – and he could taste it strongly now. 'The soul,' said Sir George appropriately, 'which is a fair field for the poet's wandering, the sea whereon he sails his barque of rhyme, his mistress of whom he sings. The soul, which is the parson's Sunday concern, is the poet's daily bread.' His daily raw potato. Enderby felt a borborygm rising.

Brrrfffp.

'I shall inflict,' twinkled Sir George, 'one of my own sonnets on you, on a theme appropriate to the occasion.' He read out, with a voice pitched high and on one tuning-fork note, a poem of fourteen lines which was certainly no sonnet. It had verdant meads in it and a sun with effulgent rays, also – for some reason – a rosy-bosomed earth. Enderby, preoccupied with the need to suppress his body's noises, heard only fragments of an exquisitely bad poem and he nodded approvingly to show that he considered Sir George to have made a very good choice of an illustrative example of very bad poetry. As the last line scrannel-piped wretchedly out, Enderby felt a particularly loud noise coming, so he covered it with a laugh.

Ha ha (perrrpf) ha.

Sir George was rather surprised than displeased. He gaped down at Enderby for five seconds and then scanned his typescript tremblingly, as if fearful that something scatological had stolen ambiguously in. Reassured, he frowned on Enderby, his patches of skin shaking, and then took breath for the peroration. As he opened his mouth, Enderby, with infelicitous timing, gave vent.

Brrrbrrrpkrrrk.

Shem Macnamara said, 'And as good and succinct a piece of criticism as ever I heard.' He had a double-chinned stormy Irish face and was shag-haired and black-shirted (to save laundry). Enderby, in his daily poet's garb, was seedy-looking, but this man was a barn-sleeping hedge-dragged sturdy beggar. The white tired faces of the other guests – which Enderby could see but dimly – moved in titters. And suddenly Sir George himself seemed to grow tired. He smiled weakly, frowned, opened his mouth as in silent joy, frowned, swallowed, said in *non sequitur*:

'And it is for this reason that it gives me pleasure to bestow on our fellow singing-bird here, er er Enderby, the Goodby gold medal.' Enderby rose to applause loud enough to drown three crackling intestinal reports. 'And a cheque,' said Sir George, with nostalgia of poet's poverty, 'that is very very small but, one trusts, will stave off pangs for a month or two.' Enderby took his trophies, shook hands, simpered, then sat down again. 'Speech,' said somebody. Enderby rose again, with a more subdued report, then realized that he was unsure of the exordial protocol. Did he say, 'Mr Chairman'? Was there a chairman? If Sir George was the chairman should he say something other than 'Mr Chairman'? Should he just say, 'Sir George, ladies and gentlemen'? But, he noticed, there seemed to be somebody with a chain of office gleaming on his chest, hovering in the dusk, a mayor or lord mayor. What should he say – 'Your Worship'? In time he saw that this was some sort of menial in charge of wine. Holding in wind, a nervously smiling Aeolus, Enderby said, loud and clear:

'St George.' There was a new stir of tittering. 'And the dragon,' Enderby now had to add. 'A British cymbal,' he continued, seeing with horror that orthographical howler in a sort of neon lights before him. 'A cymbal that tinkles in unsound brass if we are without clarity.' There were appreciative easings of buttocks and shoulders: Enderby was going to make it brief and humorous. Desperately Enderby said, 'As most of us are or are not, as the case may be. Myself included.' Sir George, he saw, was throwing up wide face-holes at him, as though he, Enderby, were on a girder above the street. 'Clarity,' said Enderby, almost in tears, 'is red wine for yodellers. And so,' he gaped aghast at himself, 'I am overjoyed to hand back this cheque to St George for charitable disposal. The gold medal he knows what he can do with.' He could have died with shock and embarrassment at what he was saying; he was hurled on to the end in killing momentum, however. 'Dross of the work-aday world,' he said, 'as our fellow-singer Goodby so adequately disproves. And so,' he said, back in the Army giving a talk on the British Way and Purpose, 'we look forward to a time when the world shall be free of the shadow of oppression, the iron heel with its swastika spur no longer grinding into the face of prone freedom, democracy a reality, a fair day's pay for a fair day's work, adequate health services and a bit of peace hovering dovelike in the declining days of the aged. And in that belief and aspiration we move forward.' He found that he could not stop. 'Forward,' he insisted, 'to a time when the world shall be free of the shadow of oppression.' Sir George had risen and was tottering out. 'A fair day's work,' said Enderby feebly, 'for a fair day's pay. Fair play for all,' he mumbled doubtfully. Sir George had gone. 'And thereto,' ended Enderby wretchedly, 'I plight thee my truth.'

The party broke up at once. Two men turned bitterly on Enderby. 'If,' said Shem Macnamara, 'you didn't want the bloody money you might at least have remembered that there's others as do. Myself included,' he mocked. He breathed, bafflingly, onions on Enderby, for onions had not formed any part of the meal. 'I didn't mean it,' said Enderby, near crying. 'I didn't know what I was saying.' Enderby's publisher said, 'Want to ruin us you do?' in a sharp rising intonation. He was a young bright man from Newport. 'Put your foot in it you have bloody nicely, man, make no mistake about it.' A small man moustached like Kipling, with the same beetle-spectacles and a heavy watch-chain, came up to Enderby and took him firmly by Arry's lapels. 'I'm Rawcliffe,' he announced. He dragged Enderby away from the table in short dance-steps, lapels

54

still held hard. Rawcliffe nodded many times, stopped nodding, cocked an ear, nodded in satisfaction, then just nodded, chewing. 'Very fibrous duck,' said Rawcliffe. 'You know me. I'm in all the anthologies. Now then, Enderby, tell me, tell me in all sincerity what you're doing at the present time.'

'Just writing, you know,' said Enderby. He was trying to think who Rawcliffe was. Uneasily he heard behind him debates in small groups on his speech and its consequences for the retail book trade.

'One would have supposed,' said Rawcliffe, tugging Arry's lapels like cow-teats, 'mildly supposed, I suppose, that you would be writing.' He chuckled, swallowed, and nodded. 'Now then, Enderby, what? What are you writing? Tell me, elm,' he laughed. 'Tale told of stem or stone, eh? James Joyce, that is. Myth-maker, what?'

'Well,' said Enderby, and, with babbling nerves, he blurted out a detailed synopsis of *The Pet Beast*.

'And the beast is really Original Sin, eh?' saw Rawcliffe. 'Without Original Sin there is no civilization, is that it? Good, good. And the title, let's have that title again.' He released the lapels, found a short pencil in a waistcoat pocket, licked the point, took out a cigarette-packet, shook it ruefully, then block-lettered Enderby's title on its bottom flap. 'Good,' he said again. 'Infinitely obleeged.' And he made off nodding. Enderby sadly watched him join a group of important poets who had not been above cynically taking a free meal – P. S. ffolliott, Peter Pitts, Albert Death-Stabbes, Rupert Tombs, or some such names. They had mostly murmured 'Well done' to him at the pre-prandial sherry-bibbing. Now he was left alone with his wind, companionless. Medalless also, and chequeless. Rather a wasted trip, really.

'Mr Enderby?' The lady panted slightly and very prettily. 'Oh, thank goodness I was in time.'

'I knew,' said Enderby, 'that Sir George would realize it was all a joke. Do, please, convey my apologies to him.'

'Sir George? Oh yes, I know who you mean. Apologize? I don't understand.' She was perhaps thirty, with fashionable stallion-flared nostrils and a model-girl's swan-neck. She wore with grace a Cardin sugar-scoop hat of beige velours, and, from the same master, a loose-jacketed suit with only a hint of flare to the peplum. An ocelot coat swung open over this. Chic shone from her demurely. Such cleanness and fragrance (*Miss Dior*), thought Enderby with deep regret, such slender and sheer-hosed glamour. A face, he decided, devoid of all obvious sensuality – no lusciousness of the underlip, the cat-green eyes very cool and intelligent, a calm high forehead shaded by the sugar-scoop brim. Enderby tightened his tie-knot and smoothed his side-pockets, saying: 'I'm sorry.' And then, 'I thought. That is to say.' She said:

'Oh.' They stood looking at each other under the glowing glass-slab signs of the hotel passage, their feet sunk in burgundy carpet. 'Well. I would like, before anything else, to tell you that I genuinely admire your work.' She spoke with the intonation of one expecting an incredulous snort. The voice was quiet, though the consonants had the sharpness of some speaker too close to a microphone, and there was the faintest tang of educated Scots. 'I wrote to you care of your publishers, ages ago. I don't think the letter could ever have reached you. If it had reached you I'm sure you would have replied.'

'Yes,' said flustered Enderby. 'Oh yes, I would. But perhaps that was forwarded by them to my old address because I'd forgotten to tell them about my new address and also, for that matter, the Post Office. Cheques,' said blabbing Enderby, 'are normally paid straight into my bank. I don't know why I'm telling you all this.' She stood in a model pose, listening coolly with lips parted, handbag hanging from right forearm, gloved left hand's thumb and index-finger lightly ringing ungloved right hand's ring-finger. 'I'm terribly sorry,' said humble Enderby. 'That may explain why I never got it.'

She finished her quiet listening and suddenly became brisk. 'Look,' she said, 'I had an invitation to that luncheon-party but I couldn't make it. Could we, do you think,' she suggested, with a kind of movement on the fringe of non-movement which was a sort of apotheosis of a working-girl's jigging up and down in a winter-day bus-queue, infinitely feminine, 'sit down somewhere for a few minutes, if you can spare the time, that is? Oh,' she said, 'I'm so stupid,' the gloved hand striking the lips in *mea culpa*, 'not telling you who I am. I'm Vesta Bainbridge. From *Fem*.'

'From what?'

'*Fem*.'

'What,' asked Enderby, with great and suspicious care, 'is that?' He had heard it as, though hardly believing it possible, something like *Phlegm*, and wondered what could be the purpose of an organization (if it was an organization) so named.

'Yes, of course, I see, of course you probably wouldn't know about that, would you? It's a magazine for women. And I,' said Vesta Bainbridge, 'am the Features Editress. Could we then, do you think? I suppose it's too early to have tea, isn't it, or is it?'

'If you would care for some tea,' said gallant Enderby, 'I should be only too happy, I should be only too delighted.'

'Oh, no,' said Vesta Bainbridge, 'you have to have it with me, you see, because it goes on my expense account. And this is a business thing, you see, connected with *Fem*.'

Enderby had once, as a poor soldier, been treated to a tea of poached egg on haddock and shortbread by a kind old lady in an Edinburgh restaurant. But by anyone so glamorous, so alluring as this, he had never thought, never dreamed. He was both shocked and awed. 'Do you, by any chance, come from Edinburgh?' he asked. 'Something in your voice –'

'Eskbank,' said Vesta Bainbridge. 'How remarkable! But, of course, you're a poet. Poets can always dig out things like that, can't they?'

'If,' said Enderby, 'you really like my poetry, which you said you did, I should really ask you to have tea with me, not you me with you. The least I could do,' said generous Enderby, fingering a half-crown in Arry's trouser-pocket.

'Come,' said Vesta Bainbridge, and she made the wraith of a gesture of taking Enderby by the arm. 'I *do* admire your work, really,' she insisted. She led him on sure high heels past the dainty boutiques that sold flowers and jewellery, the air-travel kiosk where there was busy telephoning about flights to New York and Bermuda, past the ugly and rich cocooned in an enchantment of wine-coloured snow underfoot, perfumed air all about, light drifting, dust-soft, from unseen sources in the delicate golds of fine white bordeaux. Here every breath, every footfall, thought thrifty Enderby, must cost at least a tanner. Vesta Bainbridge and he entered a vast room of huge scooped cubes of biscuit-coloured softness in which people lounged warmly cushioned. Laughter tinkled, teatrays tinkled. Enderby felt with horror his bowels prepare to comment on the scene. He looked up at a baroque ceiling with many fat-arsed cherubim in evidence. This did not help. They sank down, Vesta Bainbridge exhibiting the delicacy of exquisite shinlines, a fine moulding of ankle. A Roman waiter, lantern-jawed, took her order. Scots, she asked for a substantial spread: anchovy toast, egg sandwiches, pikelets, cakes, China tea with lemon. 'And,' said Enderby, 'do you manage to eat dinner after a tea like that?'

'Oh, yes,' said Vesta Bainbridge. 'I can't put on weight, however hard I try. The lemon tea's because that's the way I like tea, not for slimming reasons. Obviously,' she added.

'But,' said Enderby, drawn to the obvious weary compliment, 'you're surely perfect as you are.' Suddenly he saw himself, boulevardier Enderby, witty with women, graceful in flattery, roguish eyes atwinkle, taking tea. At the same time wind fought, as a picked-up naughty kitten fights, to be free. Tea free. A free tea. 'And,' he said, 'if I may ask, what precisely is this business with *Phlegm*?'

'Oh,' she said, 'isn't that funny? That's what Godfrey Wainwright calls it. He does covers, you know. *Fem*. Not, perhaps, a very good choice of name. But, you know, the market's saturated with magazines for women – *Feminocrat, Goodwife, Lilith, Glamourpuss*. The straightforward names with Woman in them were worked out long ago. It's so difficult for them to think of anything new, as you'll appreciate. But *Fem* isn't too bad, is it? It's short and sweet, and it sounds Frenchified and a bit naughty, wouldn't you agree?'

Enderby eyed her warily. Frenchified and a bit naughty, eh? 'Yes,' he said. 'And where would I come in with something like that?' Not very good, she'd said, and not too bad – both in the same breath. Perhaps not a very sincere sort of woman. Before she could answer his question the tea arrived. The Roman waiter laid it down gently on the fretted claw-footed low table – silver dish-covers steaming, tiny cakes oozing cream. He rose, bowing with sneering jowls, retiring. Vesta Bainbridge poured. She said:

'I thought somehow you'd prefer your tea like this – sugarless, milkless, lemony. Your poems are a little, shall we say, astringent, if that's the right word.' Enderby looked down sourly at the sour cup. He preferred stepmother's tea really, but she'd ordered without consulting him. 'Very nice,' he said. 'Just right.' Vesta Bainbridge began to eat with great appetite, showing fine small teeth as she bit into her anchovy toast. Enderby's heart warmed to this: he liked to see women eat, and this gusto mitigated, somehow, her lean perfection. But, he thought, she had no right, with such a figure, to have such an appetite. He felt a desire to invite her out to dinner, that same evening, to see how she would tuck into minestrone and pork chops. He feared her.

'Now,' said Vesta Bainbridge, and a rosy tongue-point

darted out, picked up a toast-crumb, then darted in again. 'I want you to know that I admire your work, and what I propose now is entirely my own idea. It's met with some opposition, mind you, because *Fem* is essentially a popular magazine. And your poetry, as you'll be proud to admit, is not exactly popular. It's not unpopular either, of course; it's just not known. Pop-singers are known and TV interviewers are known and disc-jockeys are known, but you're not known.'

'What,' asked Enderby, 'are these things? Pop-singers and so on?' She looked askance at him and noticed that his bewilderment was genuine. 'I'm afraid,' said Enderby, 'that since the war I've rather shut myself off from things.'

'Don't you have a radio or a television set?' said Vesta Bainbridge, her green eyes wide. He shook his head. 'Don't you read newspapers?'

'I used to read certain Sunday papers,' said Enderby, 'for the sake of the book reviews. But it made me so very depressed that I had to stop. The reviewers seemed so,' he frowned, 'so very *big*, if you see what I mean. They seemed to *enclose* us writers, so to speak. They seemed to know all about us, and we knew nothing about them. There was one very kind and very knowledgeable review of a volume of mine, I remember, by a man who, I suppose, is a very good man, but it was evident that he could have written my poems so much better if only he'd had the time. Those things make one feel very insignificant. Oh, I know one *is* insignificant, really, but you've got to ignore that if you're to get any work done at all. And so I've tended to cut myself off a bit, for the sake of the work. Everybody seems to be so *clever*, somehow, if you see what I mean.'

'I do and I don't,' said Vesta Bainbridge, smartly. So far she had eaten all the anchovy toast, five egg sandwiches, a couple of pikelets and one squelchy little pastry, and yet contrived to look ethereal, mountain-cool. Enderby, on the other hand, who, because of his heartburn, had only nibbled mouse-like at a square inch of damp bread and an egg-ring, was aware of himself as gross, sweating, halitotic, his viscera loaded like a nightsoil-collector's bucket. '*I* don't feel insignificant,' said Vesta Bainbridge, and 'I'm just nothing compared with you.'

'But you don't *have* to feel insignificant, do you?' said Enderby. 'I mean, you've only to look at yourself, haven't you?' He said this dispassionately, frowning.

'For a man,' said Vesta Bainbridge, 'who's cut himself from the world, you're not doing too badly. I should have thought,' she said, pouring more tea, 'that it was very unwise for a poet to do that. After all, you need images, themes, and so on, don't you? You've got to get those from the outside world.'

'There are quite enough images,' said Enderby, speaking with firm authority, 'in half a pound of New Zealand cheddar. Or in the washing-up water. Or,' he added, with even greater authority, 'in a new toilet-roll.'

'You poor man,' said Vesta Bainbridge. 'Is that how you live?'

'Everybody,' said Enderby, with perhaps diminishing dogmatism, 'uses toilet-paper.' A man in spectacles, very tall and with an open mouth, looked across from his chair as if to dispute this assertion, thought better of it, then returned to his evening paper. *Poet Refuses Medal*, said a tiny headline which Enderby caught sight of. Some other bloody fool shooting his mouth off, some other toy trumpet singing to battle.

'Anyway,' said Vesta Bainbridge, 'I think it would be an excellent thing for you to have a wider audience. Would you try it for, say, six months, a poem every week? Preferably set in the form of prose, so as not to offend anyone.'

'I thought people didn't actually find verse *offensive*,' said Enderby. 'I thought they just despised it.'

'Be that as it may,' said Vesta Bainbridge, 'what do you say to the proposal?' She shattered a sort of macaroon with a fork and, before eating, said, 'The poems would have to be, shall I say, and I hope this is the right word, ephemeral. You know, dealing with everyday things that the average woman would be interested in.'

'The dross of the workaday world,' said Enderby, 'transmuted to sheerest gold. I suppose I could do that. I know all about household chores and dishcloths and so on. Also lavatory brushes.'

'Dear me,' said Vesta Bainbridge, 'you *have* got a cloacal obsession, haven't you? No, not that sort of thing, and not too much of this sheerest gold, either. Womankind cannot bear very much reality. Love and dreams are wanted, also babies without cloacal obsessions. The mystery of the stars would come in quite nicely, especially if seen from the garden of a council-house. And marriage, perhaps.'

'Tell me,' said Enderby. 'Are you Miss Cambridge or Mrs?'

'Bainbridge, not Cambridge. *Fem*, not *Phlegm*. Mrs. Why do you want to know?'

'I have to call you something,' said Enderby, 'don't I?' She seemed at last to have finished her meal, so Enderby offered his crumpled cigarette-packet.

'I'll smoke my own,' she said, 'if you don't mind.' She took from her handbag a packet of ship's Woodbines and, before Enderby could find an unused match in his matchbox (he saved used matches, a long unfathomable habit), she had flicked her pearl-faced lighter on and then off. Her wide nostrils walrussed out two pretty blue jets.

'I take it,' said Enderby, 'that your husband's in the navy.'

'My husband,' she said, 'is dead. It shows how cut off you are, really, doesn't it? Everybody else seems to have heard of Pete Bainbridge.'

'I'm sorry,' said Enderby. 'Very sorry.'

'What for? Because he's dead, or because you've never heard of him? Never mind,' said Widow Bainbridge. 'He died in a smash four years ago, in the Monte Carlo Rally. I thought everybody knew that. It was a great loss, the papers said, to the motor-racing world. He left behind a beautiful young widow, a bride of only two years,' she said, her tone half-mocking.

'He did,' said Enderby gravely. 'He most certainly did. Beautiful, I mean. How much?'

'How much what? How much did he leave, or how much did I love him?' She seemed suddenly tired, perhaps from over-eating.

'How much do I get for doing these poems?'

'Mr Dick sets us all right,' said Vesta Bainbridge, sighing and sitting up straighter. She brushed minimal crumbs off her lap and said, 'Two guineas a poem. It's not much, but we can't manage more. We're featuring the memoirs of a pop-singer, you see – not very long memoirs, of course, because he's only nineteen – but those are costing us a pretty penny, believe me. And the memoirs have to be written for him as well. Still, the effect on the circulation should be, to say the least, stimulating. If that princely fee is all right by you I'll send you a contract. And some back numbers of *Fem*, to show you what it's like. Please remember that the vocabulary of our readers isn't very extensive, so don't go using words like "oriflamme" or "ineluctable".'

'Thank you,' said Enderby. 'I'm really most grateful that you should have thought of me like this. You're really being most kind.' He had been poking into the ashtray with a matchstick, breaking up cigarette-ends; this had necessitated a sort of crouching on the chair's edge, his bald crown presented to Mrs Bainbridge. Now he looked up sincerely, his eyes rather wet behind their glasses. She smiled.

'Look,' she said, 'you don't believe me about my liking your poetry, do you? Well, I even know one or two of them by heart.'

'Say one,' begged Enderby. She took breath and recited, quite clearly but with few nuances of tone:

'A dream, yes, but for everyone the same.
   The thought that wove it never dropped a stitch;
   The Absolute was anybody's pitch
For, when a note was struck, we knew its name'.

'Good,' said Enderby. 'This is the first time I've ever actually heard –'

> '– That dark aborted any urge to tame
>   Waters that day might prove to be a ditch
>   But then were endless growling ocean, rich
> In fish and heroes, till the dredgers came.'

'Excellent,' said Enderby. 'And now the sestet.' It excited him to hear his own verses. She went on confidently:

> '*Wachet auf!* A fretful dunghill cock
>   Flinted the noisy beacons through the shires;
> A martin's nest clogged the cathedral clock,
>   But it was morning (birds could not be liars).
> A key cleft rusty age in lock and lock;
>   Men shivered by a hundred kitchen fires.

There,' she said, taking breath. 'But I've no real idea what it means.'

'Oh,' said Enderby, 'the meaning doesn't matter all that much. I'm surprised at your liking that. It's not what I'd thought of as a woman's poem.' Suddenly the poem seemed to find its place in the real world – overseas businessmen reading financial papers, the scent of *Miss Dior* or whatever it was, the noise of London waiting to pounce outside the hotel. Spoken by her, it seemed suddenly to have a use.

'And what exactly do you mean by a woman's poem?' asked Mrs Bainbridge.

'For you,' said Enderby with disarming candour, 'something softer and yet more elegant, something with less harshness and thought and history in it. That, you see, is about the Middle Ages and the coming of the Reformation. In the sestet you get Martin Luther and the beginning of dissolution, everybody beginning to be alone, a common tradition providing no tuning-fork of reference and no way of telling the time, because the common tradition has been dredged away. Nothing sure and nothing mysterious.'

'I see,' said Vesta Bainbridge. 'I take it you're a Catholic, then.'

'Oh, no, no,' protested Enderby. 'I'm not, really I'm not.'

'All right,' said Vesta Bainbridge, smiling. 'I heard you the first time.' Protestant Enderby grinned and shut up. The Roman waiter came along, chewing gently but mournfully, with a bill. 'For me,' she said, and notes rustled in her bag like pork crackling. She paid the bill and, womanly, tipped the waiter merely adequately. Enderby said:

'I'd ask you to dine with me this evening, but I've just realized that I didn't bring very much money. I expected, you see, that I'd go straight back after lunch. I'm awfully sorry.'

'Don't be,' smiled Vesta Bainbridge. 'I'm invited out. Somewhere in Hampstead. But it was nice of you to offer. Now,' she said, looking at her tiny oyster watch, 'goodness, the time, where do I write to?' She took out a small notebook and poised a pencil to record what Enderby dictated. Somehow, the address seemed vulgar and even comic, endited primly by that slim hand. 81 Fitzherbert Avenue. He tried to hide from her the sound of the lavatory's flush, the crusted milk-bottles on the doorstep, the mice scampering through the manuscripts. 'Good,' she said, closing the book. 'Now I must go.' She settled the ocelot over her shoulders, clipped her bag shut. Enderby stood. She stood. 'It's been awfully nice,' she said. 'Oh, that's inadequate. But it's been quite a privilege, really it has. Now I really must fly.' She gave him an unexpected handshake, straight from the elbow. 'Don't bother to come to the door,' she said. Then she was off, trimly and swiftly walking a tightrope across the carpet. For the first time Enderby caught a hint of colour of her hair, upswept at the nape, a sort of penny-colour. He sighed, and turned to see the waiter looking at him. The waiter made a gesture – quick frogmouth, shrug – to indicate (a) that she was certainly elegant but much too thin, (b) that she was off to meet somebody handsomer than Enderby, (c) that women were fundamentally ungenerous, (d) that this was a hell of a life but there were always the consolations of philosophy.

Enderby nodded, the poet at ease with all classes of men, then realized with joy that he was once more alone and free. The wind that blew through him celebrated this fact.

3

Enderby was late returning home that evening. Though his perversely independent soul – the conscious Enderby shocked and gaping – had rejected the sweets of recognition, he felt that he and London had achieved more of a *rapprochement* than he could have thought possible, scratching paper and bared legs, the day before. A smart and worldly woman admired his work and had said so frankly. Lips that had been kissed by a prominent racing-driver and, Enderby presumed, by others whose teeth habitually gleamed at cameras, had recited from the *Revolutionary Sonnets* in a rich-smelling place whose denizens had passed beyond the need for the solace of poetry. Enderby, wandering the streets, was restless and had an obscure longing for adventure. Here the snow had long disappeared, but the tang of snow on the air bit sharply from the furthermost stretch of the river. London yearned back to gasflares and geese sold cheap at the end of the trading day amid raucous Cockney voices, Sherlock Holmes in Baker Stret, a widow at Windsor, all's right with the world. That was from *Pappa Pisses*. Enderby grinned sadly to himself, standing outside a music-shop, as he remembered the disastrous lecture he had once given to a Women's Institute. Victorian Literature. That was one spoonerism that his audience had passed over. But *A Sale of Two Titties* had struck Lady Fennimore as something like calculated insolence. Never again. Never, never again. He was safer in retirement, shut away in his creative lavatory. But still, this one evening, the desire for adventure was strong. Yet what did one mean by adventure these days? He gazed at the shop-window, as if for an answer. Various pictures of young louts sneered out at him from song-covers and record-sleeves – simian-foreheaded, prehensile fingers on guitar-strings, lips twisted in a song of youth. Enderby had heard of secondary modern schools and now assumed that these flat-eyed little monsters must represent their end-product. Well, for two guineas a week he was going to serve the world that these loose-lipped leerers served. What was the name of the magazine again? *Flim* or *Flam* or something. Not *Phlegm*, that was quite certain. Within the consonantal frame he tried out various vowels. And there, next door but one, outside one of Sir George Goodby's own shops, a poster put him right: 'Exclusive to *Fem*, FOR YOU, Lenny Biggs tells his own personal life story. Order your copy NOW.' And there was a picture of Lenny Biggs – a face hardly distinguishable from others of the pantheon Enderby had just viewed, though perhaps more particularly baboon-like than generally simian, with teeth as manifestly false as those of Enderby himself, sniggering with confidence at the world.

Enderby saw a man in a peaked cap dump a couple of parcels in a van lettered GOODBY'S FOR GOOD BOOKS. This van then started up contemptuously and insolently pierced the traffic. 'So,' thought Enderby, 'Sir George has already started his reprisals, has he? All copies of Enderby's poems to be withdrawn from sale, eh? Petty, a very petty-minded man.' Enderby entered the shop and was depressed to see people buying gardening books. Display studio-portraits of groomed youthful bestsellers topped piles of their bestselling novels. Enderby felt that he wanted to flee; this was as bad as reading Sunday reviews. And, to brim his misery, he realized that he had maligned Sir George: two soiled Enderby volumes sulked there on the unvisited poetry shelves. He was beneath the notice of that wealthy knight, too mean for the meanness of retaliation. Oh, well. The name Rawcliffe suddenly hurled itself, along with a pang of dyspepsia, at Enderby's breastbone. In all the anthologies, did he say? Enderby would see.

Enderby looked through *Poetry Now*, *A Tiny Garner of Modern Verse*, *Best Poets of Today*, *They Sing for You*, *Soldier's Solace* (an anthology of verse by Lieutenant-

General Phipps, v.c., d.s.o., etc., sixtieth thousand),
Voices Within, and other volumes, and found that in all
of them Rawcliffe was represented by the following artless
lyrics:

> 'Perhaps I am not wanted then,' he said.
>   'Perhaps I'd better go,'
> He said. Motionless her eyes, her head,
>   Saying not yes, not no.
>
> 'I will go then, and aim my gun of grief
>   At any man's or country's enemies.'
> He said. 'Slaughter will wreak a red relief.'
>   She said not no, not yes.
>
> And so he went to marry mud and toil,
>   Swallow in general hell his private hell.
> His salts have long drained into alien soil,
>   And she says nothing still.

Enderby looked up bitterly from the tenth selected anthology, his tenth reading of the poem. And in none of these
books was there anything by Enderby.

Enderby pulled out a spilling palmful of coin from
Arry's right trouser-pocket. Snorting, he counted it: twelve
and ninepence. In his wallet there was, he knew, one
pound note. He muttered to himself as he moved door-
wards, head down to count again. He bumped into a
young salesman who said, 'Whoops, sir. See nothing you
fancy, sir?'

'Books,' said Enderby, with proleptic drunken thickness.
'Waste of time and bloody money.' He left, saying a
soldier's goodbye to Goodby's, not one of Goodby's good
boys. There was a pub almost directly opposite, shedding
cosy Christmas-card lights through its old-time bottle-glass
windows. Enderby entered the public bar and ordered
whisky.

4

Enderby entered the public bar and ordered whisky. This was some hours later, a different pub. Not the second or third pub, but somewhere well on in the series, the xth pub or something. On the whole, benevolent and swaying Enderby decided, he had had not too bad an evening. He had met two very fat Nigerians with wide cunning smiles and many blackheads. These had cordially invited him to their country and to write an epic to celebrate its independence. He had met a Guinness-drinker with a wooden leg which, for the delectation of Enderby, he had offered to unscrew. He had met a chief petty officer of the Royal Navy who, in the friendliest spirit in the world, had been prepared to fight Enderby and, when Enderby had demurred, had given him two packets of ship's Woodbines and said that Enderby was his pal. He had met a Siamese osteopath with a collection of fighting fish. He had met a punch-drunk bruiser who said he saw visions and offered to see one then for a pint. He had met a little aggressive chinny chewing man, not unlike Rawcliffe, who swore that Shakespeare's plays had been written by Sir William Knollys, Controller of the Queen's Household. He had met a cobbler who knew the Old Testament in Hebrew, an amateur exegetist who distrusted all Biblical scholarship after 1890. He had met, seen, or heard many others too: a thin woman who had talked incessantly to a loll-tongued Alsatian; a man with the shakes who swallowed his own phlegm (*Fem, Fem*, remember that, *Fem*); a pair of hand-holding lesbians; a man who wore flower transfers on a surgical boot; callow soldiers drinking raw gin. . . . Now it was nearing closing-time and Enderby was, he thought, fairly near to Charing Cross. That meant two stops on the Underground to Victoria. There must be a nice convenient after-closing-time train to the coast.

Enderby, paying fumblingly for his whisky, saw that he had very little money left. He estimated that he had managed to consume this evening a good dozen whiskies and a draught beer or so. His return ticket was snug in Arry's left-hand inside jacket-pocket. He had cigarettes. One more drink and he would be right for home. He looked round the public bar smiling. Good honest British working-men, salt of the earth, bloodying and buggering their meagre dole of speech, horny-handed but delicate with darts. And, on a high-backed settle at right angles to the bar counter, two British working-women sat, made placid with the fumes of stout. One said:

'Starting next week, it is, in *Fem*. With free gift picture in full colour. Smashing, he is.' Enderby listened jealously. The other woman said:

'Never take it, myself. Silly sort of name it is. Makes you wonder how they think of them sometimes, really it does.'

'If,' said Enderby, 'you are referring to the magazine to which I myself am to be a contributor, I would say that that name is meant to be Frenchified and naughty.' He smiled down at them with a whiskified smirk, right elbow on the counter, left fingers on right forearm. The two women looked up doubtfully. They were probably about the same age as Vesta Bainbridge, but they had an aura of back kitchens about them, tea served to shirt-sleeved men doing their pools, the telly flicking and shouting in the corner.

'Pardon?' said one, loudly.

'Naughty,' said Enderby, with great clarity. 'Frenchi-fied.'

'What's French frieds to do with it?' said the other. 'My friend and me was just talking, do you mind?'

'Poetry is what I shall write for it,' said Enderby, 'every week.' He nodded several times, just like Rawcliffe.

'You keep your poetry to yourself, do you mind?' and she took a sharp draught of Guinness. A man came from the dart-playing part of the room, a single dart in his hand, saying:

'You all right, Edie?' He wore a decently cut suit of poor serge, but no collar or tie. His gold-headed collar-stud caught the light and dazzled Enderby. He had a gaunt

70

quick face and was as small and supple as a miner. He inspected Enderby as if invited to give an estimate on him. 'You saying something to her that you shouldn't?' he said. 'Mate?' he added, provocatively.

'He was saying,' said Edie, 'about naughty poetry. French, too.'

'Was you saying naughty poetry to my wife here?' said the man. Like Milton's Death, he shook a dreadful dart.

'I was just saying,' said smirking Enderby, 'that I was going to write for it. What they read, I mean. That is to say, Edie here, your wife, as I take it to be, doesn't read, but the other one does, you see.'

'We'll have less of that about doesn't read, do you mind?' said Edie. 'And less of using my name familiar, do you mind?'

'Look here,' said Edie's husband. 'You want to keep that for the saloon bar, where they pay a penny extra for the privilege, do you mind? We don't want your sort in here.'

'Doing no harm,' said Enderby huffily. He then poured over the huff a trickle of sweet sauce of ingratiation. 'I mean, I was just talking.' He leered. 'Just passing the time of day, if you see what I mean.'

'Well,' said the dart-man, 'don't you try to pass the time with my missis, do you mind?'

'Do you mind?' said Edie, in near-unison.

'I wouldn't want to pass the time with her,' said Enderby, proudly. 'I've other things to do, thank you very much.'

'I'll have to do you,' said the man, sincerely. 'Too much bloody hoot altogether, mate, to my way of thinking, that's what you've got. You'd better get out of here before I get really nasty. Been smelling the barmaid's apron, that's your trouble.'

Prrrfffp.

'Look,' said Enderby, 'that wasn't intended, I really had no intention, that was not meant in any way to be a comment, I assure you that is the sort of thing that could happen to any man, or woman too, for that matter, even Edie here, your wife, that is to say, yourself included.' Prrrfffp.

'Do you mind?' said Edie.

'This here's my fist,' said the man, pocketing his dart. The other customers quietened and looked interested. 'You'll get it straight in the moosh, straight up you will, if you don't get out of my bleeding sight this instant, do you mind?'

'I was just going anyway,' said dignified swaying Enderby. 'If you will allow me the privilege of finishing my drink here.'

'You've had enough, you have, mate,' said the man, more kindly. From the saloon bar came the call of 'Last orders.' 'If you want to drown your secret sorrows don't do it where me and my wife is, see, because I take the sort of thing that you've been saying very hard, see.' Enderby put down his glass, gave the dart-man a glassy but straight look, then eructed strongly and without malice. He bowed and, pushing his way courteously through the long-swallowers anxious to get one last one in, made an exit that was not without dignity. Outside in the street the heady air of a Guinness-sharp refrigerated night hit him and he staggered. The dart-man had followed him out and stood there, gauging and weighing. 'Look, mate,' he said, 'this is not for me really, because I've been like that myself often enough, God knows, but my wife insists, see, do you mind, and this is like for a keepsake.' He bowed, and while bowing swerved his torso suddenly to the left as though listening to something from that side, then he brought left fist and torso right and up and let Enderby have one, not too hard, straight in the stomach. 'There,' he said, somewhat kindly, as if the blow had been intended purely therapeutically. 'That'll do, won't it?'

Enderby gasped. The procession of the evening's whiskies and beers passed painfully through a new taste-organ that had been erected specially for this occasion. They grimaced in pain, making painful obeisance as they passed. Gas and fire shot up as from a geyser, smiting rudely the crystalline air. Premonitions of the desire to vomit huddled and fluttered. Enderby went to the wall.

'Now then,' said the man, 'where is it you want to go, eh?' Kennington you are now, see, if you didn't know.'

'Victoria,' said Enderby's stomach-gas, shaped into a word by tongue and lips. He had, at the moment, no air.

'Easy,' said the kind man. 'First to the right second to the left keep straight on brings you to Kennington Station, see. Get a train to Charing Cross, that's the second stop, Waterloo's the first, change at Charing Cross, see, Circle Line. Westminster St James's Park and then you're there, see. And the very best of luck and no hard feelings.' He patted Enderby's left shoulder and re-entered the public bar.

Enderby still gasped. This sort of thing had not happened since his student-days when he had once been beaten up by a pub pianist and his friend for being bloody sarky about the sort of pseudo-music the pub pianist had been playing. Enderby filled his coughing lungs in draught after draught, then wondered whether he really wanted to vomit. He thought, for the moment, not. The punch in the stomach still glowed and smouldered, and the name LONDON fluttered in fearful flames, a warning, as in the trailer of some film about call-girls or the end of the world. He saw himself safe in his own lavatory, at work on his poems. Never again. Never never again. Women's Institutes. Gold medals. London pubs. Traps set for poor Enderby, gins waiting for him to trip.

He reached Kennington Station without much difficulty and booked to Victoria. In the train, sitting opposite a cross-eyed man who spoke Scots to a complacent terrier on his knee, Enderby felt a shipboard motion and knew that soon he must dash to the rails. Further along on the side where he was sitting, he had the illusion that a couple of gum-chewing teenagers were discussing a play by Calderón. He strained to listen and nearly fell on his right ear. At Waterloo he was sure that the Scotsman with strabismus said 'morne plaine' to his dog. A drum beat and a bugle brayed in Enderby's stomach; here, perhaps, he must admit defeat, stagger off, be sick in a fire-bucket. Too late. The train and time marched on from Waterloo, under the river, and, thank God, there was Charing Cross. The charing-cross-eyed man got out here too, with terrier. 'A drop taken,' he said confidentially to Enderby and then marched off to the Bakerloo Line, dog trotting with twinkletoes behind, fat rump, joyous tail. Enderby now felt decidedly unwell and bewildered. He had a confused notion that the southbound platform of this Northern Line would take him whither he wanted. He staggered over and sat on a bench. Across the rail a poster showed an outdoor man draining a milk stout, his fine muscular throat corded with stout-drinker's strength. Next to that was a colour-wash sketch, vivid with steam and laughter, of a confident young man wrestling with a delighted girl for a portion of pie made with meat-extract. Next to that a ginger child, macrocephalic, went 'Ooooo!' with pleasure, his cheek gumboiled with a slab of extra-creamy toffee. Enderby retched, but memory saved him with four lines of a drinker's poem he had written in his drunken youth:

> And I have walked no way I looked
> And multitudinously puked
> Into the gutter, legs outstretched,
> Holding my head low as I . . .

That threw his present queasiness back into the past and also depersonalized it. The solace of art. And now the distant Minotaur roar of the tube-train alerted the others waiting on that platform. One man folded his evening paper and stuck it into the side-pocket of his greatcoat. *Poet Speaks Out for Fair Play,* read Enderby. Field-day for poets, this. The tube-train slammed itself into the clearing, bringing a fine gale of Arctic air which did Enderby good. He stood and felt giddy but steeled himself to travel to Victoria, seeing that, in his muzzy state, as a very large and desirable lavatory of blasts and sulphuretted hydrogen. He straddled before a not-yet-opened double-door of the train, trying to hold the unquiet platform steady, while the passengers waiting to alight stood as though for a curtain call. Then a panic of doubt clouted Enderby as the doors slid open and the alighters flooded off. 'Is this,' he called, 'all right for Victoria?' Many of the emergent did not speak English and made apologetic gestures, but a cool woman's voice said:

'This, Mr Enderby, is most certainly not all right for Victoria.' Enderby blinked at this apparition, Mrs What's-her-name of *Fem*, racing ace's widow, in semi-formal pale apple-green taffetas, sheathed at the front, and three-quarter-length Persian lamb jacket, marcasite clip as single fine dress-embellisher, tiny hoop ear-rings of marcasite, marcasite-coloured glacé kid high-heels, penny-coloured hair cleanly glowing. Enderby's mouth opened sheepishly. 'If you got this train,' she said, 'you would be travelling to Waterloo and Kennington, Tooting Bec, ultimately Morden. From the look of you, you would probably be awakened at Morden. You wouldn't like Morden very much.'

'You,' said Enderby, 'should not be here. You should be at dinner somewhere.'

'I *was* at dinner,' she said. 'I've just come back from Hampstead.' The train-doors slid together and the train moved off into its tunnel, its wind stirring her hair and making her raise her voice, so that the Scots intonation became clearer than before. 'And,' she said, her sober green eyes appraising swaying Enderby, 'I'm on my way home to Gloucester Road. Which means we can take the same train and I can make quite sure that you alight at Victoria. From Victoria on you must be commended to the protection of whatever gods look after drunken poets.' She had in her something of the thin-lipped Calvinist; in her tone was no element of amused indulgence. 'Come,' she said, and she took Enderby's arm.

'If you don't mind,' said Enderby. 'If you'll excuse me just a moment –' Green looked at green. Enderby managed to trap the brief flow in his show handkerchief. 'Oh, God,' he said. 'Oh, Jesus, Mary and Joseph.'

'Come on,' she said. 'Walk. Take deep breaths.' She led

him firmly towards the Circle Line. 'You are in a bad way, aren't you?' All her perfume could not sweeten Enderby's shame.

5

Enderby was back in 81 Fitzherbert Avenue, thoroughly sobered at last by two slips on to his bottom on the frozen way from the station. On that same sore bottom he sat on the stairs, crying. This flight ran up, starting at the side of Enderby's flat's front door, to a landing with mirror and potted palm. Then came a dark and sinister stairway, uncarpeted, to the flat above, the home of the salesman and his woman. Enderby sat crying because he had forgotten his key. He had neglected, perhaps because flustered by Mrs Meldrum's visit that morning, to transfer the key from his sports-coat pocket to the corresponding pocket of the jacket of Arry's suit. It was now after one in the morning, too late to call on Mrs Meldrum to open up for him with her master. He had no money for a hotel room; it was too cold to sleep in a shelter on the esplanade; he did not fancy begging a cell at the police station (there were criminal-looking coppers there, with wide-boy tashes). It was best to sit here on the third step up, overcoated and muffled, crying and smoking alternately.

Not that he had much left to smoke. Mrs Whatever-her-name-was of *Fem* had taken his remaining packet of ship's Woodbines (she was out of them and smoked nothing else) as a reward for her stoic Scots toleration of his wanting to be sick on the deck of the train all the way to Victoria. Enderby had five Senior Service to last him till the late winter dawn. He cried. He was weary, far beyond sleepiness. It had been a long and eventful day, excruciatingly attritive. Even on his homeward coastward train journey the entire coach had seemed to be full of wet-mouthed Irishmen singing. And now the cold stair, the long vigil. He howled like a moon-bemused hound-dog.

The door of the flat above opened creakily. 'Is that you,

Jack?' whispered the woman's voice, huskily. 'Have you come back, Jack?' Her vowels were not unlike Arry's: uvyer coom buck juck. 'I'm sorry, Jack,' she said. 'I didn't mean what I said, love. Come on to bed, Jack.'

'It's me,' said Enderby. 'Not him. Me. Without a key,' he added.

'Who are you?' asked the woman. The bulb of the landing light had long burnt out, months ago, unreplaced by Mrs Meldrum. Neither could see the other.

'Him from downstairs,' said Enderby, falling easily into demotic. 'Not him as you live with.'

'He's gone off,' came the voice down the stair-well. 'He's always said he would and now he's done it. We had a bit of a barney.'

'That's right,' said Enderby.

'What do you mean that's right? We had a bit of a barney and now he's gone off. I bet he's gone to that bitch down by the Ornamental Gardens.'

'Never mind,' said Enderby. 'He'll come back. They always do.'

'He won't. Not tonight he won't. And I'm frightened up here on my own.'

'What are you frightened of?'

'Of being on my own. Like I said. In the dark, too. It went out while we was having this barney and I couldn't see to hit him. Have you got a bob you can let me have till first thing tomorrow morning?'

'Not a sausage,' said Enderby proudly. 'I blued it all on booze in town. I think I'd better come up there,' he added, bold. 'I could sleep on the couch or something. I forgot my key, you see. It's a damn nuisance.'

'If you come up here you'd better not let Jack get hold of you.'

'Jack's gone off with this bitch down by the Ornamental Gardens,' said Enderby.

'Ah. So you seen him, did you? I thought as much. You can see the black at her roots, bitch as she is.'

'I'm coming up now,' said Enderby. 'Then you won't be

frightened of being on your own. You've got a couch up there, have you?' said Enderby, rising in pain and crawling up the stairs.

'If you think you're going to get in bed with me you've got another think coming. I've finished with all men.'

'I've no intention of getting into bed with you,' said indignant Enderby. 'I just want to lie down on the couch. I don't really feel all that good.'

'You needn't be so bloody well on your bloody high horse. I've been in bed with better men than what you'll ever hope to be. Careful,' she said, as Enderby kicked the metal pot of the palm on the landing. He clambered blind up the second flight, hugging the banister. At the top he collided with a warm bosomy shape. 'You can cut that out for a start,' she said. 'A bit too forward you are for a start.' She sniffed briskly. 'That scent's very expensive,' she said. 'Who you been with, eh? Still waters run deep, if you're really who you say you are, meaning him that lives down there.'

'Where is it?' groped Enderby. 'I just want somewhere to lie down.' His hands felt the softness and width of a sofa, the continuum broken by bottle-shapes (they clanked) and a half-full chocolate box (rustled). 'Lay down,' he corrected himself, to be more matey.

'Make yourself comfortable,' she said, bloody sarky. 'If you want anything don't hesitate to ring. At what hour of the morning would you like your morning tea?' she said, in a hot-potato chumble. 'Men,' she said, going apparently, to her bedroom. She made a contemptuous noise, worthy of Enderby himself, leaving him to the dark.

Chapter Four

1

He awoke with first light to the xylophone of milk bottles and impotent rasping of self-starters. He smacked his lips and clacked his tongue on his hard palate, feeling his mouth like – the vulgar simile swam up from his vulgar pub-crawl – an all-in wrestler's jock-strap. The vulgar simile put fingers to its nose in the gesture his stepmother had called 'fat bacon', made the old Roman sign, raspberried, and clambered off up the wall like a lizard. Enderby in his overcoat felt cold and grubby, matching the room that now emerged like a picture on a television screen when the set has at last warmed up. With the picture, noise: that woman's snoring from the next room. Enderby listened, interested. He had never realized that women could snore so loud. His stepmother had, of course, been able to blast a roof off, but she had been unique. Unique? He remembered some lavatorial writing or other about all stepmothers being women or all women stepmothers or something, and then the whole day came back, certainly not a dull day, and he caught quite clearly the name of the widow who had given him tea and taken him to the Victoria tube-stop: Vesta Bainbridge. Shame warmed all Enderby's body and then hunger hammered at him, as at a door. The shameful day marched by briskly, its nostrils widened in a silly smirk, and it carried a banner of St George. It noisily tramped off to stand at ease behind the gimcrack sideboard. Enderby put on his spectacles, seeing beer bottles and old *Daily Mirror*s with painful clarity, then creaked, groaning, to the kitchenette. This was full of small square platters that had held TV meals, also empty milk bottles with crusty archipelagoes inside them. Enderby drank water from the tap. He opened the cupboard, wiping his mouth on a dish-cloth, and found gherkins. He ate some of these crisp slugs and soon felt better.

Before leaving he called on his hostess, but she lay sprawled over the double bed, uncovered, working hard at sleep. Her bubs, like blancmanges not properly set, shivered gently under the translucent nightgown as a lorry went by. Black smoke of hair over her face lifted and fell, obedient to her snore. Enderby covered her with the eiderdown, bowed, and left. She was not so old, he decided. A fat stupid girl not really capable of ill-nature. She had given Enderby shelter; Enderby would not forget.

As Enderby went downstairs he met his own milkman: a pint for Enderby's door, a half-pint for the foot of the stairs. The milkman leered and double-clacked his tongue. So many dawns, so many betrayers. Enderby had an idea. 'Had to sleep up there,' he said. 'Locked myself out. Do you know anything about locks?'

'Love laughs at locksmiths,' said the milkman sententiously. 'I'll just see if I've got a bit of wire.'

A minute later the postman came with Littlewood's coupons for upstairs, nothing for Enderby. 'That's not quite the way,' he said critically. 'Let me have a try.' He breathed heavily over the lock, probing and fiddling. 'Coming,' he panted. 'Half a tick.' The lock sprang, Enderby turned the knob, the door opened.

'Very much obliged,' he said, 'to both you gentlemen.' He had not relished the prospect of going to see Mrs Meldrum. He gave them his last coppers and entered.

Ah, but it was a relief to be back. Enderby stripped off his overcoat and hung it by its left shoulder on the hook in the tiny hall. He took off, with slightly greater care, the suit he had borrowed from Arry and rolled it neatly in a ball. He placed this, pending the returning of it, on the unmade bed, and then he put on his turtle-neck sweater. He was dressed now for work. His bare legs twinkled into the living-room and at once he scented change. There was a letter on the table, unstamped, and the table itself had been cleared of yesterday morning's dirty dishes. Enderby kicked on the electric fire and sat down to read, his brow troubled. The letter was from Mrs Meldrum.

Dear Mr E,

You will forgive me taking a look round when you was out, as I have every right being the landlady when all said and done. Well, you have got the place disgraceful no two ways about it, what with the bath full of pieces of poetry which was never the intention of them who make baths and have them fitted in. And the carpets not swept neither, I would be ashamed to have to show anybody round it. Well, what I said still hold water, that the rent goes up from next month and you been lucky to have it so cheap for so long, what with prices of things going up everywhere. If you dont like it you know what to do, I have others who will *keep the place proper* only too anxious to move in next week. You need somebody to look after you and no mistake, it is not natural for a man of your age and with your education as you say you have, living on his own and nobody to look after the house. To be blunt about it and not to shut up about what needs to be spoke out loud you need to get married before you sink to rack and ruin, which is the true opinion of many as I have spoke to.

Yours respctfly

W. Meldrum. (Mrs)

So. Enderby scratched his knee bitterly. That's what they wanted, was it? Enderby looked after, the dishes washed properly, the beds made regularly, the bathroom a pretty dream of a place with glaucous curtains and brushes for back and nails, nylon bristles with plastic fish-shape handles, the bath always waiting for a pink healthy tubber singing la-la-la through the steam. And, for hubby Enderby, a den to write his precious poetry in, a hobby for hubby. No. Bird-voices started in his head: prudence-preaching pigeons, cautioning rooks: beware of meadows, widows. Act act act, called the ducks: drain the sacrament of choice. 'This is my choice,' said Enderby firmly, as he went to the kitchen to get breakfast (that bitch Mrs Meldrum had washed his dishes!) and brew up stepmother's tea. He would be true to that archetypal bitch, his father's second wife. She had made his life a misery; he would give no other woman that privilege.

And yet. And yet. Enderby had his breakfast of dry bread, strawberry jam, and tea, then went to his workshop. His papers lay untouched by Mrs Meldrum; his table with its legs specially shortened awaited him by the hollow seat. *The Pet Beast* was growing slowly; the volume of fifty poems, planned for the autumn, was nearly complete. The first job to be cleared out of the way was the composing of a new love lyric for the *Arry to Thelma sequence*. Enderby felt guilty about the state of Arry's suit. It had, inexplicably, collected mud round the knees; a lapel had been incontinently soiled; the knife-crease had, with incredible speed, become blunted. Arry should be mollified with something really good. He had been complaining about the subject-matter of Enderby's offerings: too many kitchen similes, the appeal to her hard heart too indirect. She had, Arry swore, been reading these poems aloud to the car salesmen, and they had been yak-yakking at them. Enderby must write something very direct, not crude, mind, but direct, telling her what Arry desired to do with her, something that she would keep under her pillow and blush when she drew it (scented with her scent) out. Enderby thought, sitting on his throne, that he might have something suitable in stock. He rummaged in the bath and found certain very early lyrics. Here was one he had written at the age of seventeen. 'The Music of the Spheres', it was called.

> I have raised and poised a fiddle
>   Which, will you lend it ears,
> Will utter music's model:
>   The music of the spheres.

> By God, I think not Purcell
>   Nor Arne could match my airs.
> Perfect beyond rehearsal
>   My music of the spheres.

Not that its virtue's vastness –
　　The terror of drift of stars.
For subtlety and softness
　　My music of the spheres.

The spheres that feed its working,
　　Their melody swells and soars
On thinking of your marking
　　My music of the spheres.

This musing and this fear's
Work of your maiden years.
Why shut longer your ears?
Look, how the live earth flowers!
The land speaks my intent:
Bear me accompaniment.

That, addressed to a supposed virgin, was manifestly
absurd for Thelma. And was not that spherical imagery
perhaps too gross for a barmaid brought up, one presumed,
respectably? Dirty jokes in the bar were one thing, but
dirty literature, even the most factitious suggestion of its
presence, was another. His stomach, still sore, attested
this.

Seventeen. The date of composition was at the foot of
the manuscript. To whom had he written that? He
brooded, scratching. To nobody, he decided glumly. But
had he not dreamed, at that romantic age, of some willow-
wand creature who, though of infinite refinement and
smelling sweet as May, would not be offended by this all
too decipherable symbolism of importunacy? He had
shaped this girl in his heart, as mystics shape God, in terms
of what she should not be, namely his stepmother; then
her positive image had arisen by dint of long brooding on
her negative attributes. She had come in a dream then,
slender and laughing and, above all, *clean. Not* a widow:
he refused to allow this re-issue of the image to take on
the colours and scents of Mrs Bainbridge.

He sighed, then began, very deliberately and coldly, as a
pure poetic exercise, to write a very erotic poem from Arry
to Thelma, full of breasts and thighs and panting longing.

When he had finished he set it aside to cool, then he went on with his building of the labyrinth, home of the Pet Beast.

2

This was the order of a usual Enderby day: he would rise at dawn or just after, winter and summer alike; he would breakfast, defecate, and then work, sometimes beginning his work while actually defecating; at ten-fifteen he would shave and prepare to go out, sometimes with a shopping-reticule; at ten-thirty he would leave the flat, walk seawards, buy a loaf, feed the gulls; immediately after that he would take his morning whisky with the aged and dying or, if Arry were not at work, with Arry in the Freemason's Arms; sometimes he would visit Arry in his kitchens, and Arry would give him scraps for his larder – a turkey-carcass, a few slices of fat pork, a bit of scrag-end for Sunday's meal; Enderby would then do such shopping as was needed – a loaf for himself, potatoes, ten cigarettes, pickles, a small meat-pie, a fourpenny custard; back home he would prepare his meal, or, if something cold was left over from the day before, eat at once, working while he ate; he would then loll somnolent in a chair or even, rolling dressed into bed, deliberately sleep. Then back to the lavatory for the last long stint of the day; after that the remains of his earlier meal, or bread with some cheap relish; stepmother's tea as a nightcap; bed. A way of life which harmed no one. Sometimes the caprices of the Muse would disrupt this pattern by hurling poems – fragmentary or fully-formed – at Enderby; then, in mid-whisky, in bed, cooking, toiling at the structures of non-lyrical works, he would have to write down at once to her hysterical or coldly vatic or telegraphic dictation. He respected his Muse but was frightened of her whims: she could be playful kitten or tiger fully-clawed, finger-sucking idiot child or haughty goddess in Regency ball-gown; her moods, like her visits, were unpredictable. More predictable were his other visitants – dyspepsia in its various forms, wind, hiccoughs. Between dispensations of celestial and visceral afflation he lived his quiet days, a solitary man, harmless. Letters and visitors rarely disturbed his door, news from the dangerous world never intruded. His dividends and tiny royalties were paid straight into the bank; the bank he visited once a month only, humbly waiting with his cash cheque made out neatly for twenty-odd pounds behind bull-necked publicans and ascetic-faced butchers who paid in, inexplicably, dull mounds of copper that took long to count. He envied nobody except the great proved dead.

His routine, already disturbed by the disastrous London trip, was further disturbed by a consequence of that trip, namely the arrival of a big parcel. The address-panel had *Fem* printed on it and the picture of a well-groomed though moronic-faced young woman, evidently a typical *Fem*-reader. Enderby, who had been deep in his poem, received the parcel trouserless and open-mouthed, then ran into the living-room with a thudding heart to open it up. There was a contract for him to sign and a brief letter from Mrs Bainbridge telling him that here was a contract to sign and here were copies of past issues of *Fem*. She wrote in thick long-strokes, was formal and business-like, but had allowed her scent to inspissate, most delicately, the writing-paper. Enderby had little nose, but he caught her very feminine image very clearly. So.

Enderby knew little of magazines. As a boy he had read *Film Fun* and *Funny Wonder*. As a young man he had known poetry periodicals and waspish left-wing week-end reviews. In the Army he had seen such things as the troops read. In professional waiting-rooms he had sat stony-faced over *Punch*. He was aware of a postwar rash of cheap journals and wondered at their range of specialization and at the number of cults they seemed to serve. There were two or three, he knew, wholly devoted to some dead film-star who had become a sort of corn-god; he had seen others which, severally, glorified young living louts with guitars

– presumably what Mrs Bainbridge had called pop-singers. There was evidently a strong religious hunger among young girls which these poor simulacra and their press-priests alone seemed available to feed. There was also, among these same young girls, money crying to be spent, for it seemed that in this age of specialists only the un-skilled and witless were at a premium. But the dreaming wives had money also. *Fem* fought screaming for their sixpences, trying to elbow out *Womanly*, kick *Lovely* in the teeth, rip the corsets off *Wifey* and tear out the hair of *Blondie* by its black roots.

He sat down eagerly to read *Fem*. Time passed, lost for ever, never to be redeemed, as he snorted adenoidally over its contents. The cover had a girl's face, generically and boringly lovely. The cover of each issue, he noted, flicking through the pile on his knees, had a young woman's face, probably always the same one, though he could not be certain. The covers of magazines for men, he fancied, pre-ferred to exploit woman from the neck down. A fair divi-sion. Enderby read readers' letters: somebody's little girl asked if God lived in an aeroplane; how to turn an old jam-jar into an elegant vase by using four different shades of nail-varnish (total cost 8s. 6d.); that sweet grateful smile was all the reward she could ask for her act of charity; the budgerigar of Mrs F. (Rotherham) could say 'Dolly loves Mummy'; how stupid men could be, couldn't they, wanting to keep potatoes in a kitchen-drawer! (Enderby read this gravely puzzled: why was that stupid?) There was a serial story called 'For Ever and a Day', illustrated opulently with a ravishing but doubtful bride. A five-page article demonstrated that it did not cost *very* much more to make your own disc-cabinet (or to get husband or boy-friend to make it) than to buy it in a shop. There were short stories called 'Heart Afire'. 'Why Did You Leave Me?', 'I Thee Wed', 'Hello, Romance', mostly garnished with pictures of couples glued together, upright. A vital-warming religious column by a popular young pop-singing parson was followed by a feature on 'Our Queen's Dogs'.

There was a chilling clinical chat on tumours, there were articles on stiletto heels, marmalade-making, being a radiant bride. Enderby sat absorbed for a long time in a Special Cookery Supplement, seeing at last a means of improving his diet (he would try Orange Goody tomorrow). He was shocked and touched by letters sent to Millicent Goodheart, a blue-haired lady with sharp red talons and a gentle smile: 'He said it was artificial respiration, but now I find I am to have his child'; 'I have only been married three months but I have fallen in love with my husband's father'. Enderby nodded approvingly at the good sense of the replies. She should not have done it; I'm terribly sorry for you, my dear, but you must remember marriage is for keeps.

Dusk fell while he was still reading, with much more reading still to do. He stole to the light-switch, feeling guilty, excusing himself for this long soaking: after all, he was going to write for them, he had to know their tastes. His belly growled its neglect. Enderby had nothing in the flat except bread, jam, pickles; he must go out and buy something. He rather fancied a dish concocted by Gillian Frobisher, Head of *Fem's* Cookery Department: Spaghetti Fromaggio Surprise.

Enderby went out with his shopping-net and returned with a pound of spaghetti, a quarter of cheese, and a large garlic for fourpence. (The recipe gave the alternative of two large onions, but Enderby had an obscure repugnance to entering a greengrocer's just to ask for two onions; garlic was a different matter, being exotic.) Panting with excitement, he took the relevant issue of *Fem* into the kitchen and followed the instructions slavishly. 'Enough for four', he read. He was but one man alone, himself, he, hungry Enderby. He must divide everything, then, by four. He took the pound of spaghetti and broke the brittle sticks into small pieces. He took his frying pan (pity that the recipe asked for a large deep one; still, never mind) and poured one tablespoonful of olive oil. (He had about a cupful of this in his cupboard, saved from sardine tins.)

He threw in about a quarter of the spaghetti, lit the gas, and cooked it slowly, turning and stirring. He then added two cupfuls of water, remembering that he was to divide by four, so threw some of the water out again. He turned, breathing heavily, to *Fem*, while the pan gently simmered. Grated cheese. He grated some with Mrs Meldrum's nutmeg-grater and threw it into the mixture. Now this question of onion or garlic. 'Two large onions chopped', said Gillian Frobisher, or 'garlic to taste'. Enderby looked at his garlic, stronger, he knew, than onions; perhaps this one would be equivalent to two of those. Should he skin it? No. The goodness was in the skin: potatoes, for instance. He sliced the garlic warpwise, then woofwise, then threw the bits into the simmering pan. And now. A greased dish. He found a cloudy Pyrex on the shelf, and he liberally coated its inside with margarine. He now had to transfer the stuff from the pan into the Pyrex. He had some difficulty in turning it out: it had stuck to the pan for some reason, and he had to gouge vigorously to detach what was willing to be detached. He flopped the mixture into the dish. 'Top with sour cream', said Gillian. There was no sour cream, but plenty of sour milk, greenish on top. He crowned the dish with generous curds, then lit the oven. It had to cook to a slow heat therein, about twenty minutes. Groaning, he placed the dish on the oven shelf, kicked the black door shut, wiped one hand on the other. There.

Damn. He had not, he realized, consistently divided by four. Never mind. And perhaps the spaghetti was meant to turn black. He had heard of smart restaurants where things were deliberately burned before one's eyes, as one sat cool and well-dressed at table. He went back to the electric fire to continue his reading of yet another issue of *Fem*. After gazing transfixed at a soup advertisement showing a cup of cold blood, and an egg advertisement in which a pallid yolk hung over the edge of the fish-slice that lifted it aslant from the pan, ready to flop in pale yellow, Enderby settled to a story called 'You're Not My Darling'. This was about an air-hostess who fell in love with the captain of her aircraft, a theme new to Enderby. He gawped on long past Gillian Frobisher's twenty minutes of cooking-time, came to with a hiccoughing start, then drew his Spaghetti Fromaggio Surprise out of the oven. Its name was not inept. He sat down to it, and savoured mingled hues of burnt farinacity and shouting brutal garlic, loud and hot as an acetylene blast; the tone of these hues was a tired tepidity. He had not quite expected this; still presumably Gillian Frobisher knew what she was doing. He ate dutifully, with many draughts of cold water. He must learn the tastes of his prospective readers.

3

Enderby awoke in the middle of the night, jerked with sergeant's roughness out of an odd dream about pokers. The pain was ghastly though it did not feel dangerous. Enderby's head was clear enough as he crawled out; he even remembered the name of the bloody woman. Gillian Frobisher. There was a photograph of her in one of the Cookery Supplements: a crisp handsome Jewish girl with an impossibly clean frying-pan. If he ever got hold of her, Enderby vowed, he would dirty that frying-pan and no mistake. He had been taken advantage of.

Bicarb shattered the pain and sent its fragments flying on the wind. Enderby sat down in his living-room and switched on the electric fire. It was, said his watch, three-ten. A ghastly hour. There was noise upstairs, a woman's voice shouting as through a muslin strainer, 'Get out, do you hear? Get out, you pig.' Then the rumble of a man's voice and the tread of heavy shoes. Jack was, apparently, back. Soon the woman's abuse grew fainter and was curiously articulated, as though from the side of the mouth, in brief bursts. Later the springs began to bounce. Enderby picked up the contract from the sofa, wondering whether he ought to sign or not. To produce a block of rhymed clichés weekly, sententious vapourings about the stars so far away, the feel of chubby baby arms round mummy's neck, being kind to those in trouble – was not this prostitution? The poems he was writing to Thelma from Arry were not that, whatever they were. Where they were not straight-forwardly sensual they were gently ironical: he needn't be ashamed of them. But this proposal of Mrs Bainbridge – was it not the fiend luring him away from proper art with the chink of guineas that, anyway, would be all for Mrs Meldrum? Enderby walked into the bathroom to survey all the tumbled years' work in the bath. He had moved, over the last decade and a half, from town to town and flat to flat, but he had thought that here he could settle it. It was not good to change one's workshop in the middle of a major creation. The mood altered under the subtle influence of a new place, the continuity was broken. And then the thought of packing all this bathful into suitcases – mice, breadcrusts and all. One lost things, one was tempted to throw things away. But Enderby, standing in bare feet, thinking hard, wondered whether perhaps he ought to make the sacrifice, move on up or down the coast, away from Mrs Meldrum and – a much more dangerous person, the widow to be enjoyed in the meadow – Mrs Bainbridge, coolly elegant, self-confessed admirer of his poems.

He saw that to some extent he was rationalizing his fear of a relationship with a woman, the possibility that what was now finishing upstairs might soon start downstairs. And yet a worry that had often nagged him – especially after scurrying away from the verge of other relationships – was that this very desire to remain uncommitted might impair his work. Love of woman had always, traditionally, played a large part in the lives of the poets. Look at Goethe, for instance, who had to have a new love affair before he could begin a new lyric. Enderby, in so far as German culture had played any part in his development, had chosen to be influenced by a much dourer personality – Schopenhauer. Spengler, too, with his promise of the undergoing of evening lands, had had something to say to him. He had needed to invoke both philosophers before writing a poem about sex and other people. He remembered the typical evening of wartime, blackout in the garrison town, horny hands groping for giggling bodies in the dark.

> Nymphs and satyrs, come away.
>> Faunus, laughing from the hill,
> Rips the blanket of the day
>> From the paunch of dirty Will.
>
> Each projector downs its snout,
>> Truffling the blackened scene,
> Till the *Wille's* lights gush out
>> *Vorstellungen* on the screen.
>
> Doxies blanch to silverwhite;
>> All their trappings of the sport,
> Lax and scattered, in this light
>> Merge and lock to smooth and taut.
>
> See! The rockets shoot afar!
>> Ah! The screen was tautest then.
> Tragic the parabola
>> When the sticks reel down again.

That was no romantic attitude to sex. Love, Schopenhauer had seemed to say, was one of the perpetual cinema performances or *Vorstellungen* organized by the evil Will, projectionist as well as manager, and these slack bodies of gum-chewing gigglers were made into stiff shining screens for the projection of what looked like reality, value. But the deflation, the reeling to earth after coitus, was frightful, and one saw the inflated words of desire – so soon after their utterance – for what they really were. The casual images of onanism could not be hurt, could not be lied to.

Enderby went back to the living-room. Heartburn, like labour pains, had started again. There was plenty of bicarbonate solution still in the glass, so, in less than half a minute, Enderby was able to growl it away hollowly:

Grerrrbrogharrrgawwwwwpffffffh.

There was an immediate response from upstairs: a shoe

of admonition was banged three times. Enderby looked up to the noise meekly, as to chiding God. It was time that he left. He heard what sounded like, 'Shut up, Enderby,' and then the woman's voice said, 'Leave him alone. He can't help it.' A row of indistinguishable words then began, ending with Jack shouting, 'Oh, he did, did he? And whose idea was that? False little bitch, aren't you?' The sadness, see, after coition. Enderby shook his head sadly and went back to bed. He would give a week's notice to Mrs Meldrum; he would sign no contract with Mrs Bainbridge. Mrs Meldrum could have her smiling bald bath-taking young man on an expense account; if there was no weekly poem from Enderby it was not likely that the strong-stomached readers of *Fem* would pine away.

4

That settled it. Morning brought a letter from Vesta Bainbridge:

Dear Mr Enderby,

Well, you do seem to have been beating it up pretty tidily on your visit to London. I have only now managed to get hold of an evening paper of that memorable day which, albeit briefly, makes it reasonably clear that you went out of your way to antagonize a certain knightly patron of your art. I must confess that, in some ways, I admire your independent attitude, though God knows how any poet nowadays can afford that Byronic luxury. Sir George, I hear, is very angry and hurt. What came over you? I just don't understand, but then I'm only a very ordinary person with no great claim to intellect, and I would never be so presumptuous as to think myself capable of fathoming a poet's brain. The fact is, and I daresay you'll hear this from your own publisher fairly soon, that your name smells to heaven with Goodby's for Good Books, so watch out.

In the circumstances, I think it would be a good plan to print your weekly effusion under or over a pseudonym. This would also give us a chance to prettify the feature with a photograph of some long-haired male model with a quill in his hand and his dreamy eyes up to heaven – you know what I mean: *The Poet*: what every housewife thinks a poet ought to look like. Can you suggest a pseudonym? Do sign that contract and return it. I *did* enjoy our tea together.

Yours,
Vesta Bainbridge

Enderby trembled with rage as he crushed the good quality writing-paper. He hurled the letter into the lavatory-pan and then pulled the chain, but the thing was too thick to flush down. He had to pick it out wet and then take it into the kitchen and put it in an old cardboard rubbish-box along with condensed-milk tins, fishbones, potato peelings and tea leaves. After an hour of brooding and trying to carry on with his work, he felt a compulsion to read it again and did so, all smothered with tea-leaves as it was. Beating pretty tidily London memorable day albeit briefly independent attitude Byronic what every housewife thinks Vesta Bainbridge. He stood frowning, reading it in the tiny hallway, squinting at the words because it was dark there. There was a sudden double-beating on the door, as on a gorilla's chest, and Enderby looked up, surprised. 'Come out, Enderby,' cried the voice of Jack. 'I want a word with you, Enderby, you bloody poet.'

'For cough,' snarled Enderby, with much of his step-mother's spirit and intonation.

'Come out of there, Enderby. Come out and fight like a man. Open that door and let me bash you, you bastard.'

'No,' said Enderby, 'I won't. If I opened that door I'd regret it. I know I would. I don't want your blood on my hands.'

'Enderby,' shouted Jack, 'I'm giving you fair warning. Open up there and let me do you in, you fornicating poet. I'll give you sleeping with my wife, you false sod.'

'It's not your wife,' said Enderby. 'And I slept on the couch. Somebody's been telling lies about me. Now you clear off before I get angry.'

'Open that door, Enderby, please,' pleaded Jack's voice. 'I want to do you in, it's only right and fair as I should, you bastard, and I'm already late for work. Open up and let's get it over.' And he thumped with both hands on the door. From above the woman's voice could be heard, and there was something about it to show clearly the image of a woman in nightdress and curlers. 'Stop it, Jack,' she cried. 'You're only making a fool of yourself.'

'Fool of myself, eh? We'll soon see. Now you shut up. You've had your turn and now it's going to be Enderby's turn.' He renewed the thundering. Enderby went to the kitchen and came back with his hare-eviscerating knife. 'Open up, Enderby. Time's getting on, you bastard.' Enderby opened up.

Jack was a youngish tough man with lined cheeks and eyes the colour of urine. If hairs be wires, black wires grew in his head. He had both fists ready, with the thumbs pitiably tucked inside. Enderby had been punched in London; he was not going to be punched here. He raised his knife. 'For cough,' he said.

'That's playing unfair,' said Jack. 'I meant clean bashing. That's not right when you get on to that stabbing lark. All I'm saying is, you leave her upstairs alone, see, and one bloody good bash in the chops and call it a day. You've no call to go fornicating with what's mine, as you ought to be first to admit. Now put that knife down like a man and take what's coming to you.'

'For cough,' said Enderby, in a murderer's stance. 'I hadn't got my key, that was all, and she let me sleep on the sofa. If you don't believe that you'll never believe anything.'

'I'll believe what I want to believe,' said Jack with great candour. 'I'm coming back to see you again. Don't think you've got away with this, because you haven't, Enderby, poet or no poet. I tell you that straight. I'm off to work now and late too, which is your fault and makes things worse.' With a sudden brisk jerk and stylish follow-through he wrested the knife from the grasp of Enderby.

'There,' he said proudly. 'Now you've had it.' Enderby swiftly slammed the door. 'I'll be back, Enderby,' called Jack. 'Make no mistake about it. You'll be done, no two ways about that, as you'll see.' He kicked Enderby's door and then thumped out of the house, crashing the great outer portal shut.

Enderby locked himself in the lavatory, trembling. *Canaille, canaglia,* with their bloody sex and blasted jealousy. Well, the time had come; all things pointed to it: out, out, out. Where to now? He sat on the seat and began to scribble: (a) Draw cash from bank; (b) Get map of south coast; (c) Send cheque and week's notice Mrs M.; (d) Write to Mrs B.; (e) see Arry. With this need to plan and the thought of the nightmare of packing still to come, he grew flustered. He tried to calm himself by writing a final consummatory poem for Arry, the end of the whole cycle. It reeked with hot hands, white flesh, hoarse desire, love, love, love. It had a certain cathartic effect on Enderby, like loud blasphemous obscenities.

> . . . And in that last delirium of lust
> Your image glows. Love is a blinding rain,
> Love crow all the cocks, love lays the dust
> Of this cracked crying throat whose thirst is pain. . . .

He wrote out a cheque for Mrs Meldrum, composed the curtest of farewells: 'Thank you for your unwanted solicitude. Take a week's notice. Yours etc.' To Mrs Bainbridge he wrote a courteous acknowledgement of her communications and regretted that, on maturer consideration, he found himself unable to find it in himself to meet the meagre poetic needs, if even these existed, of the readers of *Fem.* His compliments to Miss or Mrs Frobisher, if Mrs Bainbridge would be good enough to pass them on, and congratulations on possessing so tough-stomached a gang of followers of her culinary columns. He, Enderby, had, if it was of any interest to anyone, suffered greatly from her Spaghetti Fromaggio Surprise. He proposed to destroy the contract and distribute the copies of *Fem* to the poor.

He was hers sincerely. P.S. He was moving from the above address forthwith, whither he knew not yet. No point in her replying. Calmer now, Enderby shaved and prepared to go out. He would be safe so long as that shouter Jack was still at work.

5

Arry, in grubby cook's white, complete with white necktie and white mushroom hat, stood at the bar of the Freemason's Arms, taking time off from his kitchens. He greeted Enderby with no enthusiasm but, without asking or being asked, ordered a double whisky for him. 'That suit,' he said, 'were a right bloody mess. Ad to send it tert cleaner's.' He drank off a good three-quarters of a pint of brown ale mixed with bitter.

'I'm sorry,' said Enderby. 'It won't happen again. I shan't have to borrow from you again. I'm leaving."

'Leavin'? Goin'? Not coomin' back 'ere naw mawr?'

'That's right.'

Arry looked solemn, but that stiff crust of his expression seemed to be hiding a tiny feeling of relief; a whiff of relief escaped as through a steam-hole in the crust. He said:

'Where to?'

'I don't know,' said Enderby. 'Somewhere else along the coast. It doesn't matter where, really.'

'Thee get as far aweeeeeh,' advised Arry, prolonging his vowels, as in some primitive language, 'far aweeeeeh,' to emphasize the distance, 'far aweeeeeh,' by onomatopoeic suggestion, 'as tha can bloody get. That's naht 'ere, naht for nobody. Coom back 'ere,' he said, 'never naw mawr.' He looked with gloom at the lesbians in the corner – Gladys in glasses and leopard-skin pants sly-cuddling cross-eyed Prudence – and then with compassion at Enderby.

'This is to say good-bye, really,' said Enderby, 'and to hope that your suit prospers.'

'It'll be aw right when it cooms back fromt cleaner's.'

'I meant the other suit,' said Enderby, 'the Arry to

Thelma suit. I've brought one more poem for you, the very last of the cycle. If this doesn't do the job, nothing will.' He took the folded sheet from his pocket.

Arry shook his head. 'Naht doin',' he said, 'naht doin' at all. It were a bloody wester mah tahm.'

'My time, too,' said Enderby.

'Wan 'and int till,' said Arry, 'and toother betwinner legs. No good to man nor flamin' beast that Thelma. Oo's tecken no notice er naht av doon forrer.'

'Well,' sighed Enderby, 'that's how it is. Nobody wants poetry nowadays. All wasted.' He prepared to rip up his final fiery offering.

'Weren't wested,' said Arry. 'Ot stooff, wan or two were. *Ah* lakhed 'em. Boot oo,' he said, 'didn't 'ave bloody intelligence.' He put out a clean cook's hand to rescue Enderby's poem. He took the folded sheet and unfolded it with wan interest. He pretended to read it, then put it into his trouser-pocket. Enderby bought him a pint of brown ale and bitter. Enderby said:

'Since I've lived here you're the only one I've been in any way friendly with. That's why I wanted to shake hands with you before I go.'

'All sheck 'ands wi' thee,' said Arry, and did so. 'When will yer be clearin' off?'

'I've got to pack,' said Enderby. 'And then I've got to decide where I'm going to. Tomorrow, I should think. While Jack's out at work.'

'Oo's Jack?'

'Oh, yes, sorry. The chap who lives upstairs. He thinks I've been carrying on with the woman he lives with.'

'Ah,' said Arry, shaking his head, then looking at Enderby with renewed compassion. 'Get away as soon as yer can,' said Arry. 'Shoove yer things in a bag and then get to Victoria Station. On Victoria Station there's nameser places stoock oop on indiketters. Teck thy choice, lad. There's plenty on 'em. You choose wanner them and go straight to it. All places is the same nowadays,' he said. 'The big thing to do is to kip movin'. And,' he asked, 'what will yer do when yeu've getten wherever yer goin'? Wilt kip on wi' same game?'

'It's all I can do,' said Enderby. 'Writing verse is all I'm cut out for.'

Arry nodded and finished his pint, the fourth since Enderby's entrance. 'Dawn't write too mooch abaht spaghetti, then,' he said, frothily. 'Leave spaghetti to them as knaws summat abaht it.' He shook hands with Enderby once more. 'Moost get back now,' he said, 'tert bloody job. Special loonch for Daughters of Temperance.' He spaced out the words like a poster. 'Luke after yerself,' said Arry. He waved a white cook's arm from the door and then went out. Spaghetti coiled, puzzled, in Enderby's brain. Then a horrid thought struck him. He finished his whisky palpitating but then calmed down. He might have sent it to Mrs Meldrum. But no, he distinctly remembered pinning a cheque to a quarter-sheet of writing-paper. But that made no difference, did it? That might still have got into the wrong envelope. He'd better get out of here very, very quickly.

As he panted towards his packing down the esplanade, the gulls wheeled and wailed and climbed the blue wall of the marine winter day. For two days now he had forgotten to feed them. They planed, complained. Greedy beady eyes. Ungrateful birds. They mewed no farewell to Enderby; they would be there, waiting for his doles of bread, further up or down the coastline.

Chapter Five

1

Of what the world would call essentials, Enderby had few
to pack. It was the bathful of verse that was the trouble.
Kneeling in front of it, as though – and here he laughed
sardonically – he worshipped his own work, he began to
bundle it into the larger of his two suitcases, separating –
with reasonable care – manuscripts from sandwich-crusts,
cigarette-packets, and the cylinders of long-used toilet-
rolls. But he found so many old poems which he had quite
forgotten that he could not resist reading them through,
open-mouthed, as afternoon ticked on towards dusk. He
had modified drastically his original plan of departure, his
aim now being to catch some evening train (Jack permit-
ting) to Victoria, spend the night in a hotel, and then,
about midday, follow some new spoke to the south coast.
He had, he felt, to live near the sea, this being a great wet
slobbering stepmother or green dogmatic Church which
he could keep his eye on; nothing, at least, insidious about
it.

It was amazing what things he had written, especially
in his youth: pastiches of Whitman, Charles Doughty, an
attempted translation of the *Duino Elegies*, limericks,
even the beginning of a verse-play about Copernicus.
There was one sonnet in sprung rhythm and Alexandrines
which dated from the days of his love and envy of the
proletariat. He read the sestet with horror and wonder:

When the violet air blooms about him, then at last he can
    wipe
  His hands sheerfree of swink, monarch of hours ahead;
Hearty he eats and, full, he sits to pull at his pipe,
  Warm at the kitchen glow. The courts- and sports-news
    read,

> He argues, sups, in the Lion vault; to a plate of tripe
>   Or crisp chips home returns, then climbs to a dreamless
>   bed.

Dead on this homecoming cue Jack came home, his hands sheerfree of salesman's swink, ready for Enderby. Enderby was aroused from the past by the gorilla two-fist beat on the door.

'Come on, Enderby, out of it. On the job, Enderby. Come and be bashed, you poetic bloody nuisance.'

'Have you got my knife?'' asked Enderby, standing now behind his punished door.

'Your knife, eh? That's been put in a refuse-bin, you dirty mess as you are, you. There's going to be clean bashing only, you nasty deceitful thing. I'm giving you fair warning, Enderby. If you don't open up I'm going to get old Ma Meldrum's key. I'll say that you lost yours, lying like you lied, you nasty liar. Then I'll come in and do you. So open up like a sportsman and play the game and be bashed, you bugger, you.'

Enderby shivered with rage and immediately began to roam the flat, trembling, looking for some weapon. Meanwhile Jack, who should, by rights, have been fatigued by his work, hammered at the door and execrated nastily. In the bathroom Enderby cast around and his eyes momentarily softened as they lighted on his old friend, the lavatory-seat. It had always been somewhat loose; it was not difficult to wrench it from the pin that had held it to the pedestal. 'Coming,' called Enderby. 'Shan't be a minute.' He apologized to the wooden O as he pulled it roughly away, promising that soon he would write it a small ode of reparation. Armed with it he went to the door, pulled the door open and saw Jack's thumb-protecting fists ready for a fierce double-bang at the empty air.

'That's not fair,' he said, backing. 'You're not playing the game, Enderby. All I ask is a fair apology for ill-treating me as regards my own property.' ('Is that you back, Jack?' came the voice from above. 'Don't hurt him too hard, love.')

'There's nothing to apologize for,' said Enderby. 'If you don't believe what I told you you must take the consequences of your disbelief. I'm going to clonk you on the head with this seat here.'

'Not that,' said Jack, trying, on dancing feet, to get in odd punches. 'That's comic, that is, that's not decent. That's making a farce out of the whole thing.' Enderby parried the weak blows, slamming Jack's wrists hard with his wooden weapon. He drove him down the hallway towards the front door of the house, past the two spotted pictures on the wall, both of Highland scenery in wretched weather. Enderby raised the seat high, intended to hit Jack's wiry head with its hard border. He misjudged somewhat, and the seat came down to encircle Jack's face, so that Jack was framed like a most animated portrait in a bottom-shaped ring. His hands clawed at it, forgetting to chop at Enderby's own, which tugged down and down, Enderby's obscure aim being to pull Jack to the floor and then stamp on him. 'You bastard, you,' cried Jack. 'This isn't funny, this isn't, you sod.' He tried to lift off the wooden lei of bottom-polished smoothness, but Enderby's weight pulled down and down. 'All I ask,' panted Jack, 'is an apology for what you done, did. Give me that and I'll let you go.' Enderby swung round, still clinging to Jack's round pillory, and saw Jack's woman at the foot of the stairs. She was dressed like Hamlet in black tights, a black sweater above, inside which her bubs danced still from her descent.

'You,' sobbed Enderby, at his last gasp with all this effort, 'started all this. Tell him the truth.'

'He bashed me,' she said, 'and I did nothing wrong. Now it's only right that you get bashed.'

'Tell him the truth,' cried Enderby's dying voice.

'That won't make no difference to Jack,' she said. 'You've got to get done by Jack. Jack's like that, you see.'

'I want him to apologize,' cried Jack, still framed.

'There's nothing to apologize for,' gurgled Enderby's fading ration of air.

'Apologize for what you're doing now, then.'

'I'll stop it,' said Enderby. He let go of the wooden seat, and Jack, now pulling at nothing, went hurtling back to the hallstand, crashing into it and sending it over, still horse-collared. The little inlaid mirror tinkled; from the glove-drawer, suddenly opened, there issued letters, unforwarded, for people long shadily departed, and also highly coloured coupons representing, each, a fivepence rebate off a packet of soap-powder.

'Call it,' Enderby, bent double as though air were something to be sucked up from the floor, tried to say, 'Call it,' seeing Jack on the floor with lavatory collar still on lying beside, as a wooden mate, the crashed hall-stand, 'a day.'

'You come upstairs, love,' said the woman to Jack. 'You'll be tired after your hard day's work. I'll make you a nice cuppa.'

Jack got up, removed the collar and, panting still, handed it to Enderby. 'You got what was coming to you,' he said. 'I'm not one of those vindictive buggers, Enderby. Fair's fair's what I stand or fall by.' He dusted himself down with the hall-stand brush, still in his overcoat which was of a dull plum colour. 'Don't do it again, that's all I'm going to say now, and let it be a warning.' The woman, soothing, put her arms about him and began to lead him upstairs. Enderby, exhausted, entered his own flat, holding the lavatory-seat like a victor's wreath. It was a long long time since he'd exerted himself so much. He lay down for at least an hour on the floor of the living-room, seeing how dirty the carpet was. Under the couch were walnuts and bits of paper. He lay until the town-hall clock struck, from from afar, over the chill evening air of late January, the hour of seven. There was now no hope of leaving tonight.

When he felt better he got up from the floor and went into the kitchen to examine his store-cupboard. There was little point in, and little room for, taking these half-empty jars and bits of lard in paper, potatoes, cut spaghetti-sticks, mustard. He took down Mrs Meldrum's largest saucepan and prepared a stew of meat-paste, Oxo cubes, spaghetti, olive oil, spuds in jackets with dirt and all, pickled onions, cheese-heels, bread-crusts, dripping, half a meat pie, Branston sweet pickle, margarine, celery salt, water. At the back of the fast-emptying cupboard he found a neglected chicken carcass, a gift from Arry, which would go well. He left the stew to bubble, thrifty Enderby, and went back to the sorting and packing of his papers.

2

Enderby, fagged out by fighting, packing, and the thin and over-savoury stew he had cooked, slept later the following morning than he had intended. The work of packing and clearing-up was not yet finished. Both suitcases were crammed, but there were still many manuscripts to bundle together and put safe somewhere. Enderby, yawning, creased, and with hair in sleepy spikes, made tea with the remaining half-packet of Typhoo and coffee with the last few spoons of Blue Mountain. Taking in the milk he left a note of farewell for the milkman, several empty bottles, and a cash cheque for five shillings and fourpence. He then drank one cup of tea and emptied the rest down the lavatory, feeling the sense of virtue he always felt when he knew he had used what another man might well have wasted. Then he heated up last night's stew and felt further virtue when the gas failed half-way through the process. No waste there either. He switched on all the electric fires in the flat, ate breakfast, drank coffee, smoked. Then, in shirt and underpants (last night's nightwear, his pyjamas having been packed) he emptied the rubbish out of its cardboard box into a small dustbin outside the back-door. (Sunny, piercingly cold, gulls high-screaming.) He cleaned out this box with a copy of *Fem*, finding difficulty in dislodging corner-hugging mush of decayed peel and odd tea-leaf hieroglyphics, then lined it with two or three copies of the same magazine, collected handfuls of poems from the bath and packed them in tightly, covered with further *Fem*s then tied the box about with a discarded pair of braces and a long knotty link he made out of odd pieces of string that were lying around. He washed all dishes in (necessarily) cold water and packed them on their shelves. Then he had a cold and excruciating shave, washed quickly, and dressed in his daily working garb with corduroy trousers and a tie. The time was eleven-thirty. He could, he thought, soon now be off. The keys, of course. He went out into the hallway of the house, found that someone, probably Jack, had righted the crashed hall-stand, and then he put the keys in the glove-compartment. On a letter addressed to a long-left Mrs Arthur Porceroy (postmark 8.vi.51) he wrote, in inkpencil, KEYS EN-DERBY, and leaned this notice upright on the hallstand. While he was doing this the front door opened. A man looked in. He seemed to play an elaborate game of looking for someone everywhere except where someone was, his sad eyes roaming the entire hallway and then appearing at last to find Enderby. He nodded and smiled bleakly, as in modest self-congratulation on his success, and then said, 'Would I be addressing one of the name of Enderby?' Enderby bowed. 'Could I have the pleasure of a word with you?' the man asked. 'A question of poetry,' he added. He had a thin Uriah Heep voice. He was of less than medium height, had a long face and a fluff of whitish hair, wore a raincoat, was about Enderby's age.

'Who are you from?' asked Enderby sharply.

'From?' repeated the man. 'From nobody except me. Me being the name of Walpole. And coming to see you on a question of poetry. It's cold here in the hall,' he said. Enderby led the way into the flat.

Walpole sniffed the warm dry air, the lingering sour stew-smell, the raised dust, and then noticed Enderby's packed bags. 'Leaving, eh?' he said. 'Well, I only just got you in time, didn't I?'

'I've got to catch a train,' said Enderby, 'any minute now. Would you –?'

'Oh, I'll be quick,' said Walpole, 'very quick. What I

want to say is that I won't have you writing poetry to my wife.'

Enderby saw rush and then fade a quite unreasonable possibility. Then he smiled and said, 'I don't write poetry to anybody's wife.'

Walpole drew from his raincoat pocket a carefully folded and smoothed sheaf of sheets. 'This poetry,' he said. 'Look at it carefully and then tell me whether or not you wrote it.'

Enderby looked at it quickly. His handwriting. The Thelma poems. 'I wrote these, yes,' he said, 'but not on my own behalf. I wrote them at the request of another man. I suppose you could call him a client, really. You see, poetry is my profession.'

'If it's a profession,' said Walpole in all seriousness, 'does it have what you might call rules of professional etty kwett? More important than that, in a way of speaking, does it have a union?'

Enderby suddenly saw that he had been made a party to a proposed bed-breach. He said that he saw, ignoring Walpole's questions, saying, 'I see, I see. I'm really very sorry about all this. I knew nothing about it. I'm even more innocent than Arry. It just never crossed my mind – and I take it that it never crossed Arry's – that Thelma was a married woman.'

'Mrs Walpole,' said Walpole tautologically, 'is my wife. Thelma may or may not be her name, all according to whether she is on duty or not. At the moment she is not on duty. And this question of *Harry*' – he stressed the aitch pedantically – 'is a question that brings you in as a hypocrite and a liar, if you don't mind me saying so.' Walpole held up his hand as if taking the oath. 'I make use of those terms,' he said, 'out of reference to the conventionalities you yourself, as a boor Joyce, probably uphold. To me, in one manner of speaking, they have no proper relevance, being relics of boor Joyce morality.'

'I,' said Enderby warmly, 'object very strongly to being called a hypocrite and a liar, especially in my own house.'

'Clear your mind of cant,' said Walpole, whose reading was evidently wide. He straddled comfortably, raincoat-tails spread, in front of the electric fire. 'You are just leaving this place which is not a house and not, I presume, your property, and, moreover, what difference should it make to the effect of certain words on the individual brain whether those words are spoke in a church or in a lavatory, if you'll pardon the term, or, as it might be, here?' He made the knees-bend gesture of freeing a trouser-seat stuck in a rump-cleft.

The mention of church and lavatory went straight to Enderby's heart, also the invocation of logic. 'All right, then,' he said. 'In what way am I a hypocrite and a liar?'

'A fair question,' admitted Walpole. 'You are a hypocrite and a liar' – he pointed a *j'accuse* finger with forensic suddenness – 'because you hid your own desires under another man's cloak. Ah, yes. I have spoke to this man Harry. He admits to having sent up to Mrs Walpole plates of stewed tripe and, on one occasion, eels – both dishes to which she is not partial – but it was clear that that was in the way of colleagual friendliness, them both working in the same establishment. Both are workers, even though the place of their work is boor Joyce. Can you say the same for yourself?'

'Yes,' said Enderby, 'no.'

'Well, then,' continued Walpole, 'I have it on the word of Harry, who is a worker, that he had no adulterating intention in mind. To him it came as a shock, and I was there and I saw the shock as it came, that another man should be sending poetry to a married woman and signing it with another man's name, the name of a man who, still living in a capitalist society, is not in the same position to hit back as what *you* are.' Again the accusatory finger darted out like a chameleon's tongue.

'Why,' said stunned Enderby, aghast at such treachery on Arry's part, 'should not *he* be the liar and hypocrite? Why should you not believe me? Damn it all, I've only seen this woman once, and that was only to order a single whisky.'

'Single or double makes no difference,' said Walpole sagely. 'And there have been occasions when men, especially poets, have only seen a woman once (and I will thank you not to use that term in connexion with Mrs Walpole) or even not at all, and yet they have written reams and reams of poetry to her. There was the Italian poet who you may have heard of who wrote about Hell, and there again it was a married woman. He wrote about Hell, Mr Enderby, and not what you wrote in those shameful verses you have there and I would trouble you to hand back. There you have wrote about buttocks and breasts, which is not decent. I spent some time reading those poems, putting aside my other reading work to do so.' Enderby now detected, surfacing from the thin starved East Midland accent, the stronger tones of Anglo-Welsh. 'Indecencies,' said Walpole, 'that any man using to a married woman should be heartily ashamed of and should fear a judgement for.'

'This is absurd,' said Enderby. 'This is bloody nonsense. I wrote those poems at Arry's request. I wrote them in exchange for the loan of a suit and a few gifts of chicken and turkey carcasses. Does that not sound reasonable?'

'No,' said Walpole reasonably. 'It does not. You wrote these poems. You wrote of breasts and buttocks and even navels in connexion with Mrs Walpole and nobody else. And there the sin lies.'

'But damn it,' said angry Enderby, 'she's got them, hasn't she? She's the same as any other woman in that respect, isn't she?'

'I do not know,' said Walpole, stilling Enderby's rage with a choir-conductor's hand. 'I am no womanizer. I have had to work. I have had no time for the fripperies and dalliances of poetry. I have had to work. I have had no time for the flippancies and insincerities of women. I have had to work, night after night, after the labours of the day, reading and studying Marx and Lenin and the other writers who would lead me to a position to help my fellow-workers. Can you say as much? Where has your poetry led you? To this.' He swept a hand round Enderby's dusty living-room. 'Where have my studies led me?' He did not answer his own question; Enderby waited, but the question was definitely established as rhetorical.

'Look,' said Enderby, 'I've got to catch a train. I'm sorry that this has happened, but you can see it was all a misunderstanding. And you must take my assurance that I've had nothing to do socially with Mrs Walpole and very little more professionally. By "professionally",' added Enderby carefully, spying a possible misinterpretation, 'I mean, of course, in connexion with her profession as a barmaid.'

'That,' said Walpole, shaking his head, 'is not salaried, it is not a profession. Well,' he said, 'the question of a punishment arises. I think, to some extent, that should be a matter to let rest between you and your Maker.'

'Yes, yes,' said Enderby, too eagerly, with too much relief, 'I agree.'

'You agree, do you?' said Walpole. 'A more intelligent and more well-read man and who follows political theories would there be tempted to ask a certain simple question. What would that certain simple question be, Comrade Enderby?'

The chill honorific, with its suggestion of brain-washing and salt-mines, made Enderby's bowels react strongly: they seemed to liquefy; at the same time a solid blast prepared itself for utterance. Nevertheless he said bravely, 'People who accept dialectical materialism don't usually accept the proposition of a divine first cause.'

'And very well put, too,' said Walpole, 'though a bit old-fashioned in its circumloquaciousness. God is what you mean, Comrade Enderby, God, God, God.' He raised his eyes to the ceiling, his mouth opening and shutting on the divine name as though he were eating it. 'God, God, God,' said Walpole. As in response to a summons there was a knock on the flat-door. 'Ignore it,' said Walpole sharply.

'Here we have important things on hand and not the frip-peries of visitors. I have done it,' said Walpole, with sudden craftiness. 'I have achieved it,' he said more softly, his eyes shining with bright dementedness. 'I have discovered the sin thesis.' The knock came again. 'Ignore it,' said Walpole. 'Now then, Comrade Enderby, you should now by rights ask the question "What sin thesis?" Go on,' he said, with clenched fierceness, '*ask it*.'

'Why aren't you at work?' asked Enderby. Again the knock.

'Because,' said Walpole, 'today is Saturday. Five days shalt thou labour, as the Bible says. The seventh day is the Lord thy God's. The sixth day is for football and spreading the word and punishing and suchlike. Go on. *Ask it*.'

'What sin thesis?' asked Enderby.

'A sin thesis of *everything*,' said Walpole. 'The others left God out, but I put Him in. I found a place for Him in the universe.'

'What place?' asked Enderby, fascinated despite his bowels, his fear, the knock at the door.

'What place could it be,' said Walpole, 'except *His own place*? God's place is God's place, and you can't say fairer than that. Now,' he said, 'on your knees, Comrade Enderby. We're going to pray together to this same God, and you're going to ask for forgivenesss for all sins of fornication.' The knock came again, louder. 'QUIET,' bawled Walpole.

'I won't pray,' said Enderby. 'I've committed no fornica-tion.'

'Who hasn't,' said Walpole, 'in his heart?' And, like Enderby's boyhood picture of the Saviour, he pointed to his own. 'On your knees,' he said, 'and I shall pray with you.'

'No,' said Enderby. 'I don't accept the same God as you. I'm a Catholic.'

'All the more reason,' said Walpole. 'THERE IS ONLY ONE GOD, COMRADE!' he suddenly bawled. 'On your knees and pray and you will be let off by me, if not by the Comrade Almighty. If you don't pray I shall be the Hound of Heaven and get some of the lads from the works on the job, and bloody quick, too, even if you do think you're going off this morning. ON YOUR KNEES!' he ordered.

Enderby sighed and obeyed. His knees were stiff. Walpole knelt with the stage-fall ease of more practice. He did not close his eyes; he kept them full on Enderby. Enderby faced the electric fire's tabernacular gold. Walpole prayed:

'Comrade God, forgive the boor Joyce transgressions of Comrade Enderby here, who has been led astray by the lusts of his own body into writing phonographic poetry to Mrs Walpole, who You know, though she is stiff-necked and not one of Thy chosen. Let Your light shine upon him to make him a decent worker and good member of his union, when, him being a poet, such shall be formed. Better still, make him stop writing filthy poetry altogether and take up some decent trade at correct union rates and live in Godly righteousness, if that be Thy holy will, with some decent woman of Thy choosing in the state of holy matrimony, till such time as this boor Joyce institution is replaced by something better and more in keeping with what the proletariat will require.' Enderby now saw Walpole smile winningly at some apparition to his left, behind Enderby, at about picture-rail level. Enderby, presuming that this was God, felt no new fear. 'Just a tick,' said Walpole. 'Marvellous what prayer can do, innit? A bloody miracle, that's what it is. To finish up with, then,' he prayed, eyes now back on Enderby, 'stop this Thy comrade servant womanizing and messing about and bring him back to Your holy ways in the service of the classless society which Thou hast promisedest in the fullness of the workers' time. Thank you, Comrade God,' he said finally. 'Amen.'

Enderby, with much groaning and a posterior blast or two, got creaking to his feet. At that moment the electric fire, like some Zoroastrian deity now, having been prayed at, done with, went out. Enderby, standing, turned, blowing, and saw Mrs Bainbridge. She dangled Enderby's key in explanation of her entrance without Enderby's more direct agency, saying, 'Well, I never in all my life knew a man more capable of surprises.' She was a dream of winter bourgeois elegance: little black town suit with tiny white jabot of lace-froth; pencil skirt; three-quarter-length coat with lynx collar; long green gloves of suède; suède shoes of dull green; two shades of green in her leafy velvet hat: slim, clean, lithe-looking, delicately painted. Walpole, Marx-man of God, was clearly entranced. He handed her a small yellow throwaway poster and then, as a second thought, gave one to Enderby as well. 'GOD OR CAPI-TALISM?' it read. 'You Can't Have Both. H. Walpole will speak on this VITAL topic at the Lord Geldon Memorial Hall, Thursday, February 11th. All Welcome.'

'You come to that, lady,' said Walpole, 'and bring him along. There's good in him if only we can get at it, as you yourself will know well enough. Work on him hard, make him a decent man and stop him sending poetry to women, that's your job, I would say, and you look to me capable of tackling it.'

'Poetry to women?' said Vesta Bainbridge. 'He makes a habit of that, does he?' She gave Enderby a hard-soft green womanly look, holding her large shovel handbag in front of her, legs, as in a model pose, slightly astride.

H. Walpole was, for all his theophanic socialism, a decent man of bourgeois virtues who, now that Enderby had been thoroughly prayed for, did not want to put him in the bad with this fiancée of his here. 'That's only in a manner of speaking, as you might say,' he said. 'A very sexual man, you might say Mr Enderby is, with strong desires as must be kept down, and,' he said, 'you look to me like the one capable of doing it.'

'Thank you very much,' said Vesta Bainbridge.

'Look here,' said Enderby. The other two waited, listen-ing. Enderby had really nothing to say. Walpole said:

'Right. In his poetry if not in his private life, if you see what I mean. That's where you'd come in, comrade madam, and would give him a bigger sense of reality. May the blessings of the God of all the workers bless your union till such times as society makes something better come about.'

'Thank you very much,' said Vesta Bainbridge.

'And now,' said Walpole cheerfully, 'I take my leave. I've enjoyed our little dialectical conversation together and hope to have many more. Don't show me out, I know the way. God keep you in His care,' he said to Enderby. 'You have nothing to lose but your chains.' He blessed Enderby and his putative betrothed with a clenched fist, smiled once more, then went out. Enderby and his putative betrothed were left together, listening to Walpole's marching footsteps and cheerful whistle recede.

'Well,' said Vesta Bainbridge.

'This,' said Enderby, 'is where I live.'

'So I see. But if you live here why are you moving?'

'I don't quite get that,' said Enderby. 'Would you say that again?'

'I don't quite get *you*,' said Vesta Bainbridge. 'You send me what I suppose you'd call a verse-letter, straining at the leash with quite unequivocal suggestions, then you take fright and decide to run away. Or is it as simple as that? Obviously you thought I wouldn't get the letter till Monday morning, so it seems as though you planned to attack and retire at the same time. Actually, I always go into the office on Saturday mornings to see if there's any mail, and there I found the letter-rack practically sizzling with your little effort. I got a train right away. I was puzzled, intrigued. Also worried.'

'Worried?'

'Yes. About you.' She sniffed round the living-room with a wrinkle of distaste. 'I can see one would have cause to be worried. This place is absolutely filthy. Does nobody come in to clean it?'

'I do it myself,' said Enderby, suddenly and shamefully seeing the squalor of his life more clearly against the foil of her frightful wholesomeness. 'More or less.' He hung his schoolboy head.

'*Exactly*. And what, Harry, if I may call you that –

indeed, I *must* call you that now, mustn't I? – were you proposing to do? Where were you proposing to go?'

'Harry's not my name,' said Not-Harry Enderby. 'It's just the name at the end of the poem.'

'I know, of course, it can't really be your name, because your initials don't have an aitch in them. Still, you signed yourself Harry and Harry seems to suit you.' She surveyed him with a cocked parrot head, as though Harry were a hat. 'I repeat, *Harry*, what are you going to do?'

'I don't know,' said pseudoharry wretched Enderby. 'That was all to be thought out, you see. Where to go and whatnot. What to do and so on and so forth.'

'Well,' said Vesta Bainbridge, 'a few days ago I gave you a tea and you offered me a dinner which I couldn't accept. I think it would be a good idea if you took me out to lunch somewhere now. And after that –'

'There's one place I shan't take you,' said Enderby, betrayed and angry. 'That's quite certain. It would poison me. It would choke me. Every mouthful.'

'Very well,' soothed Vesta Bainbridge. 'You shall take me wherever you choose. And after that I'm taking you home.'

'Home?' said Enderby with sudden fear.

'Yes, home. Home, home home. You know, the place where the heart is. The place that there's no place like. You need looking after. I'm taking you home, Harry.'

Part Two

Chapter One

1

Errrrrrrrp.

Enderby was in a very small lavatory, being sick. He was also married, just. Enderby the married man. A vomiting bridegroom.

When his forehead was cooler he sat, sighing, on the little seat. All below him was June weather, June being the month for weddings. Alone in this buzzing and humming tiny lavatory he had his first leisure to feel both gratified and frightened. The bride, though only in a severe suit suitable for a registry office, had looked lovely. Sir George had said so. Sir George was friendly again. All was forgiven.

Almost the first thing she had insisted on was an apology to Sir George. Enderby had written: 'So sorry I should seem to rate your sirship as a stupid dolt, but thought you would appreciate that feeble gesture of revolt. For you yourself have tried, God wot, the awful agonizing art, and though, as poet, you are not worth the least poetaster's fart, yet you're equipped to understand what clockwork makes the poet tick and how he hates the laden hand below the empty rhetoric. . . .' That, she had said, was not really suitable, so he had tried something briefer in genuine prose, and Sir George had only been too delighted to accept the formal creaking apology.

Oh, she had begun to reorganize his life, that one. From the start, taking breakfast together in the large dining-room of her large flat, February Gloucester Road sulking outside, it was clear that things could only go one way. For what other relationship could be viable in the world's eyes than this one they were beginning now? Enderby had been forced to reject that of landlady and tenant, for he had paid no rent. The step-relationship was, with women, practically the only other one he had experienced. She was, he knew, and for this he valued her, antipodeal to a stepmother, being clean and beautiful. His father's remarriage had introduced brief squibs of step-aunts-in-law and the fable of a paragon stepsister, too good for this world and hence soon dead of a botulism, whom Enderby had always visualized as a puppet doll-dangling parody of his stepmother. Vesta was not, he had felt, a stepsister. A female Friend? He had rung that on his palate several times, upper case and all, and savoured a melancholy twilit aquarelle of Shelley and Godwin, with chorusmen's calves as if limned by Blake, holding reading-parties in a moored boat with high-waisted rather silly ladies, lovers of Gothic romances, while midges played fiddles in the sad air. Epipsychidion. Epithalamion. Ah God, that word had really started things off, for it had started off a poem.

> The cry in the clouds, the throng of migratory birds,
> The alien planet's heaven where seven moons
> Are jasper, agate, carbuncle, onyx, amethyst and blood-ruby
>   and bloodstone.
> Or else binary suns
> Wrestle like lions to a flame that we can stand,
> Bound, twisted and conjoined
> To an invertebrate love where selves are melted
> To the primal juice of a creator's joy,
> Before matter was made,
> Two spheres in a single orbit. . . .

They had drunk Orange Pekoe with breakfast and she, in a rust-coloured suit with a heavy clip of hammered pewter on the left lapel, had just gone off to work. Enderby, in the kitchenette whose pastel beauty made him feel particularly dirty and gross, had put on the kettle for stepmother's tea, and the word 'epithalamion', like the announcement of a train's approach, had set the floorboards trembling with thunder. Panting at the diningtable, he had set down words, seeing his emergent poem as a song for the celebration of the consummation of the passion of the mature – Gertrude and Claudius in *Hamlet*,

red-bearded lips on a widow's white neck. The leafy tea
had cooled beside him. Mrs Opisso the daily woman had
come in, dusky, hippy, bosomy, garlicky, moustached, leering brilliantly, a wartime Gibraltarian evacuee in whose
blood seethed Genoese, Portuguese Jewish, Saracen, Irish,
and Andalusian corpuscles, to say, interrupting sweeping,
'What are you in this house, eh? You not going out, not
doing work, true? What are you to her, eh? You tell.' It
had not been easy to tell; it was not enough to say that it
was none of her business.

> ... Swollen with cream or honey,
> The convalescent evening launches its rockets,
> Soaring above the rich man's gala day,
> In the thousand parks of the kingdom
> Which radiate from this bed....

Vesta would not necessarily think that this epithalamion
was intended for her and her guest-Male Friend-protégé,
for she had already said sardonically, 'if you intend to
write any love poetry this morning make sure you don't
send it to Sir George by mistake. This carelessness of yours
will land you into big trouble one of these days, you mark
my words.' Enderby had hung his head. She had been
irritable that morning, tired, rubbing her brow tiredly, as
in a TV commercial for some quack analgesic, under her
green eyes delicate blue arcs of tiredness. She had stood by
the door, in neat rust, a chiffon scarf in two tones of green,
a minute brown beret aslant, brown suède gloves to match
her shoes, slender, elegant and (so Enderby had divined)
menstruating quietly. Enderby had said:
'Menstruation hits some women more than others, you
know. Try gin and hot water. That's said to work wonders.'
She had blushed faintly and said, 'Where did you learn
that?'
'In *Fem*.'
Sighing, she had said, 'It's all very confusing. I must
work out, when I have time, the precise nature of our
relationship.'

Anoint the ship with wine! On ample waters,
Which always wear this ring, that the earth be humbled
Only away from cities, let it dance and ride. . . .

And again, another time, the precise nature still not
worked out, 'The question is, what's to be done with you?'

'Done with me?'

'Yes, that's the question.'

'Nothing is to be done with me.' He had looked across at
her in fear, over the shattered fragments of toast which he
had been feeding, as to a pet bird, to his mouth. 'I am,
after all, a poet.' A lorry had backfired the world's answer.

'I want to know,' Vesta had said, chill morning hands
round her breakfast-cup, 'exactly how much money you've
got.'

'Why do you want to know that?' cunning Enderby had
asked.

'Oh, please. I've got a busy day ahead of me. Let's not
have any nonsense. Please.' Enderby had begun to tell out
the contents of his left trouser-pocket. 'Not that sort of
money,' she had cut in, sharply. Enderby had said, with
care:

'Ten thousand pounds in local government loans at five
and a half per cent. For dividends. Two thousand pounds
in ICI, BMC, Butlin's. For capital appreciation.'

'Ah. And what income does all that yield?'

'About six hundred. Not a lot, really, is it?'

'It's nothing. And I suppose your poetry brings in less
than nothing.'

'Two guineas a week. From *Fem*, God bless it.' For he
had at last signed the contract and already seen in print,
over the name of Faith Fortitude, hogwash beginning, 'A
baby's cheeks, a baby's limbs are prayers to God and holy
hymns; a little baby's toothless smile does the holy saints
beguile. . . .'

'An income like yours isn't worth having, really it isn't.
So we've got to work out what's to be done with you.'

'Done with me?' prompt Enderby had flashed.

'Look,' she had said, 'I know you're a poet. But there's no need to regale us with poetic drama in the style of early Mr Eliot, is there? Not at breakfast there isn't.'

'Stichomythia,' had been learned Enderby's comment. 'But it's you who keep starting it off.'

Well, that was something not yet started off: useful employment, a *deuxième métier* for a poet. From Valentine to Pentecost he had been allowed, though not in the lavatory, to work at *The Pet Beast* peaceably. But after the honeymoon things would have to be different.

> And you whose fear of maps
> Set buzzing the long processes of power,
> Resign your limbs at length to elements
> Friendly or neutral at least,
> Mirrors of the enemy. . . .

His own bit of money had not, even before they'd started on capital purchases, been going very far ('Call in at the Lion, will you, and buy a couple of bottles of gin. Pay Mrs Opisso; I'm clean out of cash.'). And the greedy maws of Fortnum and Mason and the Army and Navy Stores. And a new wardrobe for himself, London not really favouring the casual valetudinarian garb of the seaside. Enderby's capital was going now. She, a thriftless Scot, did not believe in money, only in things. Hence the seven-thousand-pound house in Sussex in her name, this being his marriage settlement, also furniture, also a bright new Velox for Vesta to drive, Enderby when most sober managing a car like the drunkest drunk. And a mink coat, a wedding present.

Who had proposed marriage, and when? Who loved whom, if at all, and why? Enderby, in thinker's pose on the lavatory seat, frowned back to an evening when he had sat finishing his epithalamion in her twin dining-room, facing a piece of furniture he admired – a sideboard, massive and warped, proclaiming its date (1685) among carved lozenges and other tropes, fancies of the woodworker signifying his love of the great negroid ship-oak he had shaped and smoothed. Above that sideboard hung a painting of Vesta done by Gideon Dalgleish, she pearly-shouldered and haughty in a ballgown, seeming about to fly off, centrifugally, back into waiting but invisible paint-tubes. Above open bookshelves was a photograph of the late Pete Bainbridge. He grinned handsomely in a helmet, seated at the wheel of the Anselm 2.493 litre (six-cylinder; 250 b.h.p. Girling disc brakes; Weber 58 DCO carburettors, etc.) in which he had met his messy death. Enderby had started his last stanza:

> And even the dead may bring blue lips to this banquet
> And twitter like mice or birds down their corridors
> Hung with undecipherable blazons. . . .

He had felt a sudden and unwonted surge of personal, as opposed to poet's, strength: he, unworthy and ugly as he was, was at least alive, while this bright and talented handsome one had been blown to pieces. He had grinned, borrowing the shape of the grin from the dead man, in a sort of triumph. Vesta, reading some new brilliant novel by an undergraduate, had looked up from her Parker-Knoll and caught the grin. She had said:

'Why are you grinning? Have you written something funny?'

'Me? Funny? Oh, no.' Enderby had covered his manuscript with clumsy paws, as one protects one's dinner-plate from an importunate second scooping of mashed potato. 'Nothing funny at all.'

She had got up, so graceful, to see what he was writing, asking: 'What are you writing?'

'This? Oh, I don't think you'd like it. It's – Well, it's a sort of –'

She had picked up the sheet of scrawled lines and read aloud:

> . . . For two at least can deny
> That the past has any odour. They can witness
> Passion and patience rooted in one paradigm; in this music
>   recognize
> That all the world's guilt can sit like air
> On the bodies of these living.'

'You see,' Enderby had said, over-eagerly, 'it's an epithalamion. For the marriage of two mature people.' Inexplicably she had lowered her head with its sweet-smelling penny-coloured hair and kissed him. Kissed him. Him, Enderby.

'Your breath,' she had said, 'is no longer unhealthy. Sometimes it's hard for the body and mind to come to terms. You're looking better, much better.' What could he say but, 'Thanks to you'?

Airsick, seated in this aerial lavatory, he had to admit that a new Enderby had emerged out of the spring and early summer – a younger Enderby with less fat and wind, new teeth imperfect enough to look real, several smart suits, hair cunningly dressed by Trumper's of Mayfair and breathing delicately of Eucris, less gauche in company, his appetite healthier with no dyspeptic lust for spices and bread-and-jam, more carefully shaven, his skin clearer, his eyeballs glassy with contact lenses. If only Mrs Meldrum could see him now!

Who had mentioned love? Had anybody mentioned love? They had lived under one roof chaste, vestal, phoenix, and turtle, with Pete Bainbridge grinning from some Elysium of racing-drivers at the strange ménage of Friends. But one had only to chuck and see spin that worn coin on the polished floor for it to chink louder and louder music and revolve into a world. Had it been pocket or handbag? Enderby could not remember, but he was sure that one evening one of them had spoken the word in some connexion or other, perhaps denouncing its inflation in popular songs or in the hoarse speech of immediate need, perhaps discussing its personified identification with, in seventeenth-century religious poetry, the Lord. Then, by a swift process too subtle and irrational for analysis, one or other of them had whistled down the dove-hawk from safe heights of speculation to perch, blinking, on a pair of joined hands.

'I've been so lonely,' she had said. 'I've been so cold at night.'

Enderby, potential bedwarmer, still potential on this brief flight to the honeymoon, for they had been chaste till now. Till tonight. Tonight in the Albergo Tritone on the Via Nazionale. Something, gulped Enderby, to look forward to.

'Look,' said a voice, meaning 'Listen'. Enderby started from the tiny seat, listening. 'Your ticket does not entitle you to undisputed monopolization of the john.' That, Enderby considered, was well put. The voice was American and authoritative and Enderby hastened to give place, fairly sure now that he felt better. Outside the folding doors he breathed deeply, taking in a large touristy man who nodded at him, edging past. He had a steak complexion and two cameras – still and movie respectively – on his stomach at the ready. Enderby wondered if he would photograph the john. Through a porthole summer cloud shone up. Enderby walked down the aisle to his bride who sat, cool and lovely, gazing at summer cloud beneath. She looked up and smiled, asking if he felt better. She gave her hand to him as he sat. It seemed to be a new life beginning.

2

As if he were in a well-appointed bath, Enderby was struck by various liquid sensations as they descended to Rome (going down. Eternal City: pasta, old junk, monumental remnants, figleaved stone stalwarts, veal, Vatican, staircases to basement and bones of martyrs. The whole roofed in ringing silver and refreshed by fountains. And the very best of luck). He felt cold sweat as his stomach, tardy in descending, encouraged its master to view Rome in a sort of stepmother-context (Pope in picture on bedroom wall, blessing seven hills; translucent image of St Peter's embedded in cross of blancmange-coloured rosary; missal bookmark of Holy Family as middle-class spaghetti-guzzlers, printed in Rome). Then he was warmed by thrilling gushes, the chicken-skinned hand that held the hand of the bride growing smooth again, as there swam up from the *News of the World* a picture of a heavy-breasted starlet sploshing, for a lark, in the Trevi fountain. There were also weary handsome princes in sordid divorce cases and Cinecittà was greater than the Vatican. It was all right really, it would be all right, sensual, thrilling. He looked with pride on his bride and, like a distant rumour of war, felt a prick of desire, legitimate desire; she was, in a flash, identified with this new city, to be, all so legitimately, sacked and pillaged. He said to her, a few words coming back from his L. of C. days, '*Io ti amo*.' She smiled and squeezed his hand. Enderby, Latin lover.

The warmth, the excitement, the sense of rejuvenation, survived the landing (the stewardess smirked at the exit as though she herself, after the aerial gestation, had given birth to the airport; the American who had ousted Enderby from the john began clicking away desperately). In the ragged procession to the buildings, Ciampino stretching in hot honeymoon weather, Enderby felt the barren flat airfield express, like a blank page, his new freedom, this being a freedom from his old freedom. A Cassius-lean and Casca-sullen Roman customs-man zipped open roughly the overnight bag of Vesta and held up for the whole shed to see a new nightdress. He winked sullenly at Enderby, and this to Enderby was a good omen, even though the man was starved-jawed and hence untrustworthy. The fat bus-driver sang some plangent oily aria with *amore* in it, jolting up the Appian Way, thus inspiring confidence. And then, whoosh, came the cold water again as the sun clouded over above a mossy aqueduct growing in ruins out of the dry grass, over an old plinth lying like a large merd under a comic-strip-coloured petrol poster. The American from the john fed his cameras like lapdogs. Meanwhile Enderby grew oppressed with a sense of travelling through a butcher's shop of mean history, between the ribs of carcasses, already being force-fed with chunks of the carrion empire. Rostra were quietly set up just beyond his line of vision and on them settled a sort of Seneca chorus of smirking noseless ancient Romans, fat on Sicilian corndoles and gladiator's blood. They would be present at the honeymoon; it was their city.

The sun suddenly exploded, a fire in a syrup factory, as they arrived at the airline terminal on the Via Nazionale. A dwarf porter of great strength carried their cases the few doors down to the hotel and Enderby gave him a tip of over-light suspect coins. They were bowed at and greeted with insincere golden smiles in the hotel lobby. 'Signor Enderby,' said Signor Enderby, 'and Signora Bainbridge.' 'No, no, no,' said Signora Enderby. Enderby smiled. 'Not used to it yet, you see. Our honeymoon,' he explained to the receptionist. He, a dapper Roman elf, said:

'Honeymoon, eh? I maker sure everythinger quiet forer honeymoon. A longer time since I have a honeymoon,' he said regretfully. Vesta said:

'Look, I don't feel all that well. Do you think we could be taken to our –?' There were immediate calls and dartings and hoistings of bags.

'Darling,' said Enderby, concerned. 'What is it, darling?'

'Tired, that's all. I want to lie down.'

'Darling,' said Enderby. They entered a lift that was all rococo filigree-work, an airy frail cage that carried them up to a floor paved with veiny marble. Enderby saw, with interest, an open Roman lavatory, but he waved the interest away. Those days were over. They were shown into their room by a young man in a wine-coloured coat, his nose squashed flat as in desperate contradiction of the myth of Roman profiles. Enderby gave him several worthless slips of metal and asked for *vino*. (Enderby in Rome, ordering *vino*.) The young man shook hands with himself fiercely, then tensely raised the upper hand, teeth clenched as though lifting a killing weight, showing the space between to Enderby – a bottle of air with a hand-bottom and hand-top. 'Frascati,' he nodded direly, and went out, nodding. Enderby turned to his wife. She sat on the window-side of the double bed, looking out at the Via Nazionale. The little room was full of its noise – tramclanks, horse-clops, Fiats and Lambrettas. 'Tired, tired, tired,' said Vesta, blue arcs back under her eyes, her face weary in the sharp Roman light. 'I don't feel at all the thing.'

'It's not –?' asked Enderby.

'No, of course it's not. This is our wedding-day, isn't it? I'll be all right when I've had a rest.' She kicked off her shoes and then, as Enderby gulped, swiftly unhitched her stockings. He turned to the dull sights of the street: metropolitan dourness, no flashing Southern teeth, no song. Across the road a shop, as though for Enderby's own benefit, had a special display of holy pictures going cheap, ill-painted hagiographs festooned with rosary-beads. When he turned back towards the bed Vesta was already in it, her thin arms and shoulders uncovered. Not a voluptuous woman; her body pared to a decent female minimum. That was as it should be. Enderby had once caught his stepmother stripped off in the bathroom, panting with the exertion of one of her rare over-all washes, flesh-shaking, fat tits swinging like bells. He shuddered at the memory, his burring lips becoming, for the moment, those of his stepmother flinching at the cold sponge. There was a knock. Enderby had read Dante with an English crib; there was, he knew, a line which contained the word for 'come in'. He delved for it, and it came up just as the door opened. 'All hope abandon,' he called in fine Tuscan, 'you who –' A long-faced waiter peered in, doubtful, then entered with his tray, leaving without waiting (a non-waiting waiter) for a tip. Enderby, a mad Englishman, sighed and poured wine. He shouldn't have said that. It was a bad omen. It was like Byron waking on his wedding-night and thinking that the bedroom fire was hell. He said:

'Darling. Would you care for a glass of this, darling?' He gulped some thirstily. A very nice little wine. 'Help you to sleep if you're going to sleep.' She nodded tiredly. Enderby poured another glass, the urine-gold flashing in the clear light, belching as it left the bottle. He gave the glass to her and she sat up to sip it. Fair down on her upper lip, Enderby noticed in love and pity, his arm round her shoulders to support her sitting up. She drank half a glassful and at once, to Enderby's shock and horror, reacted violently. Pushing him and the glass away, she fought to leave the bed, her cheeks bulging. She ran on bare feet to the washbowl, gripped its sides, groaned and started to vomit. Enderby, much concerned, followed and stood by her, slender, defenceless in her minimal unalluring summer underwear. 'That's your lunch coming up,' said Enderby, watching. 'A bit fatty, wasn't it?' with a roar more came up. Enderby poured water from the water-bottle.

'Oh God,' she groaned. 'Oh Jesus.' She turned on both taps and began to retch again.

'Drink this,' said Enderby. 'Water.' She gulped from the proffered glass and vomited again, but this time mostly water, groaning between spasms blasphemously. 'There,' said Enderby, 'you'll be better now. That was a nasty sort of pudding they served up. All jammy.'

'Oh Jesus Christ,' retched Vesta (All jammy). Enderby watched kindly, a past master on visceral dysfunctions, as she got it all up. Then weak, wet, limp, spent, she staggered back to the bed. 'A good start,' she gasped. 'Oh God.'

'That's the worst of meals on aircraft,' said Enderby, sage after his first flight. 'They warm things up, you see. Have some more wine. That'll settle your stomach.' Fascinated by the near-rhymes, he began softly to repeat. 'That'll settle, that'll settle,' pacing the room softly, one hand in pocket, the other holding wine.

'Oh, shut up,' moaned Vesta. 'Leave me alone.'

'Yes, darling,' said Enderby, accommodating. 'Certainly, darling. You have a little sleep, darling.' He heard himself wheedling like a foreign whore, so he straightened up and said more gruffly, 'I'll go and see about traveller's cheques.' Saying that, he was standing up against the door, as if challenging it or measuring himself against it. When a knock came he was able to open it at once. The long-faced boy looked startled. His arms were full of roses, red and white. '*Fiori*,' he said, '*per la signora.*'

'Who from?' frowned Enderby, feeling for an accompanying card. 'Good God,' he said, finding it. 'Rawcliffe. And Rawcliffe's in the bar. Darling,' he called, turning. But she was asleep.

3

'Ah,' said Rawcliffe. 'You got the message, got the flowers? Good. Where,' he asked, 'is Mrs Enderby?' He was dressed as when Enderby had last seen him, in an old-fashioned heavy suit with a gold watch-chain, Kipling-moustached, beetle-goggled, drunk.

'Mrs Enderby,' said Enderby, 'is dead.'

'I beg your pardon,' said Rawcliffe. 'Already? Roman fever? How very Jamesian!'

'Oh, I see what you mean,' said Enderby. 'Sorry. She only became Mrs Enderby today, you see. It takes some getting used to. I thought you meant my stepmother.'

'I see, I see. And your stepmother's dead, is she? How very interesting!' Enderby shyly examined the bar, the shelves massed with liquors of all countries, the silver tea-urn, the espresso apparatus. Behind the bar a short fat man kept bowing. 'Have some of this Strega,' said Rawcliffe. 'Dante,' he said, and the fat un-Dantesque man came to attention. Rawcliffe then spoke most intricate Italian, full, as far as Enderby could judge, of subjunctives, but with a most English accent. 'Strega,' said Dante. 'Are you,' said Enderby nastily, 'in all the Italian anthologies, too?' He was given, with flourishes, a glass of Strega.

'Ha, ha,' said Rawcliffe, without much mirth. 'As a matter of fact, there's a very good Italian translation of that little poem of mine, you know. It goes well into Italian. Now, tell me, tell me, Enderby, what are you writing at the moment?'

'Nothing,' said Enderby. 'I finished my long poem, *The Pet Beast*. I told you about that.'

'You most certainly did,' said Rawcliffe, bowing. Dante bowed too. 'A very good idea, that was. I look forward to reading it.'

'What I'd like to know,' said Enderby, 'is what you're doing here. You don't look as though you're on holiday, not in those clothes you don't.'

Rawcliffe did something Enderby had read about but never before seen: he placed a finger against his nose. 'You're right,' he said. 'Most certainly *not* on holiday. At work. Always at work. Some more Strega?'

'With me,' said Enderby. Dante bowed and bowed, filling their glasses. 'And one for you, too,' said Enderby, expansive, on his honeymoon. Dante bowed and said to Rawcliffe, '*Americano*?'

'*Inglese*,' said Rawcliffe.

'*Americani*,' said Dante, leaning forward, confidential, 'fack you. *Mezzo mezzo*.'

'*Un poeta*,' said Rawcliffe, 'that's what he is. *Poeta*. Feminine in form, masculine in gender.'

'I beg your pardon,' said Enderby. 'Did you by any chance mean anything by that?'

'As a matter of fact,' said Rawcliffe, 'it's my belief that all we poets are really a sort of a blooming hermaphrodite. Like Tiresias, you know. And you're on your honeymoon, eh? Have some more Strega.'

'What exactly do you mean by that?' said Enderby, wary.

'Mean? You are a one for meaning, aren't you? The meaning of meaning. I. A. Richards and the Cambridge school. A lot of twaddle, if you ask my opinion. All right, if you won't have more Strega with me I'll have more Strega with you.'

'Strega,' said Enderby.

'Your Italian's coming along very nicely,' said Rawcliffe. 'A couple of nice vowels there. A couple of nice Stregas,' he said, as these appeared. 'God bless, all.' He drank. He sang, 'Who would an ender be, let him come hither.'

'How did you know we were here?' asked Enderby.

'Air terminal,' said Rawcliffe. 'Today's arrivals from

London. Always interesting. Here, they said honeymoon. Remarkable, Enderby, in a man of your age.'

'What do you mean by that?' asked Enderby.

'You gentlemen ave Strega on the ouse,' said Dante, pouring.

'*Tante grazie,*' said Rawcliffe. 'There you go, Enderby, worrying about meaning all the time.' He sang, standing to attention. 'Would you a spender be, would you a mender be, God save the Queen. No meaning there, is there? Would you a fender be. That's better still. Too much meaning in your poetry, Enderby. Always has been.' His words rode over a few drinker's belches. 'Pardon, as they say.' He drank.

'Strega,' said Enderby. '*E uno per Lei, Dante.*'

'You can't say that,' said Rawcliffe, hiccoughing. 'What bloody awful Italian you speak, Enderby! Bad as your poetry. Pardon. Fair criticism. But I will say that the monster idea of yours was a bloody good one. Too good to make a poem out of it. Ah, Rome,' he said, lyrically, 'fair, fair Rome. Remarkable place, Enderby, no place like it. Listen, Enderby. I'm going to a party tonight. At the house of the Principessa Somebody-or-other. Would you like to come? You and your missus? Or does it behove you to retire early this fair nuptial night?' He shook his head. 'La Rochefoucauld, or some other bloody scoundrel, said you mustn't do it on the first night. What did he know about it, eh? Homosexuals, the lot of them. All writers are homosexuals. They have to be. Stands to reason. To hell with writing.' He poured his last few drops of Strega on to the floor. 'That,' he said, 'is for the Lares and Penates to come and lap up. A potation, that is to say a libation. They come to lap it up like bloody big dogs. More Strega.'

'Don't you think?' said Enderby cautiously. 'I mean, if you're going to a party –'

'Not for hours yet,' said Rawcliffe. 'Hours and hours and hours. Plenty of time for you to get it over and done with several times over before it starts. If you can, that is. Shellfish are bloody good, you know. Magnificent augmenters of male potency. Scampi. Dante,' he cried, 'send for some scampi for this here signore. He is a newly married man, God bless him.' Rawcliffe swayed on his stool. Dante said:

'Today you are married? Very good. You ave Strega on the ouse.' He poured. '*Salute*,' he toasted. '*Molti bambini*,' he winked.

'Lovely grub,' said Rawcliffe, drinking. Enderby drank and said:

'What you've been saying is very indelicate. You ought by rights to be bashed.'

'Oh dear dear dear me, no,' said Rawcliffe, shaking his head, his eyes shut. 'Not on a day like this. Much too warm. *Pace, pace*, this is a city of peace.' He began to fall asleep.

'*Troppo*,' confided Dante. 'Too mash. You get im ome.'

'No,' said Enderby. 'Damn it all, I'm on my honeymoon. I don't like him, anyway, Nasty bit of work.'

'Jealous,' mumbled Rawcliffe, eyes still shut, head drooping to the counter. 'I'm in all the anthologies. He's not. Popular poet, me. Known and loved and respected by all.' He then neatly, as in a professional tumbling act, collapsed with the stool on to the deep carpet of the bar, falling, it seemed, quite slowly, in a rotary figure. The noise, though muffled, was loud enough to summon men in skimpy suits from the hotel lobby. These spoke very fast Italian and looked with hate upon Enderby. Enderby said:

'Nothing to do with me. He was drunk when I met him.' Surlily he added, 'Damn it all, I'm on my honeymoon.' Two men bent over Rawcliffe and Enderby was afforded an intimate, non-tourist's, glimpse of the city, for one man had dandruff and the other boil-scars on his nape. Rawcliffe opened one eye and said, very clearly:

'Don't trust him. He's a spy pretending to be on his honeymoon. Made me drunk to shteal official shecretsh. Overthrow of Italian government plot dishcovered, alleged. Bombs shecreted in Foro Traiano and Tempio di Vesta.'

'You leave my wife out of this,' threatened Enderby.

'Ah, wife,' said one of the men. '*Capito*.' All was clear.

Enderby had knocked Rawcliffe down in wronged husband's legitimate anger. A matter of honour. Rawcliffe now snored. The two men returned to their lobby to see about a taxi for him. Dante said to Enderby, tentatively: 'Strega?'

'Si,' said Enderby. He signed the chit and counted the number of other chits he had signed, all for Strega. Amazing. He would have to go easy, he hadn't all the money in the world. But, of course, he reflected, after this honeymoon he would start *earning* money. The capital was there to be spent; Vesta had said so.

Rawcliffe ceased snoring, smacked his lips, and said: 'Thou hast wrongedst me, O Enderby.' His eyes did not open. 'I wished no harm. Merely desired to crown your nuptials in appropriate manner.' He then gave a loud snore. A taxi-driver with a square of moustache dead under his nose entered, shook his head tolerantly, and started to lift Rawcliffe by the shoulders. Members of the hotel staff appeared, including menials in off-white jackets, and Dante struck a pose behind the bar. All were waiting for Enderby to lift Rawcliffe's feet.

Enderby said: 'I know he's *Inglese* and I'm *Inglese*, but it bloody well stops there. I can't stand him, see? *Io*,' he said, piecing the sentence together painfully, '*non voglio aiutare.*' Everybody inclined, with smiles, to show that they appreciated this attempt on the part of an Englishman to use their beautiful language, but they ignored the meaning, perhaps having been well schooled by this snoring Rawcliffe. 'I won't help,' repeated Enderby, picking up Rawcliffe's feet. (There was a hole in the left sole.) 'This is no way to be spending a bloody honeymoon,' said Enderby, helping, very awkwardly, to carry Rawcliffe out. 'Especially in Rome.' As he passed, now panting, the ranked officials of the hotel, these bowed fully or gently inclined, all with smiles.

The Via Nazionale was afire with sun and brilliant with people. The taxi throbbed, waiting, by the kerb. Enderby and the driver sweated as they pushed their way, Rawcliffe still snoring. A sort of begging friar rattled his box at Enderby. 'For cough,' said Enderby. An American, not the john one, poised his camera to shoot. 'For cough,' snarled expiring Enderby. The driver, raising his knee to support the snoring body, freed his hand to open the passenger-door. Rawcliffe, like six months' laundry, was bundled in. 'There,' said Enderby. 'All yours.'

'*Dove*?' asked the driver.

'Oh, God, yes, where to?' Enderby manhandled, still panting, the loud, still Rawcliffe, trying to shout, 'Where do you live, you bastard? Come on, tell us where.'

Rawcliffe came awake with startling briskness, as though he had merely pretended to pass out so that he might be carried. His blue eyes, quite clear, flashed patches of Roman sky at Enderby. 'Tiber, Father Tiber,' he said, 'on whom the Romans prey. The Via Mancini by the Ponte Matteotti.'

The driver eagerly drank that in. 'O world, O life, O time,' intoned Rawcliffe. 'Here lies one whose name was *not* writ in water. In all the anthologies.' He returned to a heavy sleep with louder snores than before. Enderby hesitated, then, since the whole waiting world seemed to expect it of him, roughly made room next to Rawcliffe. They drove off. The driver honked down the Via Nazionale and turned abruptly into the Via IV Novembre. Then, as they sped north up the Via del Corso, Rawcliffe came quite alive again, sat up sedately, and said:

'Have you such a thing as a cigarette on you, my dear Enderby? An English cigarette, preferably.'

'Are you all right now?' asked Enderby. 'Can I get out here and let you go home on your own?'

'Over there on the left,' pointed Rawcliffe, 'you'll find the Pantheon if you look carefully. And there' – his hand swished right, striking Enderby – 'down the street of humility, at the end, is the Fontana di Trevi. There you will throw your coin and be photographed by touts in berets. Do give me a cigarette, there's a good fellow.' Enderby offered a single crushed Senior Service. Rawcliffe took it steadily without thanks, lighting up as firm as a rock. 'We come now, Enderby, to the Piazza Colonna. There it is, the column itself, and at the top Marcus Aurelius, see.'

'I could get off here,' suggested Enderby, 'and go back to the hotel. My wife isn't too good, you know.'

'Isn't she?' said Rawcliffe. 'Not too good at what? A great admirer of poets, though. I'll say that for her. She always liked my little poem in the anthologies. It's quite likely, you know, Enderby, that you're going to be a great man. She likes to back winners. She backed one very good one, but that was in the field of sport. Poets don't get killed as racing-drivers do, you know. Look, the Piazza del Popolo. And now we're coming up to the Via Flaminia and there, you can just see, is Father Tiber himself, into whom the Romans spit.'

'What do you know about my wife?' asked Enderby. 'Who told you I'd married Vesta Bainbridge?'

'It was in the popular papers,' said Rawcliffe. 'Didn't you see? Perhaps she kept them from you. Pete Bainbridge's widow to remarry, they said. The popular papers didn't seem to know very much about you. But when you're dead there'll be biographies, you know. There haven't been any biographies of Pete Bainbridge, so there's a lot to be said for not being known to the readers of the *Daily Mirror*. Ah, here is the Via Mancini.' He banged the glass partition and made grotesque boxing gestures at the driver. The driver nodded, swerved madly, and came to rest before a small drinking-shop. 'This is where I have my humble lodging,' said Rawcliffe. 'Above here.'

'Do you really believe that?' asked Enderby. 'I thought perhaps I appealed to a sort of protective instinct in her. And I'm very fond of her. Very, very fond. In love,' said Enderby. Rawcliffe nodded and nodded, paying the driver. He seemed to have recovered completely from his Stregabout. The two poets stood in the warm street, cooled by river air. Enderby let the taxi go and said, 'Damn. I've let that taxi go. I ought to get back to my wife.' He reminded himself that he disliked Rawcliffe because he was in all the anthologies. 'It strikes me,' said Enderby, 'that you were swinging the bloody lead. I needn't have come with you at all.'

'Strega,' said Rawcliffe, nodding, 'passes through my system very quickly. I think, now we're here, we'll have some more. Or perhaps a litre or so of Frascati.'

'I must get back. She may be all right now. She may be wondering where I am.'

'There's no hurry. The bride's supposed to wait, you know. Supposed to lie in cool sheets smelling of lavender while the bridegroom gets drunk and impotent. The Toby night, you know. That's what it used to be called. After Tobias in the Apocrypha. Come on, Enderby, I'm lonely. A brother poet is lonely. And I have things to tell you.'

'About Vesta?'

'Oh, no. Much more interesting. About you and your poetic destiny.'

They entered the little shop. It was dark and warm. On the walls were vulgar mosaics, pseudo-Etruscan, of prancing men and women in profile. There were glass jars of wine and cloudy tumblers. An old man from the age of Victor Emmanuel sucked an ample moustache; two sincere-eyed rogues, round-faced and, despite the heat, in overcoats, whispered roguery to each other. A champing old woman, each step an effort, brought a litre of urine to two English poets. 'Salute,' said Rawcliffe. He shuddered at the first draught, found the second blander. 'Tell me, Enderby,' he said, 'how old would you say I am?'

'Old? Oh, about fifty.'

'Fifty-two. And when do you think I stopped writing?'

'I didn't know you *had* stopped.'

'Oh, yes, a long time, a long, long time. I haven't written a line of verse, Enderby, since I was twenty-seven. There, that surprises you, doesn't it? But writing verse is so diffi-cult, Enderby, so so difficult. The only people who can write verse after the age of thirty are the people who do the competitions, you know, in the week-end papers. You can add to that, of course, the monkey-gland boys, of whom Yeats was one, but that's not playing the game, by God. The greatest senile poet of the age, by God, by grace of this bloody man Voronoff. But the rest of us? There are no dramatic poets left, Enderby, and, ha ha, certainly no epic poets. We're all lyric poets, then, and how long does the lyric urge last? No bloody time at all, my boy, ten years at the most. It's no accident, you know, that they all died young, mainly, for some reason, in Mediterranean lands. Dylan, of course, died in America, but the Atlantic's a sort of Mediterranean, when you come to think of it. What I mean is, American civilization's a sort of seaboard civilization, when you come to think of it, and not a river civilization at all.' Rawcliffe shook his head in a fuddled gesture, the Frascati having wakened the sleeping Strega. 'What I mean is, Enderby, that you're bloody lucky to be writing poetry at all at the age of – what is your age?'

'Forty-five.'

'At the age of forty-five, Enderby. What I mean is, what are you looking forward to now? Eh?' He let more Frascati stagger into his glass. Outside, the Roman daylight flashed and rippled. 'Don't kid yourself, my dear boy, about long bloody narrative poems, or plays, or any of that nonsense. You're a lyric poet, and the time is coming for the lyric gift to die. Who knows? Perhaps it's died already.' He looked narrowly at Enderby over the glass flask of Frascati swimming and dancing in his grip. 'Don't expect any more epiphanies, any more mad dawn inspirations, Enderby. That poem of mine, the one in the anthologies, the one I'll live by if I'm going to live at all, I wrote that bugger, you know, Enderby, at the age of twenty-one. Youth. It's the only thing worth having.' He nodded sadly. As in a film, an easy symbol of youth orchestrated his words, passing by outside, a very head-high girl of Rome with black hair and smoky sideburns, thrust breasts, liquid waist like Harry Ploughman's, animal haunches. 'Yes, yes,' said Rawcliffe, 'youth.' He drank Frascati and sighed. 'Haven't you felt, Enderby, that your gift is dying? It's a gift appropriate to youth, you know, owing nothing to experience or learning. An athletic gift, really, a *sportif* gift.' Rawcliffe dropped his jaw at Enderby, disclosing crooked teeth of various colours. 'What are you going to do, Enderby, what are you going to do? To the world, of course, all this is nothing. If the world should enter and hear us mourning the death of Enderby's lyric gift, the world, Enderby, would deem us not merely mad. They would consider us, Enderby, to be, Enderby' – he leaned forward, hissing – 'really talking about something else in the guise of the harmless. They would think us, perhaps, to be *Communists*.'

'And,' said Enderby, frightened by this vision of coming impotence, impotence perhaps already arrived, 'what do *you* do?'

'I?' Rawcliffe was already drunk again. He shoulder-jerked spastically and munched the air like spaghetti. 'I, Enderby, am the great diluter. Nothing can be taken neat any more. The question is this: do we live, or do we partly live? Or,' he said, 'do we,' and he was suddenly blinking in the killing lights, before the cranking cameras, jerking upright to stand against the wall, as against, with spread thin arms, a rockcliff, a rawface, 'die?' He then collapsed on the table, like a Hollywood absinthe-drinker, but none of the Romans took any notice.

4

'And,' said Vesta, 'what exactly do you think you've been doing? Where exactly do you think you've been?' Enderby felt a sort of stepson's guilt, the only kind he really knew, looking at her, head hung. She was brilliant in a wide-skirted daffodil-yellow dress, penny-coloured hair smooth and shining, skin summer-honeyed, healthy again, her eyes green, wide, nasty, a most formidable and desirable woman. Enderby said, mumbling: 'It was Rawcliffe, you see.'

She folded her bare arms. 'You know Rawcliffe,'

chumbled Enderby and, a humble and hopeful attempt at palliation of his crime or crimes, 'he's in all the anthologies.'

'In all the bars, most likely, if I know anything about Rawcliffe. And you've been with him. I'm giving you fair warning, Harry. You keep out of the way of people like Rawcliffe. What's he doing in Rome, anyway? It all sounds very suspicious to me. What did he say? What was he telling you?'

'He said that being a lyric poet was really like being a racing motorist and that you've only lowered yourself to marry me because you'll be in all the biographies and will share in my eternal fame and glory, and he said that my poetic gift was dying and then what was I going to do? Then he passed out and I had to help carry him upstairs and that made me very thirsty. Then I couldn't find a taxi for a long time and I couldn't remember the name of the hotel. So that's why I'm late. But,' said Enderby, 'you didn't say anything about what time to be back, did you? You didn't say anything at all.'

'You said you were going to cash traveller's cheques,' said Vesta. 'It was your duty to stay here, with me. A fine start to a honeymoon this is, isn't it, you going off with people like Rawcliffe to get drunk and listen to lies about your wife.'

'What lies?'

'The man's a born liar. He was always trying to make passes at me.'

'When? How do you know him?'

'Oh, he's been a journalist of sorts,' said Vesta. 'Always messing round on the fringes of things. He's probably here in films, I should think, just messing round. Look,' she said very sternly, 'in future you're not to go anywhere without me, do you understand? You just don't know the world, you're just too innocent to live. My job is to look after you, take charge of things for you.'

'And *my* job?' said Enderby.

She smiled faintly. Enderby noticed that the bottle of

Frascati, three-quarters full when he had left the bedroom, was now empty. She had certainly recovered. Outside was gentle Roman early evening. 'What do we do now?' asked Enderby.

'We go and eat.'

'It's a bit early for that, isn't it? Don't you think we ought to drink a little before eating?'

'You've drunk enough.'

'Well,' said Enderby, looking again at the empty Frascati bottle, 'you haven't done too badly yourself. On an empty stomach, too.'

'Oh, I sent down for some pizza and then a couple of club sandwiches,' said Vesta. 'I was starving. I still am.' She took from the wardrobe a stole, daffodil-yellow, to cover her bare shoulders against evening cold or Italian lust. She had unpacked, Enderby noticed; she couldn't have been ill for very long. They left the bedroom and went down by the stairs, mistrusting the frail filigree charm of the lift. In the corridors, in the hotel lobby, men frankly admired Vesta. Bottom-pinchers, suddenly realized Enderby, all Italians were blasted bottom-pinchers; that raised a problem. And surely duels of honour were still fought in this backward country? Out on the Via Nazionale, Enderby walked a pace behind Vesta, smiling sourly up at the SPQR shields on the lamp standards. He didn't want any trouble. He hadn't before quite realized what a responsibility a wife was. 'I was told,' said Vesta, 'that there's a little place on the Via Torino. Harry, why are you walking behind? Don't be silly; people are looking at you.'

Enderby skipped to her side, but, invisible to her, his open hand was spread six inches behind her walking rump, as though warming itself at a fire. 'Who told you?'

'Gillian Frobisher.'

'That,' said Enderby, 'is the woman who nearly killed me with her Spaghetti Surprise.'

'It was your own fault. We turn right here.'

The restaurant was full of smeary mirrors and smelt

strongly of cellar-damp and very old breadcrumbs. Enderby read the menu in gloom. The waiter was blue-jawed,
lantern-jawed, untrustworthy, trying to peer, slyly, into
Vesta's *décolletage*. Enderby wondered why such glamour
surrounded the Italian cuisine. After all, it consisted only
of a few allomorphs of paste, the odd sauce or so; the only
Italian meat was veal. Nevertheless Enderby read 'bifstek'
and, with faint hope, ordered it. Vesta, starving, had
worked through minestrone, a ravioli dish, some spaghetti
mess or other, and was dipping artichoke leaves into oily
vinegar, Enderby had begun to glow on a half-litre of
Frascati when the alleged steak arrived. It was thin, white,
on a cold plate. Enderby said to the waiter :

'*Questo é vitello.*' He, who had, before his life with
Vesta, subsisted on ghastly stews and dips in the jampot,
now became steak-faced with thwarted gastronome's anger.

'*Si, é vitelo, signore.*'

'I ordered beefsteak,' cried furious Enderby, uncouth
Englishman abroad, 'not bloody veal. Not that it is bloody
veal,' he added, with poetic concern for verbal accuracy.
'Fetch the manager.'

'Now, Harry,' rebuked Vesta. 'We've had enough
naughtiness for one day, haven't we? See, people are looking at you.' The Roman eaters all round were shovelling
away, swollen-eyed, sincerely voluble with each other.
They ignored Enderby; they had seen his type before. The
manager came, fat, small, shiftily black-eyed, breathing
hard with suppressed indignation at Enderby.

'I ordered,' said Enderby, 'a steak. This is veal.'

'Is a same thing,' said the manager. 'Veal is a cow. Beef
is a cow. Ergo, beef is a veal.'

'Are you,' said Enderby, enraged by this syllogism, 'trying to teach me what is a beefsteak and what is not? Are
you trying to teach me my own bloody language?'

'Language, Harry, language,' said Vesta ineptly.

'Yes, my own bloody language,' cried Enderby. 'He
thinks he knows better than I do. Are you going to stick
up for him?'

'Is a true,' said the manager. 'You not a eat, you pay just a same. What a you a order you a pay.'

Enderby stood up, saying, 'Oh, no. Oh, most certainly bloody well no.' He looked down at Vesta, before whom frothed a zabaglione. 'I'm not,' he said, 'paying for what I didn't order, and what I didn't order was that pallid apology down there. I'm going to eat somewhere else.'

'Harry,' she ordered, 'sit down. Eat what you're given.' She pinged her zabaglione glass pettishly with her spoon. 'Don't make such a fuss over nothing.'

'I don't like throwing money away,' said Enderby, 'and I don't like being insulted by foreigners.'

'You,' said Vesta, 'are the foreigner. Now *sit down*.'

Enderby grumpily sat down. The manager sneered in foreigner's triumph, ready to depart, having resolved the stupid fuss, meat being veal anyway, no argument about it. Enderby saw the sneer and stood up again, angrier. 'I won't bloody well sit down,' he said, 'and he knows what he can do with this bloodless stuff here. If you're staying, I'm not.'

Vesta's eyes changed from expression to expression rapidly, like the number-indicator of a bus being changed by the conductor. 'All right,' she said, 'dear. Leave me some money to pay for my own meal. I'll see you in fifteen minutes in that open-air café place.'

'Where?'

'On the Piazza di what's-its-name,' she said, pointing.

'Repubblica,' said the waiter, helpful.

'You keep your bloody nose out of this,' said Enderby. 'All right, then. I'll see you there.' He left with her a large note for several thousand or million lire. From it the face of some allegorical lady looked up at Enderby in mute appeal.

Fifteen minutes later Enderby, gazing glumly at the colour-lit fountain, watching the Vespas and the Fiats and the sober crowds, sat near the end of a bottle of Frascati. It had come to him warm, and he had said to the terrace waiter. '*Non freddo*.' The waiter had agreed that the bottle was *non freddo* and had gone off smiling. Now the bottle was less *freddo* than ever. It was a warm evening. Enderby felt a sudden strong longing for his old life, the stewed tea, the poetry in the lavatory, onanistic sex. Then, wanting to blubber, he realized that he was being very childish. It was right that a man should marry and be honeymooning among the fountains of Rome; it was right to want to be mature. But Rawcliffe had said something about poetry being a youthful gift, hence immature, cognate with the gifts of speed and alertness that made a man into a racing-driver. Was it possible that the gift was already leaving him, having stayed perhaps longer than was right? If so, what was he, what would he turn into?

Vesta arrived, a *Vogue* vision of beauty against the flood-lit fountain. Fluttered and suddenly proud, Enderby stood up. She sat down, saying, 'I was really ashamed of you in there. You behaved absolutely disgracefully. Naturally, I paid for the meal you ordered. I hate these petty wrangles over money.'

'My money,' said Enderby. 'You shouldn't have done it.'

'All right, your money. But, please remember, *my* dignity. I don't allow you or any man to make a fool out of me.' She softened. 'Oh, Harry, how could you, how could you behave like that? On the first day of our honeymoon, too. Oh, Harry, you upset me dreadfully.'

'Have some wine,' said Enderby. The waiter inclined with a Roman sneer, bold eyes of admiration for the *signora*. 'That last lot,' said Enderby, 'was bloody *caldo*. This time I want it *freddo*, see? Bloody *freddo*.' The waiter went, sneering and leering. 'How I hate this bloody town!' said Enderby, suddenly shivering. Vesta began to snivel quietly. 'What's the trouble?' asked Enderby.

'Oh, I thought things would be different. I thought you'd be different.' Suddenly she stiffened, staring straight ahead of her, as though waiting for some psychic visitation. Enderby looked at her, his mouth open. Her mouth opened, too, and, as from the mouth of a spiritualistic medium, there was emitted what sounded like the greeting of a Red Indian 'control':

Haaaaooooo.

Enderby listened in silent wonder, his mouth open wider. It was a belch.

'Oh,' she said, 'sorry. I couldn't help that at all, really I couldn't.'

'Let it come,' said Enderby kindly. 'You can always say excuse-me.'

Barrrrrp.

'I *do* beg your pardon,' said Vesta. 'You know, I don't think I feel frightfully well. I don't think this change of food is agreeing with me.' Rorrrrp. Auuuuu.

'Would you like to go back to the hotel?' asked Enderby eagerly.

'I think I'll have to.' Borrrrphhh. 'We're having the most unfortunate day, aren't we?'

'The Toby night,' said Enderby with relief. 'Like Tobias in the Apocrypha.' He took her arm.

Chapter Two

1

'Piazza San Pietro,' said the guide. 'St Peter's Square.' He was a young Roman with a crewcut, insolent, bold eyes for the ladies. 'Place Saint Pierre. St Peter's Platz.' Vulgar, decided Enderby. Pretentious. The guide saw Enderby's sourness, saw he was not impressed. 'Plaza San Pedro,' he said, as though playing a trump card.

It was a real scorcher, and Vesta was dressed for a real scorcher in beige linen, something austere and expensive by Berhanyer. She had amazing powers of recuperation. Last night her stomach upset had jabbered and frothed away like an idiot child even when, eventually, she had got to sleep. Enderby had lain in clean pyjamas listening tolerantly, her slim back and haunches visible through the diaphanous nightdress, neat but unseductive, heaving occasionally with new accessions of wind, the bedclothes having been kicked away by Enderby because of the warmth of the night. The bedside lamp out, she had become a mere parcel of noises which had filled Enderby with weak nostalgia for his single days, so that he had gone to sleep to dream of stewpans and the craft of verse, the sea. At three-thirty by his luminous wristwatch (a wedding-present), he had awakened with his heart punch-balling desperately because of Strega and Frascati to hear her still fizzing and pooping healthily away. But, waking at nine o'clock to the peevish traffic of the Via Nazionale, he had seen her at the window, eating.

An essential task had not yet been accomplished. Enderby, blinking and squinting, noting that he had slept with his teeth in, wondering where he had put his contact lenses, was emboldened by morning chordee to say, 'Oughtn't you to come back to bed for a while? What I mean is, you ought really.' Impromptu verses, wittily gross, came into his head to give the lie to Rawcliffe's raised finger of doom; the Muse was still very much with him:

> The marriage contract was designed,
>   Despite what all the notaries think,
> To be by only one pen signed,
>   And that is mine, and full of ink.

Enderby hesitated about saying these verses aloud. Anyway, Vesta said:

'I've been up for hours. I had a ham omelette in the restaurant and now I'm eating the breakfast I ordered for you. But it's only *croissants* and jam and things. Look, we're going on a little excursion. I thought it might be fun. We're going to see Rome. The coach calls here at nine-thirty, so you'd better hurry.' Waving the excursion tickets in a shaft of Roman sun, then cracking a kind of hard bread: 'You don't seem very enthusiastic. Don't you want to see Rome?'

'No.' Ask a straight question and you get a straight answer.

'You call yourself a poet. Poets are supposed to be full of curiosity. I don't understand you at all.'

Anyway, here they were, stepping out of the coach in full noon, to inspect the Obelisk of Nero's Circus. The guide, who had decided that Enderby was a Spaniard, said ingratiatingly, 'Obelisco del Circo de Nerón.' '*Sí*,' said Enderby, unenticed, 'Look,' he said to Vesta, 'I'm parched. I must have a drink.' It was all the solids they'd been forced to eat – the Pincian Gate and the Borghese Gallery and the Pincio Terrace and the Mausoleum of Caesar Augustus and the Pantheon and the Senate House and the Palace of Justice and the Castle of St Angelo and the Via della Conciazione. Enderby remembered what the great poet Clough had said about Rome. Rubbishy, he had called it. Enderby was always ready to defer to the judgement of a great poet. 'Rubbishy,' he quoted.

'You know,' said Vesta, 'I do believe you're really quite a philistine.'

'A thirsty one.'

'All right. It's nearly the end of the tour, anyway.' Enderby, who had developed in less than a day a sightless instinct for drinking shops, led Vesta down the Road of Conciliation. Soon they were sitting very cool and drinking Frascati. Vesta sighed and said:

'Peace.'

Enderby choked on his wine. 'I beg your pardon?'

'That's what we all want, isn't it? Peace. Peace and order. Certitude. Certainty. The mind quiet and at peace in the presence of order.' Her skin was so clear, so youthful, under the widebrimmed hat (also from the Madrid workshop of the crafty young Berhanyer), and her body so elegantly decked; exquisite the stallion-flared nostrils and honest and yet clever the green eyes. 'Peace,' she said again, then sighed once more. 'Och.'

'What was that word?' asked Enderby.

'Peace.'

'No, no, the one after.'

'I didn't say anything after. You're hearing things, Harry boy.'

'What did you call me then?'

'Really, what *is* the matter with you? Rome's peculiar magic seems to be having a curious influence. . . . And you're drinking far far more than you drink in England.'

'You cured my stomach,' said Enderby ungrudgingly. 'I find I can down any quantity of this stuff without any ill effects. That diet you put me on certainly worked wonders.' He nodded cheerily at her and poured more wine from the flask.

Vesta looked slightly disgusted; she flared her nostrils further, saying, 'I talk about peace and you talk about stomachs.'

'One stomach,' said Enderby. 'Poets talk about stomachs and *Fem* editors talk about peace. That seems a fair division.'

'We can look forward to so much peace,' said Vesta, 'the two of us. That beautiful house in Sussex, overlooking the downs. It breathes peace, doesn't it?'

'You're too young to want peace,' said Enderby. 'Peace is for the old.'

'Och, we all want it,' said Vesta fiercely. 'And I feel it here, you know, in Rome. A big big peace.'

'A big piece of peace,' said Enderby. '*Pax Romana*. Where they made a desolation they called it a peace. What absolute nonsense! It was a nasty, vulgar sort of civilization, only dignified by being hidden under a lot of declensions. Peace? They didn't know what peace was. The release of the vomitorium after fieldfares in syrup and quail's brains in aspic and a go at a little slave-boy between courses. They knew that. They knew the catharsis after seeing women torn apart by mangy starved lions in an arena. But they didn't know peace. If they'd been quiet and reposeful for thirty seconds they'd have heard too many voices telling them that the Empire was all a bloody swindle. Don't talk to me about the bloody *pax Romana*.'

Enderby snorted, not quite knowing why he was so moved.

Vesta smiled in tolerance. 'That's not real Rome. That's Hollywood Rome.'

'Real Rome *was* Hollywood Rome, only more so,' said Enderby. 'And what's really left of it now? Mouldering studio-lots. Big vulgar broken columns. The imperial publicity of P. Virgil Maro, yes-man to Augustus and all his triumphal arches, now dropped. Boots boots boots boots marching up and down again. Rome.' Enderby made, appropriately but vulgarly, the old Roman sign. 'A big maggoty cheese, with too many irregular verbs.'

Vesta was still smiling, somewhat like Our Lady in the vision Enderby had had that slippery day, travelling to London with a poem to give birth to. 'You just don't listen, do you? You just don't give me a chance to say what I want to say.'

'Bloody Roman peace,' snorted Enderby.

'I didn't mean that Empire. I meant the other one being nourished in the catacombs.'

'Oh God, no,' murmured Enderby.

Vesta drank some wine and then, quite gently, belched. She did not say excuse me; she did not seem to notice. Enderby stared. She said, 'Doesn't it seem to you to be a bit like coming home? You know – the return of the prodigal? You opted out of the Empire and have regretted it ever since. It's no good denying it; it's there in your poems all the time.'

Enderby breathed deeply. 'In a way,' he said, 'we all regret the death of universal order. A big smile of teeth. But that smile is a smile of dead teeth. No, not even just dead. False. It never began to be alive. Not for me, anyway.'

'Liar.'

'What do you know about it?' said Enderby, truculent.

'Oh, more than you think.' She sipped her Frascati as though it were very hot tea. 'You've never been much interested in me, have you? Not really. You've never troubled to find out anything about me.'

'We haven't known each other very long,' said Enderby, somewhat guiltily.

'Long enough to get married. No, be honest. To Enderby, Enderby's always been the important thing. Enderby the end of Enderby.'

'That's not really true,' said Enderby doubtfully. 'I've regarded my work as important, I suppose. But not myself. I've not cared very much for my own comfort or honour or glory.'

'Exactly. You've been too interested in yourself to be interested in those things. Enderby in a void. Enderby spinning round and round in an eternal lavatory.'

'That's not fair. That's not true at all.'

'You see? You're getting really interested. You're prepared for a good long talk about Enderby. Supposing we talk about me instead.'

'Gladly,' said Enderby, settling himself in resignation. Vesta pushed her wine-glass away and, with slim hands folded on the table, said:

'How do you think I was brought up?'

'Oh,' said Enderby, 'we know all about that, don't we? Good Scottish home. Calvinist. Another imperial dream to be opted out of.'

'Oh, no,' said Vesta, 'not at all. Not Calvinist. Catholic. Just like you.' She smiled sweetly.

'What?' squawked Enderby, aghast.

'Yes,' said Vesta, 'Catholic. There are Catholics in Scotland, you know. Lots and lots of them. It was intended that I should be a nun. There, that's a surprise for you, isn't it?'

'Not really,' said Enderby. 'Granted that original premiss, which I'm still trying to digest, not at all a surprise. You wear your clothes like a nun.'

'What a very odd thing to say!' said Vesta. 'What, I wonder, do you mean by that?'

'Why didn't you tell me before?' asked Enderby, agitated. 'I mean, we've lived under the same roof for, oh, for months, and you've never breathed a word about it.'

'Why should I have done? It never seemed relevant to anything we ever talked about. And you never showed any curiosity about me. As I've already said, you have, for a poet, surprisingly little curiosity.'

Enderby looked at her, definitely curiously: by rights, this revelation should have modified her appearance, but she still seemed a slim Protestant beauty, cognate with his adolescent vision, an angel of release.

She said, 'Anyway, it makes no difference. I left the Church when I was, oh, when I married Pete. He, as everybody but you knows, had already been married and divorced. I was drifting anyway; I didn't believe any more. Pete believed in motor engines, I'll say that for him, and he used to pray before racing, though I don't know what to; perhaps to some archetypal internal combustion engine. Pete was a nice boy.' She drained her glass.

'Have some more wine,' said Enderby.

'Yes, I will, just a little. Rome has a peculiar atmosphere, hasn't it? Don't you feel that? It makes me, somehow, feel that I'm empty, empty of belief and so on.'

'Be careful,' said Enderby, very clearly, leaning across. 'Be very careful indeed of feeling like that. Rome's just a city like anywhere else. A vastly overrated city, I'd say. It trades on belief just as Stratford trades on Shakespeare. But don't you start thinking that it's a great pure mother calling you home. You can't go home, anyway. You're living in sin. We were only married in a registry office, remember.'

'And are we living in sin?' asked Vesta coolly. 'I haven't noticed particularly.'

'Well,' said Enderby, confused, 'that's what the world would think if the world happened to know and to be Catholic. We're not, of course, really, as you say, living in sin at all.'

'You've contracted out of everything in your time, haven't you? Out of the Church, out of society, out of the family –'

'Damn it all, I am, after all, a poet –'

'Everything goes into the lavatory, everything. Even the act of love.'

Enderby flushed flea-coloured. 'What do you mean by that? What do you know about that? I'm just the same as anybody else, except that I'm not accustomed, except that it's been a long time, except that I'm ugly and shy and –'

'Everything's going to be put right. You just wait. You'll see.' She gave him, forgiving, a kind cool hand. Anything he might then have wanted to say was snatched from his very lungs by a massive silver plunging of claws, swallowed, as all sounds of angelic noontime were swallowed, by a sudden boisterous revelry of bells, huge throats of white metal baying, snarling, hurling, fuming at the sky, the heavens of Rome a nickel and aluminium flame of bells.

2

After sauced pasta and a straw-harnessed globe of Chianti, Vesta's proposal seemed reasonable enough. Because she spoke of the process rather than the end: cool breezes stirred by the fan of the moving coach; the stop for tasting the wines of the Frascati vineyards; the wide sheet of lake and the *albergo* on its shore. And then the rolling back to Rome in early evening. It was more than a proposal, anyway. When Enderby said yes she promptly pulled the tickets out of her handbag. 'But,' said Enderby, 'are we to spend all our time in Rome riding in coaches?'

'There's a lot to see, isn't there? And you'd better see it all just so you can confirm that it's rubbishy.'

'It is rubbishy, too.' And Enderby, in after-lunch somnolence, thought particularly of that ghastly Arco di Costantino which was like a petrified and sempiternal page of the *Daily Mirror*, all cartoons and lapidary headlines. But a lake would be, especially in this cruel mounting heat, different altogether. Rome was really best taken in liquid form – wine, fountains and Aqua Sacra. Enderby approved of Aqua Sacra. Charged with a wide selection of windy

151

chemicals, it brought the wind up lovely and contrived a civilized evacuation of the bowels. In these terms he recommended it seriously to Vesta.

Enderby was surprised that this lake was to be visited by so many. Boarding the coach at the hotel, he had immediately prepared for sleep; almost at once they, and the jabbering polyglot others, had been told to get out. They were at some nameless piazza, sweltering and bone-dry, mocked by a fountain. There, their metal blistering in the sun, stood a fleet of coaches. Men with numbered placards stuck on sticks yelled for their squads, and obedient people, frowning and wrinkling in the huge light, marched on to markers. 'We're Number Six,' said Vesta. They marched.

Heat was intense in the coach; it had cooked to a turn in a slow oven. Even Vesta glowed. Enderby became a kind of fountain, his bursting sweat almost audible. And a worried man came on to the coach, calling, 'Where is Dr Buchwald?' in many languages, so that a kind of fidgety sense of responsibility for this missing one pervaded the coach and engendered scratchiness. In front of Enderby a Portuguese snored, his head on the shoulder of a Frenchman, a stranger; Americans camera-recorded everything, like the scene of a crime; there were two chortling Negroes; a large ham-pink German family spoke of Rome in serious and regretful cadences, churning the sights and sounds into long compound sausage-words. Enderby closed his eyes.

Vaguely, through the haze of his doze, he was aware of comforting wind fanned in by the movement of the coach. 'A very popular lake,' he said sleepily to Vesta; 'must be. All these people.' The convoy was rolling south. Through the coach loudspeaker came the voice of the guide, in Italian, French, German and American, and the intermittent drone was finneganswaked by lightly sleeping Enderby into a parachronic lullaby chronicle, containing Constantine the grandgross and battlebottles fought by lakes which were full of lager. He awoke, laughing, to see villas and vineyards and burning country, then slept again, carrying into deeper sleep a coin-image of Vesta looking on him protectively with the protectiveness of a farmer's wife carrying a pig to market.

He was awakened, smacking dry lips, to a small town of great charm and cleanliness, napkin-carrying waiters waiting on a wide terrace full of tables. Stiff stretching coach-loads got out to drink. Here, Enderby understood, they were very near to Frascati, and that wine that was so shy of travel had travelled the least possible distance. White dust, heat, the shimmering flask on the table. Enderby felt suddenly well and happy. He smiled at Vesta and took her hand, saying:

'Queer that we're both renegade Catholics, isn't it? You were right when you said that it's a bit like coming home. What I mean is, we understand a country like this better than the Protestants. We belong to its traditions.' He indicated, with a kind smile, a couple of hungry-eyed children at the foot of the terrace steps, the elder of the two solemnly nose-picking. 'Even if you don't believe any longer,' said Enderby, 'you're bound to find England a bit strange, a bit inimical. I mean, take all the churches they stole from us. I mean, they can keep them for all I care, but they ought to be reminded occasionally that they're really still ours.' He looked round the full drinking terrace happily, soothed by the jabber of alien phonemes.

Vesta smiled somewhat sourly and said: 'I wish you wouldn't talk in your sleep. Not in public, anyway.'

'Why, what was I saying?'

'You were saying, "Down with the Pope", or words to that effect. It's a good thing that not many people on this trip can understand English.'

'That's funny,' said Enderby. 'I wasn't even thinking of the Pope. That's very curious. Amazing what the subconscious mind can get up to, isn't it?'

'Perhaps you'd better stay awake on this leg of the journey,' ordered Vesta. 'It's the last leg.'

'I mean, it isn't as though anybody mentioned the Pope,

or anything, is it?' puzzled Enderby. 'Look, people are climbing aboard.'

They followed the chatter, smiling faintly at their fellow-passengers as they moved down the aisle of the coach. There had been some changing-round of seats, but that didn't matter: at the very furthest, you could not be more than one seat away from the window. A paunched small cocky Frenchman, however, linen-suited and with panama as though resident in a colony, hurled and fluted sharp words at a German who, he alleged, had taken his seat. The German barked and sobbed indignant denial. A tipsy lean Portuguese, thus encouraged by a fellow-Latin, started on an innocent red cheese of a Dutchman: a claim had, at the outset, been staked to that seat nearest the driver and renewed at this stop for refreshment – see, your fat Dutch arse is sitting on it, my map of Rome and environs. Europe now warred with itself, so that a keen-eyed Texan called, 'Aw, pipe down.' The guide came aboard and spoke French, saying that as a little infant at school he had been taught to keep to the first seat allotted to him. Enderby nodded; in French that sounded reasonable and civilized. The guide translated into American, saying, 'Like you were in school, stick to your own seat and don't try and grab somebody else's. Okay?'

Enderby felt himself growing instantly red and mad. He cried: 'Who the hell do you think you are – the Pope?' It was an Englishman's never-never-never protest against foreign overbearingness. Vesta said, 'Why don't you keep your big mouth –' The words of Enderby were translated swiftly into many tongues, and faces turned to look at Enderby, some wondering, others doubtful, yet others fearful. But one elderly man, a grey and dapper *raisonneur*-type, stood to say, in English. 'We are rebuked. He reminds us of the purpose of our journey. Catholic Europe must not be divided.' He sat down, and people began to look more warmly on Enderby, one wizened brownish woman offering him a piece of Belgian chocolate. 'What did he mean by that?' asked Enderby of Vesta. 'The purpose o our journey, he said. We're going to see this lake, aren't we? What's a lake got to do with Catholic Europe?' 'You'll see,' soothed Vesta, and then, 'I think, after all, it might be better if you *did* have a little sleep.'

But Enderby could not now doze. The countryside slid past, brilliant distant townships on high sunlit plateaux, olive, vine, and cypress, villas, browned fields, endless blue sky. And at length came the lake, a wide white sheet of waters in laky air, the heat of the day mitigated by it, and the little inn close by. The guide, who had sulked and been silent since Enderby's blast of brash Britishry in rebuke, now stood up to say, 'We stay here two hours. The coach will be parked in the parking-place for coaches.' He indicated, with a sketchy squizzle of his Roman fingers, roughly where that might be. He frowned at the Enderbys as they came down the coach-aisle, a blue-jawed lean Roman's frown despite Enderby's 'No hard feelings? Eh?' He was even stonier when Enderby said, '*Ma é vero che Lei ha parlato un poco pontificalmente.*' 'Come on,' said Vesta.

The wide silver water breathed coolness. But, to Enderby's fresh surprise, nobody seemed anxious to savour it. Crowds were leaving coaches and toiling up a hill towards what seemed to be a walled township. Coach after coach came up, disgorging unfestive people, grave, some pious with rosaries. There were carved Africans, a gaggle of Chinese, a piscatorium of Finns, a rotary chew of Americans, Frenchmen haussing their *épaules*, rare blond Vikings and their goddesses, all going up the hill. 'We,' said Vesta, 'are also going up there.'

'What,' asked Enderby carefully, 'lies up yonder hill?'

'Come on.' Vesta took his arm. 'A little poetic curiosity, please. Come and find out.'

Enderby now half-knew what lay at the top of the hill-street they now began to ascend, dodging new squealing arriving coaches, but he suffered himself to be led, passing smiling sellers of fruit and holy pictures. Enderby paused for a moment aghast, seeing a playing-card-sized portrait repeated more than fifty-two times: it seemed at first to be his stepmother in the guise of a holy man blessing his portrait-painter. And then it was not she.

Panting, he was led up to massy gates and a courtyard already thronged and electric. Behind himself and Vesta crowds still moved purposefully up. A trap, a trap: he would not be able to get out. But now there was a holy roar, tremendous, hill-shaking, and an amplified voice began to speak very fast Italian. The voice had no owner: the open ecstatic mouths drank the air, their black eyes searching for the voice above the high stucco buff walls, the window-shutters thrown open for the heat, trees and sky. Joy suffused their stubbled faces at the loud indistinct words. The cry started – '*Viva, viva, viva!*' – and was caught up. 'So,' said Enderby to Vesta, 'it's him, is it?' She nodded. And now the French became excited, ear-cocking, lips parted in joy, as the voice seemed to announce fantastic departures by air: Toulon, Marseilles, Bordeaux, Avignon. '*Bravo!*' The vales redoubled to the hills, and they to heaven. '*Bravo, bravo!*' Enderby was terrified, bewildered. 'What exactly is going on?' he cried. Now the voice began to speak American, welcoming contingents of pilgrims from Illinois, Ohio, New Jersey, Massachusetts, Delaware. And Enderby felt chill hands clasp his hot body all over as he saw the rhythmical signals of a cheer-leader, a young man in a new jersey with a large blue-woven P.

'Rhode Island,' said the voice. 'Kentucky, Texas.'

'Rah, rah, rah!' came the cheers. 'The Pope, the Pope, the Pope!'

'Oh God, no,' moaned Enderby. 'For Christ's sake let me get out of here.' He tried to push, with feeble excuse-mes, but the crowd behind was dense, the eyes up to the hills, and he trod on a little French girl's foot and made her cry. 'Harry,' said Vesta sharply, 'you just stay where you are.'

'Mississippi, California, Oklahoma.' It was like something from a sort of holy Walt Whitman.

'Rah, rah, rah! The Pope, the Pope, the Pope!'

'Oh Christ,' sobbed Enderby, 'please let me get out, please. I'm not well, I'm ill, I've got to get to a lavatory.'

'The Church Militant is here,' said Vesta nastily, 'and all you want is a lavatory.'

'I do, I do.' Enderby, his eyes full of tears, was now grappling with a redolent Spaniard who would not let him pass. The French child still cried, pointing up at Enderby. Suddenly there was a sort of exordium to prayer and everybody began to kneel in the dust of the courtyard. Enderby became a kind of raging schoolmaster in a sea of stunted children. She too knelt; Vesta knelt; she got down on her knees with the rest of them. 'Get up!' bawled Enderby, and, like a sergeant, 'Get off your bloody knees!'

'Kneel down,' she ordered, her eyes like powerful green poisons. 'Kneel down. Everybody's looking at you.'

'Oh my God,' wept Enderby, praying against the current, and he began to try to get out again, lifting his legs as though striding through treacle. He trod on knees, skirts, even shoulders, and was cursed roundly even by some who prayed with frightening sincerity, their eyes dewy with prayer. Stumbling, himself cursing, goose-stepping clumsily, laying episcopal palms on heads, he cut through the vast cake of kneelers and reached, almost vomiting, blind with sweat, the gate and the hill-road. As he staggered down the hill, past the smiling vendors, he muttered to himself, 'I was a bloody fool to come.' From the top of the hill came the sound of a great Amen.

3

'*Cefil Uensdi*,' said the man. '*Totnam Otispar. Cardiff Siti.*' He had a surprised lion-face, though hairless, with a few wavy filaments crawling over his otherwise bare scalp. Staring all the time at Enderby as though convinced Enderby wished to mesmerize him and too polite (a) to object that he did not wish to be mesmerized and (b) to announce that the mesmerism was ineffectual, he ever and anon brought, with a bold arm gesture, a cigarette-end to his lips, drawing on this with a desperate groan as if it were a sole source of oxygen and he dying.

'*Tutti buoni*,' nodded Enderby over his wine. 'All football very good.'

The man gripped Enderby's left forearm and gave a mirthless grin of deep deep blood-brotherhood's understanding. They were sitting at rough trestle-tables in the open air. Here Frascati had reached its last gasp of cheapness – golden gallons for a few bits of tinkly metal. '*Ues Bromic*,' the man went on in his litany. '*Mancesita lunaiti. Uolveramiton Uanarar*.' This, though more heartening than the geographical manifests up the hill, was beginning to weary Enderby. He wondered vaguely if perhaps that was what Etruscan had sounded like. Up on the main road, beyond the dark and nameless trees that were a wall to this sky-roofed tavern, the pilgrims could be heard coming back to their buses, walking slowly and with dignity now after the comic freewheeling down the hill. If Vesta had any sense at all she would know where to find him. Not that, in his present mood, he cared much whether she found him or not. Next to the lion-faced man with the football litany lolled a patriot who did not believe that Mussolini was really dead: like King Arthur he would rise with unsheathed sword to avenge his country's new wrongs. This man said that the English had always been the friends of Mussolini; Italian and Briton together had fought to expel the foul Tedesco. He bunched one side of his face often at Enderby, raising his thumb like an emperor at the games, winking in complicity. There were other drinkers on the periphery, some with bad unsouthern teeth, one carrying on his shoulder an ill-kempt parrot that squawked part of a Bellini aria. There was also a very buxom girl, a country beauty called Bice, who brought round the wine. Enderby did not, would not, lack company. He only wished his Italian were better. But 'Blackburn Rovers' he fed to the litanist and 'Newcastle United'; to the patriot 'Addis Ababa' and 'La Fanciulla del Golden West'. Meanwhile thunder flapped with extreme gentleness on the other side of the lake. 'Garibaldi,' he said. 'Long live Italian Africa!'

When Vesta at last arrived the pleasant dirty drinking-yard at once was disinfected into a background for a *Vogue* fashion pose. She looked tired, but her calm and elegance fluttered all present, making even the roughest drinkers consider removing their caps. Some, remembering that they were Italian, said dutifully, '*Molto bella*' and made poulterer's pinching gestures to the air. Without preamble she said to Enderby, 'I knew I'd find you in some such place as this. I'm fed up. I'm sick to death. You seem to be doing your utmost to make a farce out of our honeymoon and a fool out of me.'

'Sit down,' invited Enderby. 'Do sit down. Have some of this nice Frascati.' He bowed her towards a dry and fairly clean part of the bench on which he had been sitting. The litanist, grasping that she was *Inglese*, assuming a passion for football in her accordingly, said, ingratiatingly, 'Arse an all,' meaning a football team. Vesta would not sit. She said :

'No. You're to come with me and look for this coach. What I have to say to you must wait till we get back to Rome. I don't want to risk breaking down in public.'

'Peace,' mocked Enderby. 'Peace and order. You played a very mean trick on me, and I shan't forget it in a hurry. A really dirty trick.'

'Come on. Some of the coaches are going already. Leave that wine and come on.' Enderby saw that there still remained a half-litre of this precious golden urine. He filled his glass and said, '*Salute*.' His swallow excited cries of '*Bravo*', as enthusiastic as those heard up the sacred hill, though not then for Enderby. 'Right,' said Enderby, waving farewell. 'We're late,' said Vesta. 'Late for that coach. We wouldn't have been late if I hadn't had to come looking for you.'

'It was a mean trick,' repeated Enderby. 'Why didn't you tell me that we were being taken to the Vatican?'

'Oh, don't be so stupid. That's not the Vatican; that's his summer residence. Now where on earth is this coach?'

There was a bewildering number of coaches, all looking

alike. The pilgrims had nestled snugly and smugly in
them; some of them were impatiently roaring off. Coaches
had settled everywhere – by the roadside, down small hilly
streets – like big bugs in bed-crevices. Vesta and Enderby
began to examine coaches swiftly but intently, as though
they proposed to buy them, passengers and all. None
looked familiar, and Vesta made noises of distress. Listening through his thick curtain of wine, Enderby thought he
heard the veneers and inlays of Received English stripped
roughly off, so that something like raw Lallans became
audible, as spicy as home-pickled onions with its gut-
turals and glottal stops. She was really worried. Enderby
said:
   'Damn it all, if they do leave us behind there's no great
harm done. There must be a bus service or trains or taxis
or something. It's not as though we're lost in the jungle
or anything.'
   'You insulted him,' complained Vesta. 'It was blasphemous, too. These people take their religion very seriously,
you know.'
   'Nonsense,' said Enderby. Stealthily the sky had, above
their searching heads, been clouding over. There was a
greenish look in the atmosphere as though the atmosphere
proposed, sooner or later, to be sick. From beyond the lake
care renewed gentle drummings, as of finger-tips on tim-
pani. 'It's going to rain,' wailed Vesta. 'Och, we'll be
caught in it. We'll be drenched.' But Enderby, in imper-
meable of wine, said not to worry, they would catch that
blasted bus.
   But they did not catch it. As soon as they approached a
coach, the coach skittishly started up, its gears grinding a
derisive expletive all for Enderby. Faces looked down,
grinning pilgrims, and some hands waved. It was as though
Vesta and Enderby were host and hostess after some huge
party, seeing off loads of quite unappreciative guests. 'He's
done it deliberately,' cried Vesta. 'He's getting his own
back. Oh, you *are* a nuisance.' They hurried towards another coach and, like a kitten in chase-me play, it at once

began to move off. There were very few left now, but Enderby was fairly sure that, from one of these few, a Roman face, the ignoble face of a Roman guide, leered and Roman fingers made a complicated gesture of mean triumph.

The timpanists across the lake picked up their felt sticks and rolled for a few bars, while the coaches, as though they could thus escape from bad weather, sang off to the city. The lake underwent complex metallurgical changes and the sky, cloaking hot and fearsome lights, began to sweat, then cry. 'Oh Jesus,' called Vesta, 'here it comes.' And indeed there it came while they were still half a mile from shelter other than that of trees: the sky cracked open like a waterbutt, and the air became vertical glass down which pail after pail was poured. They dashed blindly towards the lakeside inn, Vesta tottering on her smart spikes, Enderby gripping her elbow as though her arm were a pair of blackboard dividers, already too wet really to be all that urgent about seeking shelter. The deluge made Enderby's scalp prickle with dandruff, and his fawn summer suit was soaked. But she, poor girl, was already a wreck: hat comically flopping, hair in rat-tails, mascara running, her face that of a crying old crone as though she wept over the disintegration of her *chic*. 'In here,' gasped Enderby, steering her straight into a room smelling of size and new paint, empty chairs and tables in it, a sleek boy-waiter admiring the free show of the rain. 'I think,' panted Enderby, 'that we'll have to take a room, if they have one. The first thing to do is to get dry. Perhaps they'll –' The waiter called a name, then turned his young empty face back on these two wet ones. Enderby said, '*Una camera. Si é possible.*' The boy called again, an unbroken boy's yelp under the drumming water. A woman came, creamily fat in a flowered frock, clucked commiseration, took in in a swift look Vesta's ringed finger, said there was a *camera* with one *letto*. Beside her smiling hugeness Vesta looked a snivelling waif. '*Grazie,*' said Enderby. Lightning cracked momentarily the late-sky, the timpanists counted half a bar and came in with a fine peal, rolling cosmic Berlioz chords. Vesta made the sign of the cross. She was shivering.

'What,' asked Enderby, 'did you do that for?'

'Oh God,' she said, 'it scares me. I can't stand thunder.' Enderby felt his stomach turn over when she said that.

4

Up in the bedroom they confronted each other naked. Somehow, for some reason, Enderby had not expected that, when they had stripped off their drenched clothes and dumped them outside the door, they would confront each other naked. Naked confrontation was supposed to come about otherwise: deliberately, in desire or duty. Enderby had been trying to digest too many other things to foresee this prelapsarian picture (and there up the hill, so neatly fitting into the pattern, was a great postlapsarian witness), for the room was very much like his own as a boy – pictures of St John the Baptist, the Sacred Heart, the B.V.M., a melodramatic Golgotha; a smell of unclean bedclothes, dust, boots, and stale holy water; a stringy unbeaten carpet; a narrow bed. This reproduction of the main stage-set for so many adolescent monodramas, here in Italy under rain, did not depress him: that bedroom had always been an enclave of revolt in stepmother country. Very clearly, lines of an unpublished poem came back to him:

... There were times, misunderstood by the family,
   When you, at fifteen, on your summer evening bed
Believed there were ancient towns you might anciently visit.
   There might be a neglected platform on some station
And a ticket bought when the clock was off its guard.
   Oh, who can dismember the past? The boy on the friendly
     bed
Lay on the unpossessed mother, the bosom of history,
   And is gathered to her at last. And tears I suppose
Still hunger for that reeking unwashed pillow,
   That bed ingrained with all the dirt of the past,
The mess and lice and stupidity of the Golden Age,
   But a mother and loving, ultimately Eden. ...

He nodded several times, standing there naked in rainy Italy, thinking that it was a mother he had always wanted, not a stepmother, and he had made that mother himself in his bedroom, made her out of the past, history, myth, the craft of verse. When she was made she became slimmer, younger, more like a mistress; she became the Muse.

Lightning again shivered the firmament and then, after a careful count, the laughing drummers knocked hell out of their resonant membranes. Vesta gave a little scream, put her arms round Enderby's trunk, and then seemed to try to push herself inside him as though he were a disemboweled rabbit of great size and she a mound of palpitating stuffing. 'There, there,' said Enderby, kindly but disturbed: she had no right to bring these stepmother terrors into his adolescent bedroom. Then he sweated, seeing more than a mere fear of thunder. Still, he clasped her to him and soothed her shoulder-blades, thinking how such naked contacts had an essential unalluring core of *heartiness*: the slap of palm on buttock; the jelly sound of two moist segments of flesh drawing apart. She shivered: the air had cooled considerably.

'You'd better,' said Enderby, 'get into bed.'

'Yes,' she shuddered, 'yes. Into bed.' And she pulled him towards bed, her grip on him unrelaxed, so that they shambled to it as though clumsily dancing. As soon as they were in it, a skein of lightning lay an instant against the sky, like a stunned man against a cliff, and then the drums whammed out from hi-fi loudspeakers all over the heavens. She again seemed to try to enter him in fear, a rather soft rock of ages, and he smelt her terror, as familiar a smell as that faintly oily one of the coverlet.

'There,' he said again, clasping her, stroking and soothing. It was a very narrow bed. This, he kept reminding himself, was his bride, an intelligent and desirable young woman and it was time, under the thunder and rain, to be thinking of performing, that is to say consummating, that is to say. He stealthily felt his way down to find out what was his body's view of this constatation, but all was quiet there, as though he were calmly reading Jane Austen.

The rain eased and the thunder was trundled, grumbling, off. Enderby felt her body relax and seem, somehow, to grow moister and more expectant. She gripped him still, though there was no more thunder to fear. Enderby's engines, rusty and sluggish, tried to wake up and respond to various quite unoriginal ganglionic stimuli, but there were certain difficulties which were secret and shameful. Enderby had been spoiled by too many pictures; it was a long time since he had held a real woman in his arms like this; he had possessed in imagination houri after houri of a beauty, passivity, voluptuousness no real woman could ever touch. Perhaps, he now felt, if this body he held could become – just for twenty or thirty seconds – one of those harem dreams of his, pampered, pouting, perfumed, steatopygous, he could, he was sure, achieve what it was a plain duty, apart from all questions of gratification, to achieve. But the body of his bride was spare, barely cushioned. With a desperate effort he conjured a gross tit-swinging image, saw whose image it was, then, making the retching noises of a child trying to disgust, he swung out of the bed with unwonted agility and stood shivering on the worn mat. 'What's the matter?' she called. 'What is it? Don't you feel well?' Forgetting that he was naked, Enderby dashed out of the room without replying. Two doors down the corridor was the sign *Gabinetto*, and Enderby, re-living the past, entered it and locked its door. To his horror he found that the lavatory was not a sane comfortable English WC but a Continental crouch-hole with a right-hand hand-rail and a toilet-roll-fitting on the same side. Once, many years ago, he had fallen into one of these holes. He almost cried for the security of his old seaside lavatory but, unlocking the door to leave, the tears froze as he heard two female Italian voices on the corridor. One of these, saying loud passing greetings to the other, was now right up against the *gabinetto* door and trying the handle. Enderby swiftly re-locked himself in. The voice spoke urgently, saying, for all

Enderby knew, that its owner was in a bad way, desperate, and couldn't wait too long. Enderby seated himself on the edge of the low crouch-hole dais, saying, 'Go away. Go away,' and, as an afterthought, '*Io sono nudo, completamente nudo*', wondering if that was correct Italian. Correct or not, the voice was silenced and apparently carried back down the corridor. Enderby the completely naked sat on, in thinking pose, feeling at his lowest ebb.

5

Like an Arab thief, though not so slippery, Enderby darted back to the bedroom. Vesta was sitting up in the bed, smoking a ship's (or export) Woodbine through a holder and, because of that, looking more naked than she was, though this, reflected Enderby, was not really possible. 'Now then,' she said. 'We're going to have this whole thing out.'

'No,' mumbled Enderby. 'Not like this.' He sat shamefacedly down on the cane chair in the corner, wriggling and wincing as odd prickly cane thorns assaulted his bottom. 'Not,' said Enderby, 'with no clothes on. It's not right.' He joined his hands as for prayer and, with this frail cage of fingers, hid his genitals from the smoking woman in the bed. 'I mean,' said Enderby, 'one can't really talk about anything naked.'

'Who are you to say that?' she said fiercely. 'What do you know about the world? My first husband and I once belonged to a nudist camp –' (Enderby whimpered at the sudden formality of 'first husband') '– and there used to be *really* prominent men and women there, and they didn't have any *pudeur* about talking. And they, I might add,' she added acidly, 'could talk about rather more than lavatories and stomachs and how rotten the Roman Empire must have been.' Enderby gazed glumly out of the window, seeing that the rain had stopped and the June warmth, encouraged, was creeping back into the Italian evening. Then he was granted a brief image of a fat sack-bellied middle-aged female nudist don, breasts hanging like tripe, discoursing on aesthetic values. This cheered him up a little, so he turned boldly on Vesta to say:

'All right then. Let's have it out, the whole damned thing. What exactly do you think you're playing at?'

'I don't understand you,' she said. 'I'm playing at nothing. I'm working hard, with absolutely no co-operation from you, to try and build a marriage.'

'And your idea of building a marriage is to try to drag me back into the Church, is that it?' said Enderby, half-uncovering his genitals so as to gesticulate with one hand. 'And in a nasty sly way too. Not saying anything about being a Catholic yourself, and even being quite ready to have a registry office wedding, even though you know that that sort of wedding means nothing at all.'

'Oh,' she said, 'you admit that, do you? You admit that it means nothing at all? In other words, you admit that a Catholic wedding is the only valid one?'

'I don't admit anything,' cried Enderby. 'All I'm saying is that I'm confused, completely confused about what's supposed to be going on. What I mean is, we've only been married a couple of days, and everything seems to have changed. You weren't like this before, were you? You weren't like this when we were living in your flat in London, were you? Everything was all right then. You were on my side, and you were getting on with your job and I was getting on with mine, and it was all nice and pleasant and not a care in the world. But now look at things. Since we got married, and that's only a couple of days ago, mind you, only a couple of days –' (two fingers held up, five on his genitals) '– you've been doing your damnedest to turn into my stepmother.'

Vesta's mouth opened and smoke wandered out. 'To what, did you say? To turn into what?'

'My stepmother, bitch as she was. You're not fat yet, but I suppose you soon will be. You keep belching away all the time and saying "Och" and going on at me – natter and nag, nag and natter – and you're scared of the bloody thunder and you're trying to get me to go back into the Church. Why? That's what I want to know. Why? What's your motive? What are you getting at? What are you trying to do?'

'This,' she said heavily, 'is fantastic. This is the most incredible – this is the most incredible fantastic –' She started to get out of bed. Enderby, seeing this, saw that there would be too much visible nakedness about the room, so he lunged across from the cane chair, genitals swinging, and pushed her back into bed and pulled the clothes over her. He said:

'We'll have less frivolity, if you don't mind, and less nonsense. Before we got married – listen to me, I'm talking – before we got married you were what I'd dreamed of, ever since I was a boy. You were everything she wasn't; you were a release; you were a way out. You were something that would kill her for good and all. And now look at you.' He pointed sternly. She, as though he were a stranger who had just broken in, pulled the grey sheet over her bosom and looked fearful. 'You're trying to drag me back into that old world, aren't you? Back to the bloody Church and female smells all over the place –'

'You're drunk,' she said. 'You're mad.' There was a knock at the door and Enderby, gesticulating, went to answer it, now wearing his nakedness as unconsciously as if it were a suit. 'Drunk, eh?' he said. 'Mad, eh? You've made me drunk, that's what it is.' He opened the door, and the lady of the house presented a pressed pile of dried clothes. '*Tante grazie,*' said Enderby, and then, turning back on his wife, he presented his bottom to the *signora*; she slammed the door and went off speaking loud Italian. 'Things,' said Enderby, 'already,' dumping the clothes on the bed, 'have not worked out at all as I expected. It's been a bloody big mistake, that's what it's been.'

She reached over for her clothes, angrily fussily trembling, saying, 'A mistake, you say? That's gratitude, I must say, gratitude.' She paused, one hand on her clothes, breathing deeply as if a stethoscope had begun to wander down her back, eyes downcast, seeking self-control. Then she said, calmly, 'I'm keeping my temper, you notice. Somebody has to be rational.' Enderby began, in a sort of hopping dance, to put on his underpants. 'Listen to me,' she said, 'listen. You're like a child, you know so little about life. When I first met you, it looked horrible that a man of so much talent should be living the way you did. No, let me speak, let me keep my temper.' Enderby, from inside his shirt was mumbling something. 'You had nothing to do with women,' she continued, 'and no faith in anything, and no sense of responsibility to society. Oh, I know you had substitutes for all those things,' she said bitterly. 'Dirty photographs instead of flesh and blood.' Enderby repeated the hopping dance, this time with his trousers, scowling and blushing. 'Society,' she said, with loud eloquence, 'shrunk to the smallest room in the house. Is that any life for a man?' she asked strongly. 'Is that any life for a poet? Is that the way you expect to make great poetry?'

'Poetry,' said Enderby. 'Don't you start telling me about poetry. I know all about poetry, thank you very much,' he said with a bull-snort. 'But let me tell you this. There's no obligation to accept society or women or religion or anything else, not for anyone there isn't. And as for poetry, that's a job for anarchs. Poetry's made by rebels and exiles and outsiders, it's made by people on their own, not by sheep baaing bravo to the Pope. Poets don't need religion and they don't need bloody little cocktail-party gossip either; it's they who make language and make myths. Poets don't need anybody except themselves.'

Vesta picked up her brassière and wearily dropped herself into it as though it were some necessary instrument of penance. 'You seemed,' she said, 'to like going to parties. You seemed to think it was a good thing to wear a decent suit and talk with people. You said it was civilized. You gave me, one evening you may have forgotten, a long dull lecture on the Poet and Society. You even went to the trouble of thanking me for having rescued you from your old life. Some day,' she sighed, 'you'll make it absolutely clear to people what exactly you *do* want.'

'Oh,' said Enderby, 'it was all right, I suppose. It made a nice change. It was nice to be clean and smart, you see, and hear educated accents. It was, you see, so different from my stepmother.' Now fully dressed, he sat with greater confidence on the cane-bottomed chair in the corner. 'But,' he said, 'if society means going back to the Church, I don't want anything to do with society. As far as I'm concerned, the Church is all tied up with that bitch, superstitious and nasty and unclean.'

'Oh, you're so stupid,' said Vesta, having put on her dress swiftly and neatly. 'You're so *uneducated*. Some of the best modern brains are in the Church – poets, novelists, philosophers. Just because a silly illiterate woman made a nonsense out of it for you doesn't mean that it *is* a nonsense. You're a fool, but you surely aren't such a fool as all that. Anyway,' she said, clicking her handbag open and rummaging for a comb, 'nobody's asking you to go back into the Church. The Church, presumably, can get on very well without you. But if I'm going back, you might at least have the courtesy and decency to go through the form of going back with me.'

'You mean,' said Enderby, 'that we'll have to get properly married? By a priest in a church? Look,' he said, folding his arms and crossing his legs, 'why didn't you think about all this before? Why do you have to wait till our honeymoon before you decided to baa back to the fold? Don't answer, because I know the answer. It's because you want to go down to posterity as the woman who reorganized Enderby's life, faith and works. It's what Rawcliffe said, and I hadn't thought of it before, because I really believed that you had some affection for me, but, looking at it more soberly, I can see now that was impossible, me being ugly and middle-aged and, as you're kind enough to say, stupid. All right, then; now we know how we stand.'

She was combing her hair, gritting her teeth at the tangles, and the penny-colour shone out, crackling, renewed after its rat-tailed dullness. 'Fool, fool,' she said. 'My idea was that we could make a go of marriage. We still can. Of course, if you think that Rawcliffe's more trust-worthy than I am (and remember that Rawcliffe's jealous as hell of you) then that's your own affair and you can get on with it. The fact is that, for all your stupidity, I'm very fond of you and, at the same time, I feel that I can make you happy by making you more normal, more sane.'

'There you are, you see,' said Enderby in triumph.

'Oh, nonsense. What I mean is this: an artist needs a place in the world, he needs to be committed to something, and he needs to be in touch with the current of life. Surely the trouble with all your work is that it reads as though it's cut off from the current?'

'Very interesting,' said Enderby, his arms still folded. 'Very, very fascinating.'

'Och,' she said, drooping as though suddenly very weary. 'What does it matter? Who's going to care whether you write great poetry or not? The feeblest teenage pop-singer is a million times more regarded than you are. You sell only a handful of copies of every book you write. There's going to be a nuclear war and the libraries will be destroyed. What's the use? What good can it all possibly be if one doesn't believe in God?' She sat on the bed, quite dispirited, and began to cry softly. Enderby came softly over to her and said:

'I'm sorry, I'm terribly sorry. But I think I'm too old to learn really, too old to change. Perhaps we'd better admit it's all a mistake and go back to things as they were before. No real harm's been done, not yet, has it? I mean, we're not even properly married, are we?'

She looked up sternly and said, 'You're like a child. A child who doesn't like his first morning at school so says he doesn't think he'll go back in the afternoon.' She wiped her eyes and became hard, self-possessed again. 'Nobody makes a fool of me,' she said. 'Nobody throws me over.'

'You could have the marriage annulled,' said Enderby.

170

'On the grounds of non-consummation. Because it won't ever be consummated, you know.'

'You think,' said Vesta, 'that you'll go back to living on a tiny but adequate income, writing your poetry in the lavatory. But you won't. What little bit of capital you've got left I shall have. I'll make sure of that. And the things you've bought are on my name. Nobody makes a fool out of me.'

'I can get a job,' said Enderby, growing angry. 'I'm not reliant on anybody. I can be independent.' Then he felt tears of self-pity coming. 'The poet,' he said, whimpering, 'is best left to live on his own.' Through his tears he had confused images of Dantesque eagles flitting round lightning-shot peaks. He left the edge of the bed and went to stand in a corner. 'The poet,' he said, blubbing like that seven-year-old Elizabethan bridegroom who had cried to go home with his father.

Chapter Three

1

'My main purpose,' said swaying Rawcliffe, 'was to present you with –' He swayed and fumbled in various pockets, drawing out filthy old papers decaying at their folds, two half-used tubes of stomach tablets which were dust-fluffy, a referee's whistle, a dry rattle of ball-points, finally a quite clean envelope. '– these. Tickets for a première. I think, my dear old Enderby, you should be reasonably amused. I have no further interest in the film in question, having been so closely involved in it. And, let me tell you, Enderby, it is a cheap film, a film made on a shoestring, a film made very quickly, with bits borrowed – quite without permission, you know – from other films. Strega,' he said suddenly to Dante behind the bar. The bar was, as at their first meeting in it, empty except for them. Enderby felt worn and old, his mouth seeming to taste of cascara-coated motoring chocolate. It was mid-morning, the day after the day of their return from the papal township by the lake, and Vesta had gone to see a woman called Princess Irene Galitzine, a Roman lady famed for her boutique models or couture designs or something. Vesta was spending money fast. 'And,' said Rawcliffe, 'there are, of course, for this the world expects of Italy, several *sfacciate donne Fiorentine*, except that they're not Florentine but Roman, *mostrando con le poppe il petto*. There, Enderby, you see: brazen-faced bitches showing breasts with paps. Dante was a great prophet; he foresaw the Italian film industry. Dante.'

Dante behind the bar bowed. 'Same a name,' he said confidentially to Enderby.

'Bloody big coincidence, eh?' swayed Rawcliffe. 'You'll find everything in Dante, Enderby, if you look long enough. Even the film you're going to see derives its title from the *Purgatorio*. I found that title, Enderby, I, an English poet, for none of these unholy Romans has even so much as glanced at Dante since leaving school, if any of them ever went to school.' Enderby took from the envelope the cards of invitation and saw that the film was named *L'Animal Binato*. It meant nothing to him. He turned to the bottle of Frascati on the counter and poured himself a tumbler. 'Drinking hard, I see, Enderby,' said Rawcliffe. 'If I may make so lewd a guess, it is because you are using muscles you never used before. Venus catches cold without Bacchus and Ceres, although you can leave out that goddess of breakfast foods for all I care. Strega,' he called again, nodding vigorously.

'Look,' said Enderby, 'I'm not taking you home again. You were a damned nuisance last time, Rawcliffe, and you made a real fool out of me. If you're going to pass out here, you can stay passed out, is that clear? I've got worries of my own without having to look after –'

'He talks in rhyme,' said Rawcliffe in exaggerated wonder. 'He is still very much the poet, is he not? But for how much longer now, eh?' he said sinisterly, slitting his eyes.

'The Muse, O Enderby. Has the Muse yet been in to tell you that she has booked her one-way flight to Parnassus or wherever Muses live? She has done her long stint with Enderby and the time has come for Enderby to abjure this rough magic and pack it in, the Muse, unlike Ariel, being no airy slave of indeterminate sex but a woman, very much a woman.' Rawcliffe now made himself look shrunken and very old. 'Perhaps, Enderby, I was destined never to be much of a success with that particular woman because of – you know, because of – that is to say, a certain, shall I say, indeterminate attitude towards sex.' He sighed in a litre or so of Roman bar air. He drank down a centilitre or less of Strega. 'And now, you see, Enderby, I'm on the move again. This afternoon, to be precise. So, you see, you won't have to carry me home or anywhere. The BEA men will come and collect me, excellent fellows. They will get me on that plane. Where am I going, Enderby?' He leered roguishly, wagging a finger. 'Ah, I'm not telling you. I am, suffice it to say, on my way further south. I have picked up my little packet here.' He tapped, winking, the right breast of his coat. 'And now little Marco and Mario and that bloody Piedmontese, to quote Milton, can go and stuff themselves. I have finished, Enderby, with the lot. Finish, Enderby,' he said loudly and with emphatic fists on the counter, 'with the lot. You, I mean. Get wise to yourself, as they say. Wake up. A poet must be alone.'

Enderby pouted, pouring himself the last of his bottle. He felt that it was not up to Rawcliffe to tell him that he must be alone. He took from his inside jacket-pocket a piece of paper on which he had been doing sums. 'Did you know,' he said, 'how much mink costs? Mink,' he repeated. 'I have it here,' he said carefully. 'One Black Diamond mink coat: one thousand four hundred and ninety-five pounds. One hip-length jacket: five hundred and ninety-five pounds. One pastel mink bolero: three hundred and ninety-five pounds. We leave out of account,' said Enderby, 'as being too inexpensive for serious consideration, a pastel stole at two hundred pounds. That's a frippery, a mere nugacity.' He smiled sillily. 'What,' he asked, 'can a poet do with no money, eh? How does a poet live?'

'Well,' said Rawcliffe, both hands round his new Strega as if it were something to be strangled, 'there are jobs, you know. All sorts of jobs. Only the very luckiest of poets can be professional poets. You could teach or write for the papers or do film scripts or advertising slogans or lecture for the British Council or get unskilled work in a factory. Lots of things to be done.'

'But,' objected Enderby, 'suppose one is no good at anything except writing poetry? Suppose one makes a bloody fool of oneself at anything else?'

'Oh,' said Rawcliffe reasonably, 'I don't think that anybody could make such a bloody fool of himself that it would really matter. Now, if I were you, I should leave everything in the hands of Auntie Vesta. She'll fix you up with something nice and easy.'

'But,' protested Enderby, 'only a minute ago you were telling me that I've got to be alone.'

'I see,' said Rawcliffe, seeing into his Strega. 'Well, in that case it's all a bit of a mess, isn't it, Enderby? But don't worry me with your worries, Enderby, because I've got worries of my own, you see. You sort out things for yourself.' He seemed suddenly sober and rather cold despite the June warmth. He downed his Strega and shivered exaggeratedly, as if he had taken a wholesome but bitter medicine. 'Perhaps,' he said, 'I should have started this heavy drinking business earlier. I might possibly be dead by now instead of having putatively fathered or foster-fathered or helped with the illegitimate fathering of *L'Animal Binato*, alive and healthy and almost impervious to the more deadly effects of alcohol. I should, by rights, Enderby, have considered seeing myself off when I found that the lyric gift had departed from me. I could at least have contrived to be careless crossing the road, couldn't I? And, instead of that propaganda job during the war, I could perhaps have volunteered for something more genuinely lethal.'

'What,' asked Enderby morbidly, 'did it feel like? I

mean, when the lyric gift departed?' Rawcliffe looked up so morosely, fixing Enderby with an eye so baleful, that Enderby began to smile nervously. Rawcliffe said:

'Blast your mean little soul, it's no laughing matter, even in retrospect.' Then he came nearer to Enderby and gave him a close-up of bad teeth and worse breath. 'It was like everything going all dead,' said Rawcliffe. 'It was like going dumb. I could see quite clearly what had to be said, but I couldn't say it. I could perceive that an imaginative relationship existed between disparate objects but I couldn't tell what the relationship was. I used to sit for hours with paper in front of me, hours and hours, Enderby, and then I would at last get something down. But what I got down somehow – don't laugh at me – had a smell of decay about it. What I got down was *evil*, and I used to shudder when I crumpled it up and threw it in the fire. And then, at night, in bed, I used to wake up to hear mocking laughter. And then,' tottered Rawcliffe, 'one night there was the sound of an awful *click*, and then everything in the bedroom seemed cold, somehow, cold and obscene. I knew, Enderby, it was all over. Thenceforward I should be outside the Garden, useless to anyone, a mess and, moreover, Enderby, in some indefinable way *evil*. Like an unfrocked priest, Enderby. The unfrocked priest does not become a mere neuter harmless human being; he becomes *evil*. He has to be used by something, for supernature abhors a supervacuum, so he becomes *evil*, Enderby.' He swigged more Strega and staggered, as it were, against the ropes, saying, 'And all that is left for the poet, Enderby, when the inspiration is departed, Enderby, is the travesty, the plagiarism, the popularization, the debasement, the curse. He has drunk the milk of paradise, but it has long passed through his system, Enderby, and, unfortunately for him, he remembers the taste.' Rawcliffe shut weary eyes, saying, '*Ara vos prec,*' and then 'be mindful in due time of my pain.' I translate, Enderby, because you would not understand the original Provençal. That is the poet Arnaut Daniel in Purgatory. He was a lucky bugger, or is, Enderby, a lucky bugger to be in Purgatory. Not like some of us.' At this point, Rawcliffe went quite gently to sleep standing up, his head reposing on arms he had folded on the counter. Dante said: 'Better e slip.' There was a plum-plush settee against the wall; to this Dante and Enderby carried, led, pushed, dragged Rawcliffe. 'Too mash fackin Strega,' diagnosed Dante. Sighing, Enderby sat next to Rawcliffe, a fresh bottle of Frascati and a tumbler on the table in front of him, and he continued to do sums on bits of paper. At intervals Rawcliffe gave gnomic utterance, often obscure, from his sleep; reports from the first crazed space-traveller:

'No expense of breath in falling downstairs.'

'Mario, put that bread-knife away.'

'You are a naughty boy, but not undelectable.'

'In all the antholololologies.'

'This will make Enderby feel very sick.'

Indeed, Enderby felt very sick when he had worked out his sums and found that his credit balance in the bank stood at, taking the most liberal computation, little more than four hundred and ninety pounds. It was pointless asking himself where the money had gone to, for he knew all too well: it had flowed back to its source: his stepmother had given and his stepmother had, in a youthful, well-spoken, dove-soft, spring-smelling, highly improbable disguise, taken away again. From his sleep Rawcliffe called:

'Aha! Man not the boats, but woman-and-child them. I'll shoot all else. Back, you brute, back. The rash, smart, sloggering Hopkinsian brine. Enderby was a very inferior poet. Very wise of him to pack up.'

Enderby spoke sternly to this dark voice. 'I am not packing up,' he said. This silenced Rawcliffe's sleep-persona temporarily. To himself Enderby said, 'If I can keep the relationship on the most superficial of levels, for superficially I am quite fond of her, then it should be possible to contrive some sort of satisfactory co-existence. But I will not be ordered about. And she has, after all, a good job and I could, at a pinch, refuse to get a job of my own or have a job found for me. The Sussex house has many rooms. My stomach is better.' Rawcliffe's sleeping voice spoke again from outer space:

'You will do as I say, Vincent. I will not have you calling Reggy an old queen. He is not old.' And then, 'God should feel highly flattered that we have invented Him.' And finally, before falling into serious speechless sleep, in the voice of Yeats speaking with the voice of Swift speaking with the voice of Job: *'Let the day perish wherein I was born.'* Enderby shuddered, the wine seeming sharper than usual.

2

They arrived late for the film première. The cinema was in an obscure street somewhere off the Viale Aventino, and the taxi-driver had difficulty in finding it. He at first denied, in the manner of taxi-drivers, the existence of what he himself did not know existed, until Enderby waved a ticket of invitation in his moustached face. The façade of the cinema rather let down the rest of Rome, thought Enderby, as he helped Vesta out of the cab.

Sculpturally and architecturally, the rest of Rome was rubbishy, yet rubbishy on a baroque and hypnotic scale, like the delusions of grandeur of some gibbering G.P.I. patient. But here was authentic fleapit, from the look of it, epitome of every bughouse that Enderby had, as a child, queued outside on Saturday afternoons, sticky paw clutching twopence, filthy-jerseyed other children clinging to him aromatically lest they lose him in the scrimmage of entrance, Enderby being the only one of their lot who could read. The old silent film had, Enderby reflected, been, in one facet, an extension of literature. He said now to Vesta, 'This is one of those places where you go in with a blouse and come out with a jumper.' He tweaked her elbow jocularly, but she looked queenlily blank. 'Blouse?' she said. 'I'm not wearing a blouse.' She was, in fact, wearing black silk from her Roman-lady *couturière*, sleeveless,

the back *décolleté*, the skirt slim, tails of mink dripping
from her shoulders against the night's cool. Enderby was
in white tuxedo, black silk in breast pocket to match tie.
But it looked as though he needn't have taken so much
trouble: there were no adoring crowds, no gleaming stars'
mouths of coral and ivory in maniacal abandon to the
flashbulbs, no jostle of Cadillacs and Bentleys. There were
a few decent Fiats, unattended, evidently owner-driven; a
painted banner across the deplorable rococo façade said,
in the midst of cheap coloured bulbs, L'ANIMAL
BINATO. The man who took their cards of invitation
chewed something morosely and his lantern-jaw was ill-
shaven. It let down Vesta as much as it let down Rome.
Little, of course, thought Enderby, could let down
Enderby.

They were flashlamped to their seats. Enderby felt torn
cheap plush beneath him and smelt a strong citrus tang
through the dark. Orange, too, bloodless orange, was the
light which warmed the worn stage curtains. These now,
as if they had been waiting only for Enderby and his wife,
parted to the noise of loud cinema music, banal, conven-
tionally sinister. Enderby peered through the dark: there
did not, by the feel and sound of things, seem to be a very
large audience. The screen said L'ANIMAL BINATO and
followed this with jerkily dissolved frames of the names
of the conspirators: Alberto Formica; Giorgio Farfalla;
Maria Vacca; A. F. Corvo; P. Ranocchio; Giacomo Capra;
Beatrice Pappagallo; R. Coniglio; Giovanni Chiocciola;
Gina Gatto. Rawcliffe's name appeared near the end,
Italianized to, as far as Enderby could tell, something like
Raucliffo. 'Serve him right,' thought Enderby, and told
Vesta so. She said shhhhh. The film began.

Night, very much night, with tortured cypresses lit by
lightning. Thunder (Vesta dug her nails into Enderby's
hand). Tempestuous wind. Camera tracks to steps of terrace, handsome woman standing thereon, much of Italian
bosom exposed to lightning. She raises arms, cornily, to
stormy heavens in crash of thunder. Camera swings up

178

towards sky. Another stock shot of lightning cracking cloud like a teacup. Thunder (Vesta's nails). New camera angle shows a something speeding down the firmament, a white flashing something. Cut to wooden effigy of cow, lightning-lit. Handsome bosomed woman seen walking through tempest, statelily, towards wooden cow. Lightning shows her doing something obscure, pulling some lever or other, then creaking music accompanies shot of wooden cow opening, two hollow half-cows, woman climbing into upright half, cow closing up, woman imprisoned in cow. Cut to white bull, snorting against the thunder, tearing down the sky, bull-lust from heaven.

'You know,' said Enderby with wonder, 'this is really an astonishing coincidence.'

'Shhhhh,' said Vesta. Enderby, his eyes now accustomed to the dark, looked round to find the cinema half-empty, but next to him was a huge man, jowled and bag-eyed in lightning from the screen, a cigar slowly burning towards his fingers, already asleep and snoring slightly.

Day. Ruritanian palace, moustached handsome king in late middle age conferring with deferential bearded (false-bearded) counsellors. Fanfare. Palaver is ended. One counsellor stays behind, ingratiating Iago-type, to talk to the king. The king's eyes cornily cloud with suspicion. Odd Italian words that Enderby can understand snap out from the sound-track: queen, cow, Dedalo. Dedalo ordered to be brought in. Cut to Dedalo's workshop. Dedalo and Icaro, Dedalo's crisp-haired son, are building aeroplanes. Dedalo very old skinny man. Summoned by servant, he pulls down shirt-sleeves, dons jacket period 1860, follows down labyrinthine corridors, a kind old man with clever eyes and deep face-furrows. He enters royal presence. Long unintelligible Italian colloquy with much eloquent arm-waving. Dedalo struck on aged face by angry king. Iago-type goes off, bowing, oily, leaving royal face in royal hands. Dedalo hauled off for torture.

Enderby now began to feel an emotion other than wonder; his stomach heaved and pricked with apprehension:

this was more than coincidence. 'Don't you think,' he said to Vesta, 'this is just a little too much like my poem? Don't you think –'

'Shhhhh,' she said. The snoring man next to Enderby said, in his sleep, '*Tace.*' Enderby, reminded of the sleep-talking Raucliffo, said, '*Tace* your arse.' And to Vesta, 'This is just like *The Pet Beast.*' He then remembered that she hadn't yet read it, had not, in fact, yet shown any desire to read it. He grimly watched the screen, the further un-winding of Raucliffo's infamy.

Day. Pregnant queen in exile, sitting in mean cottage with old crone. Colloquy. Labour-pains. Then dissolve to shot of doctor galloping in from afar. He enters cottage. From bedroom door come bellowing noises. He enters bed-room. Close-up of doctor's face. Horror, incredulity, nausea, syncope. Close-up, with foul discord of what doctor sees: head of bull-calf on child's body.

'That's mine,' said Enderby. 'It's mine, I tell you. If I find that blasted Rawcliffe –'

'It's nobody's,' said Vesta. 'It's just a myth. Even I know that.'

'*Tace,*' snored Enderby's pone.

Calf-child, in montage series, grows to bull-man, hideous, muscular, fire-breathing, gigantic. Having stolen piece of raw meat from kitchen, bull-man makes discovery of carni-vorous nature. Kills old crone and eats her. Tries to kill mother, too, but mother escapes, falls over cliff screaming but uneaten. Good clean fun. Bull-man totters, tall as ten houses, to capital city, leaving bone-trail behind. Cut to palace gardens where Princess Ariadne, with sizeable bosom-show, is playing ball with giggling bosom-showing alleged maidens. Close-up of beast drooling through thicket. Screams, scatter, Ariadne carried off on beast's back. Beast, drooling, carries her, screaming, to cellars of metropolitan museum. Shots of priceless pictures, rare books, stately sculptures, sounds of great music as bull-man bellows his-its way to hide-out deep beneath eternal monu-ments of culture. Ariadne shows more bosom, screams more loudly. Bull-man does not, however, wish to eat her, not yet anyway.

Enderby clenched his fists tight, their knuckles gleaming in the light that flashed, intermittently, from the screen. Dénouement. Alpine-Italian hero, Mussolini-headed, crashes into deep cellars, wanders through dark, hears bull-bellow and princess-scream, finds monster and victim, shoots, finds bullets of no avail as bull-man is, on sire's side, thing from outer space. Ariadne escapes, screaming, showing allowable limit of Roman bosom, as howling chest-beating beast advances on hero. Hero, like Count Belisarius, has pepper-bag. He hurls its contents, temporarily blinding beast. To sneezes-bellows-howls, hero escapes. Lo, a prodigy: Dedalo and Icaro in flying-machine some decades ahead of its time drop bomb on metropolitan museum. Howls of dying bull-man, crash of statuary, flap and rustle of books caught alight, Mona Lisa with burnt-out smile, harp-strings pinging as they crack. Death of culture, death of the past, a rational future, embracing lovers. Dedalo and Icaro have engine-trouble. They crash in sea, against glorious sunrise. Heavenly voices. End.

'If,' trembled Enderby, 'I could lay my hands on that bloody Rawcliffe –'

'Stop it, do you hear?' said Vesta very sharply indeed. 'I can't take you anywhere, can I? Nothing satisfies you, nothing. I thought it was quite a nice little horror film, and all you can do is to say that it's been stolen from you. Are you getting delusions of grandeur or something?'

'I tell you,' said Enderby, with angry patience, 'that that bastard Rawcliffe –' The house-lights, all sick sweet orange, came gently up, disclosing applauding people crying *bravo, brava,* and *bravi,* as for the Pope's whole family. The fat man next to Enderby, now radiantly awake, lighted his long-gone-out cigar and then openly laughed at Enderby's clenched fists. Enderby prepared twelve obscene English words as a ground-row (variations and embellishments to follow), but, like a blow on the occiput, it suddenly came to him that he had had enough of words, obscene or otherwise. He smiled with fierce saccharinity on Vesta and said, so that she searched his whole face for sarcasm, 'Shall we be going now, dear?'

3

Late at night, thought Enderby, meant in England after the shutting of the pubs. Here there were no pubs to shut, so it was not yet late. He and Vesta picked up a horse-cab or *carrozza* or whatever it was called on the Via Marmorata, and this clopped along by the side of the Tiber while Enderby fed sedative words to his wife, saying, 'I'm honestly going to make an effort, really I am. My maturity's been much delayed, as you realize. I'm really terribly grateful for everything you've done for me. I promise to try to grow up, and I know you'll help me there as you've helped me in everything else. That film tonight has convinced me that I've got to make a real effort to live in public.' Vesta, beautiful in the June Roman aromatic night, her hair stirred but gently by the bland wind of their passage, gave him a wary look but said nothing. 'What I mean is,' said Enderby, 'that it's no use living in the lavatory on a tiny income. You were quite right to insist on spending all my capital. I've got to *earn* a place in the world; I've got to come to terms with the public and give the public, within reason, what it wants. I mean, how many people would want to read *The Pet Beast*? A couple of hundred at the outside, whereas this film will be seen by millions. I see, I see it all.' He reminded himself of the main protagonist of a drink-cure advertisement in *Old Moore's Almanac*: the medicine cunningly mixed with the drunkard's tea; the immediate result – the drunkard's raising a hand to heaven, wife hanging, sobbing with relief, round his neck. Too much ham altogether. Vesta, still with the wary look, said:

'I hope you mean what you say. I don't mean about the film; I mean about trying to be a bit more *normal*. There's a lot in life that you've missed, isn't there?' She gave him her hand as a cool token. 'Oh, I know it must sound a little pretentious, but I feel that I've got a duty to you; not the ordinary duty of a wife to a husband, but a bigger one. I've been entrusted with the care of a great poet.' The horse should, rightly, have neighed; massed trumpets should have brayed from the Isola Tiberina.

'And you were quite right,' said Enderby, 'to bring me to Rome. I see that too. The Eternal City.' He was almost enjoying this. 'Symbol of public life, symbol of spiritual regeneration. But,' he said, slyly, 'when are we going back? I'm so anxious,' he said, 'to go back, so we can *really* start our life together. I long,' he said, 'to be with you in our own home, just the two of us. Let's,' he said, bouncing suddenly with schoolboy eagerness, 'go back tomorrow. It should be possible to get a couple of seats on some plane or other, shouldn't it? Oh, do let's go back.'

She withdrew her hand from his, and Enderby had a pang of fear, not unlike heartburn, that perhaps she was seeing through this performance. But she said:

'Well, no, we can't go back. Not just yet. Not for a week or so, anyway. You see, I have something arranged. It was meant to be a surprise, really, but now I'd better tell you. I thought it would be a good idea for us to be married, here in Rome, married properly. I don't mean a nuptial mass or anything, of course, but just the plain ceremony.'

'Oh,' gleamed Enderby, swallowing bolus after bolus of anger and nausea, 'what a very good idea!'

'And there's a very good priest, Father Agnello I believe his name is, and he'll be coming to see you tomorrow. I met him yesterday at Princess Vittoria Corombona's.' She trilled the name with relish, dearly loving a title.

False Enderby breathed hard with the effort of pushing True Enderby back into the cupboard. 'What,' he asked, 'was a priest doing in a dress-shop?'

'Oh, silly,' smiled Vesta. 'Princess Vittoria Corombona doesn't run a dress-shop. She does film-gossip for *Fem*. Father Agnello is very intellectual. He's spent a lot of time in the United States and he speaks English perfectly.

Strangely enough, he's read one of your poems – the blasphemous one about the Virgin Mary – and he's very anxious to have a couple of good long talks with you. Then, of course, he'll hear your confession.'

'Well,' smiled Enderby, 'it's good to know that everything's being taken care of. It's such a relief. I am really, you know, most grateful.' He squeezed her hand as they turned into the Via Nazionale: lights, lights; the Snack Bar Americano; the Bank of the Holy Spirit; shop after shop after shop; the air terminal, alight and busy; the hotel. The fat horse clomped to a ragged halt and snorted, not specifically at Enderby. The driver swore that his taxi-meter was wrong, a mechanical fault hard to repair, it showed too little. Enderby would not argue. He gave five hundred lire more than the clocked amount, saying 'Sod you too' to the driver. Rome; how he loved Rome!

Enderby watched and waited carefully in the hotel bar. There were late coffee-drinkers at the little tables, voluble speakers of fast foreign tongues, ten or a dozen all told, and Enderby would have given them all for Rawcliffe. He wished yesterday morning could be shunted back for just five minutes, he and Dante and Rawcliffe alone in the bar, one damned good crack on the proleptically bloody nose. *L'Animal Binato*, indeed. The Muse would be very annoyed now, fuming, a harpy, with all that work wasted. Enderby watched Vesta lovely over her glass of Pernod, waited till his third glass of Frascati, then writhed in simulated stomach-ache. 'Ugggggh,' said Enderby, 'blast it. Arrrrgh.' Vesta said:

'You've been drinking too much, that's your trouble. Come on, we're going to bed.' Enderby, artist to the end, made a harrowing borborygm, just like old times. Grerrrrkhrapshhhhh. She rose in concern. Enderby said:

'No. You wait here. There's a lavatory on the ground floor. Really, it's nothing.' He smiled, the liar, through his agony, motioning her to sit down again. He gargoyle-bulged his cheeks, nodded vigorously to show that this showed what it seemed to show, then left the bar smartly, urrping and arrrkhing to the surprise of the coffee-drinkers, into the lobby. To the insincerely gold-grinning dapper receptionist, framed in tubes of light at his desk, Enderby said urgently, 'I have to return to London. Just for a couple of days. Business. My wife will stay on here. I don't want you to think,' added Enderby guiltily, 'that I'm running away or anything like that. If you wish, I'll pay my bill up to date. But I'm leaving my luggage. All except one small overnight case. I take it that that will be all right, will it?' He almost prepared to give the receptionist a thousand-lire note of hush-money but, in time, thought better of it. The receptionist, with a graceful head-inclination as of one bending to hear the tick of a watch in an invisible man's waistcoat pocket, said that everything would be quite all right, but Signor Enderby must understand that there could be no rebate in respect of the time that Signor Enderby would be away. Signor Enderby gladly understood. 'I want,' he said, 'to ring up the air terminal, the one on this street. Could you give me the number?' The receptionist would be only too pleased to ring up for him; he could take the call in one of those boxes over there.

From the box Enderby could just see Vesta eating a ham sandwich. It must be ham, because she was stroking each sliver with what must be, from the shape of the jar, mustard. Enderby tried, which was not difficult, to look very ill in case she should glance up and see him. If she came over he would have to pretend that he had blindly dashed in here because it had the outward appearance of a lavatory; if she saw him urgently mouthing into the telephone he would have to pretend he was calling a doctor. A voice now spoke in English to Enderby, and Enderby said furtively, 'Enderby here.' The name, understandably, meant nothing to the suave clerkly voice. Enderby said, 'I want to travel to London by the next possible plane. Very urgent. I already have a first-class ticket, but my booking, you see, is for the twenty-fifth or twenty-sixth or something – I can't quite remember the exact date. This is very

very urgent. Business. And my mother's dying.' There was no cluck of condolence: hard bastards these Romans. The voice said, above the rustle of ledger-pages, that it thought there might be empty seats on the BOAC plane from Cape Town, due at Rome at five-thirty in the morning. The voice would ring back to confirm or deny. 'A matter of life and death,' said Enderby. The voice, however, seemed to know that Enderby was about to run away from his wife.

Vesta had finished her sandwiches and was picking her front teeth with an old London tube ticket she had taken from her bag. The bag was open, very untidy, but in it Enderby saw a bunch of keys. Those keys he would require: in the Gloucester Road flat were certain things he needed. Seeing the teeth-picking, Enderby nodded: another thing marshalling him the way that he was going. 'How do you feel now?' she asked.

'A good deal better,' smiled Enderby. 'I got a lot of it up.' With what was still in the bank, with what he thought he could legitimately filch from her (mink, chiefly), he considered it was possible for him to return for a year or two to something like his old life: the lone poet in some sordid attic or other with thin stews and bread, trying to make it up to his Muse. He did not repine at the loss of his capital. Not any longer. It was, after all, his stepmother's money, and here, now pulling a ham-fibre from her molars, though with grace and without ostentation, sat his stepmother, all too able to use that money. The interest, of course, was another matter. The Church had always condemned the lending out of money at interest, so no good Catholic had a right to claim the increment it had earned when the return of the loan was made. Enderby, though determined to be just, was also determined to be strictly Protestant here. As he smiled to himself he was suddenly jolted by the calling of his name over a loudspeaker.

'Who on earth,' said Vesta, 'can be ringing you up at this hour of the evening? You stay there, I'll take it. You're still looking a bit pale.' And she rose.

'No, no, no,' protested Enderby, pushing her roughly back into her cane armchair. 'It's something you're not supposed to know about. A surprise,' he tried to smile. She grimaced and, taking a hair-clip from her bag, began to clean her left ear. Enderby was delighted to see that.

The clerkly voice was pleased to be able to confirm a booking on the plane from Cape Town. Enderby was to report at the terminal at four; the clerk then on duty would alter his ticket for him. '*Deo gratias*,' breathed Enderby, meaning *grazie*. But only that liturgical gratitude, he reflected, could express his relief at the prospect of getting out of, with all its detonations and connotations, Rome.

'It's arranged,' he smirked at Vesta. 'Don't ask me what, but it's all arranged.' As they rose to go to their room he saw on the table a hair-clip; its bend of bifurcation was stuffed with ear-wax. He took Vesta's arm with something like love.

4

Staying awake till three-thirty was not really difficult. Really difficult was getting the packing done on a night when Vesta, normally a good solid Scots sleeper, had decided to be restless and somniloquent. Enderby watched her warily as she lay prone, having kicked the clothes off the bed, her nates silvered by the Roman moonlight to the likeness of a meringue. Delectable, yes, but from now on for somebody else's delectation. Enderby stole about the silvered room in his socks, suddenly stiffening as in a statue dance each time she burbled in her sleep, rushing to the dark corner by the window to stand as if for his height to be taken when she pettishly whisked from the prone to the supine. Supine, she uttered strange words to the ceiling and then chuckled, but Enderby would not permit himself to be scared. Taking his passport and air ticket from the top drawer of the chest of drawers he also, after a few seconds of ethical thought, decided to take hers. Thus, if she woke to a realization of Enderby's desertion, she would not be able to follow at once. But he placed several thousand or million lire on the mantelpiece, and he knew that she had traveller's cheques of her own. Although she and Rome went so beautifully together, he could not, in all decency, condemn her to too long an enforced stay; he hoped he still had enough humanity not to wish that on his worst enemy.

One suitcase was enough for Enderby's clothes and shaving gear. The lotions and creams and sprays she had made him buy – these he decided to leave behind: no one would ever want to smell him any more. Now there was the question of that key to the flat; he had left a couple of boxes there, stuffed with drafts and notes. The typescript of *The Pet Beast* was locked in the drawer of her own escritoire, and there it could stay. Its interest, he admitted glumly, was one of content more than form, and the content had been filched and distorted. Let that be a lesson to him. Enderby now squinted in the moonlight for Vesta's bag, a flat silver envelope into which, that evening, she had poured the entire load of rubbish from a black bag from a grey bag from a white bag from a blue bag, a woman who, with residual Scots thrift, could not bear to throw anything away. Enderby saw this silver bag, further silvered by the light, lying on her bedside table. He stalked over for it, like some clumsy ballerina on her points, and, as he made to pick it up, Vesta swiftly pronated, diagonal across the bed, and a bare slim arm flopped over the table to hold the bag down like a silver bar. Enderby hesitated now, standing with breathing suspended, wondering whether he dare risk. But then she, with the same swiftness, lurched her body to the supine, though with her left arm still across the table, and began to speak out of some profound dream. She said:

'Pete. Do it again, Pete. Och, Pete, that was bloody marvellous.' It was a coarse accent, suggesting the Gorbals rather than Eskbank, and, to match it, the sleeping Vesta began to use coarse terms suggesting an extremity of abandon. Enderby listened horrified, at last calming his nerves by reflecting that anything, even necrophily, was allowed to the dreamer. He did not now try to extract the bag from under her silver arm; he could perhaps get into the flat without a key. Effect an entrance, as they say. He now wished to effect an exit, and quickly.

As he fumbled at the door-handle, hidden under the mink coat that hung from the door-hook, he had the impression that she was about to lift herself out of sleep, some warning bell having shrilled at the end of one of the long corridors of the cerebral cortex. He calmed her with words and a noise:

'Brarrrkh. Just going to the lavatory.' His last words to her as he softly folded the mink over his arm. She grunted, smacked her lips, then, seeming satisfied, started to lower herself into deeper levels of sleep. Enderby opened the door and went out. Standing an instant to quieten his loud heart, he felt cautiously elated that soon, on the aircraft, he would be able to feel fully and uninhibitedly elated.

A poem began to twitch as he weighed his suitcase and paid his embarkation fee and bought his bus ticket:

Stepmother of the West . . .

Enderby waited with excitement for the images to come into focus – Emperor and Pope the same pantomime dame, no more red meat since spate of it in snaring arena, old bitch she-wolf with hanging dugs, the big backyard of broken columns for the refuse-collector; Enderby waited with impatience for the rhymes to line up. City, titty. Beyond that was nothing.

Stepmother of the West, of venal cities
  Most venal something something she-wolf bitch
Romulus Remus something something titties
  Something something something something rich which
    ditch pitch

On the bus to Ciampino Enderby, frowning, called on his Muse to do something about this ragged *donnée*. On the aircraft, placed next to a Negro clergyman, Enderby muttered and grimaced so that the stewardess came up to ask if everything was all right. A suspicious character, muttering and frowning, a mink coat on the luggage rack overhead, Enderby looked down on Rome. He had forgotten all about Vesta already. He had expected that he would be able to recite, under his breath, at least a stanza of this poem in valediction. Thwarted and somewhat apprehensive, remembering the prophecy of the traitor Rawcliffe, he could only devise a farewell that went beyond words but which the Negro clergyman apparently took to be an adverse comment on his colour.

Fffffrrrrrerrrrrpshhhhhh.

Part Three

Chapter One

'You've got absolutely nothing to worry about there,' said Dr Preston Hawkes. 'The plates are negative: no TB, no carcinoma, nothing.' He held up a couple of cloudy portraits of the inner Enderby. 'That's the lot, then.' He had a loud Northern voice, some of the vowels home-made approximations to Received Standard. 'You can go away with a contented mind.' He was young and highly dentate, tanned, and tousled as though to advertise, for a side-line, the healthful properties of the resort where he practised. 'If bicarb helps that dyspepsia, you just stick to bicarb. But fundamentally your stomach and guts are perfectly sound.'

'You would say, would you,' said Enderby, 'that I'm quite unlikely to die in the near future?'

'Oh, my dear fellow,' said Dr Preston Hawkes, 'none of us can ever know that. Apart from the normal hazards of living – getting run over or electrocuted or slipping in the bathroom – there must always be some unknown factor that doesn't yield to examination. We know a lot,' he confided, 'but we don't know everything. But, as far as I can see, you're physically sound and likely to live for many years.' He glowed at Enderby like a frying slice of potato. 'Of course,' he said, 'your tone isn't as good as it might be. Take exercise: tennis, golf, walks. You could do with paring yourself down a bit. Keep off fried things; don't eat too much starch. You're a sedentary worker, aren't you? A clerk or something?'

'Perhaps in the older sense,' said Enderby. 'I am,' he explained sadly, 'a poet.'

'You mean,' said Dr Preston Hawkes incredulously, 'that's your job?'

'It was,' said Enderby. 'That's really why I came to see you. You see, I'm not writing any more poems.'

'Oh.' Dr Preston Hawkes became agitated; he tapped contrary-motion five-finger exercises on his desk, his smile fixed and nervous. He spoke now slackly, bubbling. 'Well, I hardly think – I mean, that's nothing to do with me, is it? I mean, I should have thought – That is to say, if you don't propose writing any more poetry, well, good luck to you. The very best of luck and all that sort of thing. But that's entirely your own affair, isn't it? That's what I'd say, anyway.' He now began to perform, though ineptly, the ritual of a man whose time is valuable: a syndrome of nervous grubbing among papers, looking at his watch, peering exophthalmically above Enderby's head as though the next patient was due to squeeze in between door and lintel.

'No,' said Enderby, 'you've got that wrong. What I mean is that I can't write poetry any more. I try and try, but nothing happens, nothing will come. Can you understand what I mean?'

'Oh, yes,' said the doctor, smiling warily. 'I quite see that. Well, I shouldn't worry too much about it if I were you. I mean, there are other things in life, aren't there? The sun is shining, the children are playing.' That was literally true; Dr Preston Hawkes lifted a hand as if he himself were conjuring the warm evening shaft through the window, the noise of an infant squabble on the road to the beach. 'I mean, writing poetry isn't the whole of life, is it? You're bound to find something else to do. Life is still all before you. The best is yet to be.'

'What,' asked Enderby, 'is the purpose of life?'

The doctor brightened at this question. He was young enough to have answers to it, answers clearly remembered from pipe-puffing student discussions. 'The purpose of life,' he said promptly, 'is the living of it. Life itself is the end of life. Life is here and now and what you can get out of it. Life is living by the square inch and the round minute. The end is the process. Life is what you make it. I now what I'm talking about, believe you me. I am, after all, a doctor.' He smiled towards something framed on the wall, his duly certified twin baccalaureate.

Enderby shook his head in vigorous gloom. 'I don't think Keats would have given you that answer. Or Shelley. Or Byron. Or Chatterton. Man,' said Enderby, 'is a tree. He bears fruit. When he stops bearing fruit life cuts him down. That's why I wanted to know whether I was going to die.'

'Look,' said the doctor sharply, 'this is all a lot of morbid nonsense. It's everybody's duty to *live*. That's what the National Health Service is for. To help people to live. You're a healthy man with years of life ahead of you, and you ought to be very glad and very grateful. Otherwise, let's face it, you're blaspheming against life and God and, yes, democracy and the National Health Service. That's hardly fair, is it?'

'But what do I live for?' asked Enderby.

'I've told you what you live for,' said the doctor, more sharply. 'You weren't paying attention, were you? You live for the sake of living. And, yes, you live for others, of course. You live for your wife and children.' He granted himself a two-second smirk of fondness at the photograph on his desk: Mrs Preston Hawkes playing with Master Preston Hawkes, Master Preston Hawkes playing with teddy-bear.

'I had a wife,' said Enderby, 'for a very short time. I left her nearly a year ago. In Rome it was. We just didn't get on. I'm quite sure I have no children. I think I can say that I'm absolutely sure about that.'

'Well, all right then,' said the doctor. 'But there are lots of other people who need you, surely. Friends and so on. I take it,' he said cautiously, 'that there are still people left who like to read poetry.'

'That,' said Enderby, 'is written. They've got that. There won't be any more. And,' he said, 'I'm not the sort of man who has friends. The poet has to be alone.' This platitude, delivered rhetorically in spite of himself, brought a glassy look to his eyes; he got up stiffly from his chair. The doctor, who had seen television plays, thought he descried in Enderby the lineaments of impending suicide. He was not a bad doctor. He said:

'You don't propose to do anything silly, do you? I mean, it wouldn't do anybody any good, would it, that sort of thing? I mean, especially after you've been to see me and so on. Life,' he said, less certainly than before, 'has to be lived. We all have a duty. I'll get the police on to you, you know. Don't start doing anything you shouldn't be doing. Look, I'll arrange an appointment with a psychiatrist, if you like.' He made the gesture of reaching at once for the telephone, of being prepared to tap, at once, all the riches of the National Health Service for the benefit of Enderby.

'You needn't worry,' said Enderby soothingly. 'I shan't do anything I'd consider silly. I promise you that.'

'Get around a bit,' said the doctor desperately. 'Meet people. Watch the telly. Have the odd drink in a pub, all right in moderation. Go to the pictures. Go and see this horror film round the corner. That'll take you out of yourself.'

'I saw it in Rome,' said Enderby. 'The world première.' Here in England *L'Animal Binato* or *The Two-Natured Animal* had become *Son of the Beast from Outer Space*. 'As a matter of fact,' said Enderby, 'I wrote it. That is to say, it was stolen from me.'

'Look,' said Dr Preston Hawkes, now standing up. 'It would be no trouble at all for me to fix up an appointment for you. I think you'd feel a lot happier if you talked with Dr Greenslade. He's a very good man, you know, very good, very sympathetic. I could ring up the hospital now. No trouble at all. He could probably see you first thing in the morning.'

'Now,' said Enderby, 'don't worry. Take life as it comes. Live it by the square yard or whatever it was you said.'

'I'm not at all happy about what you might do,' said Dr Preston Hawkes. 'It wouldn't be fair for you to go back ome and do yourself in straight after coming to see me. 'd feel happier if you'd see Dr Greenslade. I could ring up ow. I could get a bed for you straight away. I'm not sure at it's right for you to be going off on your own. Not in our present state of mind, that is.' He stood confused and oung, mumbling, 'I mean, after all, we've all got a duty to ach other –'

'I'm perfectly sane,' soothed Enderby, 'if that's what ou're worrying about. And I promise you again not to do nything silly. You can have that in writing if you like. 'll send you a letter. I'll write it as soon as I get back to my igs.' Dr Preston Hawkes bit his lip from end to end and ack again, as though testing it for durability. He looked arkly and uncertainly at Enderby, not liking the sound of etter' in this context. 'Everything,' said Enderby, with a reat smile of reassurance, 'is going to be all right.' They ad exchanged roles. It was with a doctor's jauntiness that nderby said, 'Nothing to worry about at all.' Then he eft swiftly.

He passed through a waiting-room full of people who, rom the look of them, could not write poetry either. Some vere in sporting kit, as if prepared to be tried out at the ets by Dr Preston Hawkes, wearing their ailments as ightly as a blazer-badge; others, dressed more formally, aw disease as a kind of church. Enderby had to squint his vay out. He had lost his contact-lenses somewhere; the lasses he had formerly worn were, he supposed, still in he Gloucester Road flat. Unless, of course, she had thrown ut all that was his. Walking through the rich marine ight he regurgitated the word 'police'. If this doctor pro-osed to put the police on to him it would be necessary to ct quickly. In imagination he heard what the world called anity as something in heavy clumsy hoofing boots. He emembered the boots that chased him when, just back rom Rome, he had tried to break into the flat by the win-low and been suddenly transfixed in the beam of a opper's lantern. He could have stayed to explain, of ourse, but the police might well, with their professional tendency to suspicion, have held him till the eventual arrival of Vesta. That mink coat, left behind in the scamper, would have taken some explaining away. So he had swung his suitcase into the constable's groin and, between a starting-line and finishing-tape of whistles, dodged about till – to his surprise, for he had thought such things only possible in films – he had managed to escape by skidding down a sidestreet and into an alley, waiting there till the whistles peeped, like lost tropical birds, forlornly in the distance.

The May sun whizzed over the sea, and spread over the sea was a sort of blinding silver-shred marmalade. It was not the sea near to whose roar he had laboured, to so little purpose, at *The Pet Beast*, but its north-western brother. It fed a louder and more vulgar resort than Enderby's former Channel home: there was more gusto in the pubs, the vowels were broader, jugs of tea could be bought to take on the sands, a pleasure-beach was hysterical with violent machines of pleasure, an open-air concert party had a comedian who told his feed that if his brains were elastic he wouldn't have enough to make a canary a pair of garters. 'I've got blue blood in my veins,' said the feed. 'What do you think I've got in mine?' said the comedian. 'Dandelion and burdock?' It was an odd place, so posterity might think, in which to choose to die.

On this lovely evening there were queues, Enderby peeringly noticed, for *Son of the Beast from Outer Space*. Next door but two to the cinema was a cool cavern of a chemist's, full of the smell of soap, holiday laughter in place of medicines, the prints of beach snapshots being collected, sunburnt arms and necks. Enderby had to wait till a holiday woman had been served with hair-clips, skin cream, hydrogen peroxide and other life-enhancers before he could ask for the means of death. At last the white-coated girl put her head on one side at him:

'Yes, sir?'

He felt as embarrassed as if he were buying condoms. 'Aspirin, please.'

'Which size, sir?' There were, it seemed, various sizes. Enderby said:

'Fairly small ones, please. I have to take rather a lot.' She opened her mouth at him so he said, 'Not a lethal dose, of course.' He smiled winningly.

'Ha ha, sir. I should hope not. Not on a lovely evening like this.' He was quite a one.

Enderby went out with a bottle of a hundred. He had exactly twopence left in the world. 'Good,' he thought, 'timing.'

'A queer year,' reflected Enderby, potential death in his pocket, turning off the warm gay beery candy-flossy promenade into Boggart Road. It had been a queer empty year, or near-year.

June had been the month of marriage, honeymoon, desertion. He had drawn out from his London bank ninety pictures of clavigerous lions. He had bought a sponge-bag, stuffed the lions into it, wound the string of the bag round a trouser-button, then hung the bag inside his trousers. There it had walked and sat with him, a big comforting scrotum. Every man's fly his own bank; cheerful disbursements at all hours; no interest (though, of course, no overdrafts); frugal needs met without formality. He had travelled to this Northern resort once mentioned with approval by Arry (far from South, London, Vesta). He had found a homely attic with a gas-ring (share lavatory and bathroom) at Mrs Bamber's, Butterworth Avenue, a permanent apex above the transient holiday guests.

In July and August he had put together laboriously a volume of fifty lyric poems (the fair copies and late drafts had fortunately been in his suitcase taken to and from Rome; a mass of other, rougher, material was still in, or else had been thrown out of, the Gloucester Road flat and was, presumably, no longer recoverable). The title of the volume was *The Circular Pavane*. Having been turned into typescript by a little woman at a typing bureau in Manchester, it had been delivered to, and received with little enthusiasm by, his publisher. In public lavatory cabinets, where privacy could be bought for a penny, he had planned a long autobiographical poem in blank verse, a sort of *Prelude*. The sponge-bag inside trousers still fat, he was able to afford to wait for the torpid or sulking Muse to wake up and see sense. The few autobiographical poetic lines achieved had been destroyed, re-written, destroyed, re-written, destroyed, re-written, slept on, read, re-read, re-written, destroyed. Through August and September the resort had been big-mouthed with cheerful visitors wearing comic caps with slogans (Try Me I'm The Easy Sort; Have A Go Joe Your Mother Won't Know), sticky with kisses, brine, ale, candy, rock. There had been no news of Vesta or anyone. Sitting in a public lavatory one sunny morning, hearing the cheerful bucket-and-spade-clanking children on their way to the beach, he had savoured, like Frascati, his renewed aloneness. It was a pity he could not write anything, however. He had abandoned the idea of the long autobiographical poem; how about an epic on King Arthur or Lord Rutherford or Alcock and Brown? A verse drama, perhaps? He had spent long grubbing hours in the public library, pretending that he was really working, building foundations, gathering material. He had written nothing.

October, November, brought a whiff of foreboding. This was getting past a joke. He had money enough still, of course, but less and less to do with his time. Walking through the sea-deafening deserted streets, overcoat-collar round his ears, trying to crank up a poem, returning to hopelessness, stew, Mrs Bamber insisting on coming up to his attic, sitting there, talking about her own past redolent of oyster-bars and Yates's Wine Lodge.

If, he vowed at Christmas, if he were given some sort of token of assurance that he would be able to start writing again, then, when his money ran out, he would willingly take some futile occupation or other, becoming a part-time poet, keeping alive for his Muse.

Towards the end of January he awoke to a morning clamped in frost, a poem singing in his ears. Thank God, the relief. He wrote the gnomic telegraphic message down and spent the morning refining it to a final shape:

You being the gate
Where the army went through
Would you renew the triumph and have them decorate
The arch and stone again?
Surely those flowers are withered, the army
Now on a distant plain.

Reading it, he saw, his hair bristling, that it was a private message, a message from her to himself.

But some morning when you are washing up,
Or some afternoon, taking a cup
Of tea, possibly you will see
The heavens opening and a lot
Of saints singing, with bells swinging.
But then again, possibly not.

He had felt a clammy glair of sweat settle on him, his diaphragm start to liquefy. A poem of farewell.

In March came publication of *The Circular Pavane*. Reviews followed: '. . . Pleasant and lucid verse in the tradition . . .'; 'Mr Enderby has lost none of his old cunning; it is a pity, however, that we see no signs of new cunning, new directions. It is a cunningly blended mixture, but it is very much the mixture as before . . .'; '. . . One remembers with a sigh the old lyrical perfection. It is a relief to turn to the work of two young Oxford poets . . .' And one that was surely by Rawcliffe: 'Mr Enderby is undoubtedly enough of a realist not to regret the passing of the lyric gift. It cannot last for ever, and with Mr Enderby it has lasted longer than with most. Many of his contemporaries have already elected for the dignified silence of remembered achievement, and one may predict that Mr Enderby, after this not unexpectedly disappointing volume, will join their cloistral seclusion. . . .' In *Fem* there was, of course, no review.

Enderby had spent April brooding over a pain in his chest. In May, now, this month, three days ago, he had decided to go to a doctor. The doctor, after palpation and auscultation, had more or less decided that nothing was really wrong but, to be on the safe side, had sent Enderby to the hospital for radiography. But, before that, with 'nothing wrong' in his ears, Enderby had sat down in his warm attic to write out a list of possible ways to die:

> Slash wrists in warm bath
> Overdose of sedative
> Hang from picture rail in dining-room
> Jump in sea from jetty

This was early summer, and Mrs Bamber's house had a fair number of early summer visitors, mostly, as far as Enderby could judge from the noise, teams of galloping children ineptly driven by whoaing but disregarded young parents. It would not be right, Enderby thought, to make his suicide a public affair. It was no way to start a holiday morning to find a corpse swinging with its tongue out at the cornflakes laid the night before, or else dreaming cold in a bath of cold red ink. Too public, of course, to upset anyone might have been the jump from the jetty at the end of Central Pier, but some swimmer, bored already with his holiday, might have splashed too swiftly to the rescue. The overdose was best: clean and quiet, clean and quiet, by something something and dreamy something. Kingsley, jocular Christian.

Enderby, non-Christian stoic, climbed the vanilla-coloured steps of 17 Butterworth Avenue. The front door was open and on the hat-stand were buckets and spades, the smell of feet and sand in the whole dark seaweedy hall. All the guests were out, perhaps at *Son of the Beast from Outer Space*, but from her kitchen Mrs Bamber sang, the merry widow of a tram-driver, a song smelling of oysters and ruby port. Mounting the stairs, Enderby was suddenly transfixed by a line from, he thought, *Ulysses*, which seemed to him, with his lethal dose in his pocket, to be the most poignant line (though it was not really a line – only, so far as he could remember, a splinter of Bloom's interior monologue), the most pregnantly regretful line he had ever heard:

. . . And lie no more in her warm bed.

He shook his head as images clustered round it, images he was no longer capable of translating into words and rhythms: the horses under starter's orders, the champagne tent, the sun on the back of the neck, the omelette made with a hundred eggs and a bottle of Napoleon brandy, life.

. . . And lie no more in her warm bed.

Enderby climbed higher, climbed to the top, where there was only a roof between him and the sun. This garret of his was, like the sea, warming up for the summer. He entered and sat on his bed, panting after the climb. Then his stomach, living its own life, decided it was hungry, so Enderby put to warm on the gas-ring the remains of a simple stew. While it bubbled, he turned over and over the sizeable bottle of aspirin he had bought: he had read, or heard, that a hundred should be enough. Mrs Bamber, he felt sure, would be efficient at coping with the unexpected corpse of Enderby: she was a Lancashire woman, and Lancashire people rather enjoyed death. It would, anyway, be a clean corpse lying, jaw dropped as in astonishment at being dead, between the sheets. (He reminded himself to effect, as far as was possible, a total evacuation of his body before making it a corpse.) The holiday guests would not be disturbed; the Chief Constable and the Town Clerk would want no publicity; everything would be done quietly at night, and then cornflakes would be shuffled on to plates for the morning. Enderby now sat down, with something like appetite, to his last supper, a thin but savoury viaticum. He felt excited, as though after supper he were going to see a film that everybody had been talking about and the critics had highly praised.

Enderby was in his pyjamas. It was still light, a May evening, and he had a fugitive impression of being a child again, sent to bed while the life of day was beating strongly without. He had washed his feet and scrubbed his dentures, scoured his few pots and pans, eaten a piece of chocolate left over from some weeks back, and poured water from the jug on the wash-stand into a clean milk-bottle. (He had no tumbler, and would need a good long draught to speed the aspirin down.) Now, with the cotton-wool stopper removed and the tablets clinking discreetly, the aspirin bottle began to dramatize itself, drawing evening light from all angles, becoming almost grail-like, so that the hand that held it shook. Enderby carried it over to his bed, and it made a tiny dry castanet-noise all the way. From the bed, which he now entered, he could look down on Mrs Bamber's back-yard. He dredged it hungrily, squinting, for symbols of life, but there were only a dust-bin, a cardboard box full of cinders, dandelions growing up from the flag-cracks, an old bicycle discarded by Mrs Bamber's son, Tom. Beyond were three-storey houses with bathing costumes drying on window-sills, beyond again the sea, above all a primrose sky. 'Now,' said Enderby aloud.

One shaking hand shook out a shaking palmful of aspirin. He gave the white seeds to his mouth like a golly-wog money-box feeding in a penny. He drank water from the milk-bottle, still shaking. Aspen, aspirin. Was there a connexion?

An aspen hand aspiring now to death

He finished off the bottle in six or seven more handfuls, washing them down carefully. Then, sighing, he lay back. There was nothing to do now except wait. He had committed suicide. He had killed himself. Self-slaughter was of all sins the most reprehensible, being the most cowardly. What punishment awaited suicide? If Rawcliffe were there now he would be able to quote from the *Inferno*, lavishly, that man who had added to Italian art. Enderby could vaguely remember that suicide belonged to Nether Hell, the Second Ring, between those who had been violent against their neighbours and those who had been violent against God and art and nature. There, in that Third Ring, Rawcliffe rightly belonged, perhaps there already. All these were, Enderby thought, Sins of the Lion. He closed his eyes and saw, quite clearly, the bleeding trees that were the suicides, harpies fluttering about with a rattle of dry wings like the magnified noise of a shaken aspirin bottle. He frowned. All this seemed very unfair. He had, after all, chosen the way of the Second Ring to avoid the way of the Third, and yet both sins were tucked together in the same round slice of Nether Hell.

With infinite care and delicacy the day wormed itself through a continuum of darker and darker greys. The watch on his wrist ticked on healthily, the too-efficient servant that would announce death as coldly as day and breakfast. Enderby began to feel a great tiredness and to hear a loud buzzing in his ears.

A fanfare of loud farts, a cosmic swish of lavatory-flushings. The dark in front of his eyes was cut away in rough slice after rough slice, like black bread, right down to the heel of the loaf. This then began to turn slowly, brightening with each revolution until it became blinding like the sun. Enderby found it an insuperable effort to interpose blankets or hands or eyelids. The circle cracked with intolerable luminosity, and then Enderby seemed to be dragged, with hearty, though somehow archangelic, tug-of-war cries towards some ineffable hidden Presence. Suddenly this Presence, at first humorously offering Itself as a datum for mere intellection, erupted into a tingling ultimate blow at all the senses, and Enderby staggered back.

There she was, welcoming him in, farting prrrrrrp like ten thousand earthquakes, belching arrrp and og like a million volcanoes, while the whole universe roared with approving laughter. She swung tits like sagging moons at him, drew from black teeth an endless snake of bacon-rind, pelted him with balls of ear-wax and snuffled green snot in his direction. The thrones roared and the powers were helpless. Enderby was suffocated by smells: sulphuretted hydrogen, unwashed armpits, halitosis, faeces, standing urine, putrefying meat – all thrust into his mouth and nostrils in squelchy balls. 'Help,' he tried to call. 'Help help help.' He fell, crawled, crying, 'Help, help.' The black, which was solid laughter and filth, closed on him. He gave one last scream before yielding to it.

Chapter Two

1

'And,' said Dr Greenslade the psychiatrist, 'we won't try that sort of thing again, will we? For, as we can now see, it only causes lots and lots of worry and trouble to other people.' He beamed, a fat youngish man in a white coat not too clean, with the unhealthy complexion of a sweet-eater. 'For example, it didn't do our poor old landlady's heart any good, did it? She had to run up the stairs and then down the stairs' – he illustrated this with up-and-then-down-the-air wiggling fingers – 'and she was most agitated when the ambulance finally got there. We must consider others, mustn't we? The world wasn't made just for us and nobody else.'

Enderby cringed from the nanny-like substitution of first plural for second singular. 'Everybody gives trouble when they're dying,' he mumbled. 'That can't be avoided.'

'Ah,' pounced Dr Greenslade, 'but you didn't die. When people die in the normal decent way they give a normal decent *leisurely* kind of trouble which harms no one. But you were just caught more or less in the act of sailing off. That meant rushing about and worry for everybody, particularly for your poor old landlady. Besides' – he leaned forward, hushed – 'it wasn't just a matter of straightforward dying with you, was it? It was' – he whispered the dirty words – '*attempted suicide.*'

Enderby bowed his head, this being the required stock response. Then he said, 'I'm sorry I made a mess of it. I don't know what came over me. Well, I do in a way, of course, but if I'd been braver, if I'd stuck it out, I think I could have sailed straight through, if you see what I mean. What I mean is that that was just a vision of Hell meant to frighten me. Bogies and so on. It wasn't real.'

Dr Greenslade rubbed his hands discreetly. 'I can see,' he said, 'that a lot of fun lies ahead. Though not for me, unfortunately. Still, I'll be getting Wapenshaw's reports. It's a lovely place,' he said dreamily, 'especially lovely at this time of year. You'll like it.'

'Where?' said Enderby with suspicion. 'What?' Dr Greenslade had sounded like some Dickens character talking about a beloved idiot-child's grave. 'I thought I was being discharged.'

'Oh, dear me, no,' said shocked Dr Greenslade. 'Healthy people don't try to commit suicide, you know. Not coldly and deliberately they don't. And you'd planned this, you know. Preston Hawkes told me you'd planned it. It wasn't just a mad impulse.'

'No, it wasn't,' said Enderby stoutly. 'It was logical. I knew perfectly well what I was doing and I've given you perfectly logical reasons for doing it.' He belched acidulously: Greeeeekh. 'This hospital food's bloody awful,' he said.

'The food at Flitchley is excellent,' dreamed Dr Greenslade. 'Everything's excellent there. Lovely grounds to walk in. Table tennis. Television. A library of sedative books. Congenial company. You'll be sorry to leave.'

'Look,' said Enderby quietly, 'I'm not going, see? You've got no right to keep me here or send me anywhere. I'm perfectly all right, see? I demand my freedom.'

'Now,' said Dr Greenslade harshly, changing from nanny to schoolmaster, 'let's get one or two things absolutely clear, shall we? There are certain laws in this country appertaining to mental derangement, laws of restraint, certificates and so on. Those laws have, in your case, already been invoked. We can't have people wandering all over the country trying to kill themselves.' Enderby closed his eyes to see England swarming, as a log swarms with woodlice, with peripatetic suicides. 'You're a danger to yourself,' said Dr Greenslade, 'and a danger to the community. A man who doesn't respect his own life isn't likely to respect anybody else's. That's logical, isn't it?'

'No,' said Enderby promptly.

'Oh, well,' said Dr Greenslade sarcastically, 'you, of course, are the big expert on logic.'

'I don't pretend to be anything,' said Enderby loudly, 'except a poet whose inspiration has departed. I'm an empty eggshell.'

'You are,' said Dr Greenslade sternly, 'a man of education and culture who can be of great value to the community. When you're made fit again, that is. Empty eggshells, indeed,' he poohed. 'Poets,' he near-sneered. 'Those days are past, those wide-eyed romantic days. We're living in a realistic age now,' he said. 'Science is making giant strides. And as for poets,' he said, with sudden bubbling intimacy, 'I met a poet once. He was a nice decent fellow with no big ideas about himself. He wrote very nice poetry, too, which was not too difficult to understand.' He looked at Enderby as though Enderby's poetry was both not nice and not intelligible. 'This man,' said Dr Greenslade, 'didn't have your advantages. No private income for him, no cosy little flat in a seaside resort. He had a wife and family, and he wasn't ashamed of working for them. He wrote his poetry at week-ends.' He nodded at Enderby, week-day poet. 'And there was nothing abnormal about him, nothing at all. He didn't go about with a lobster on a string or marry his own sister or eat pepper before drinking claret. He was a decent family man whom nobody would have taken for a poet at all.' Enderby groaned frightfully. 'And,' added Dr Greenslade, 'he had a poem in all the anthologies.' Enderby held back a loud howl. Then he said:

'If he was so normal, why did you have anything to do with him?'

'This,' smiled Dr Greenslade in large triumph, 'was a purely social acquaintance. Now,' he said, looking at the clock above Enderby's head, 'you'd better get back to your ward.' Enderby stood up. He was in hospital pyjamas, dressing-gown, slippers, and felt grey, shrunken, a pauper. He shambled out of the electro-cardiogram room into the corridor, hesitated at the stairs with their WAY OUT notice, remembered that they had locked his clothes away, and then, resigned, shuffled into the Medical Ward. He had been brought here to sleep it off after the stomach-pumping in the Emergency Ward, had lain for two days starved in a sort of big cot with iron bars at the sides, and now was allowed to pout about the ward in his dressing-gown. If a fellow-patient said, 'What's wrong with you, mate?' he replied, on the ward sister's instructions, 'Acetyl-salicylic poisoning.' But these rough men, all with impressively visible illnesses, knew better than that. This here one had had a go at doing himself in. As Enderby, hands in dressing-gown pockets, bowed towards his bed (ring-worm to the left of it, to the right a broken femur), a dwarf of a working-man hopped towards him on crutches. ' 'Ere,' said the dwarf.

'Yes?' said Enderby. The dwarf cleared his nasopharynx via his oesophagus and said, conspiratorially:

'Trick cyclist been 'avin a go at you, eh? I seen 'im come in. Ridin' all over you, eh?'

'That's right,' said Enderby.

'Should be a law against that, I reckon. Draggin' out secrets from the back of your mind, like. Not decent, way I see it. 'Ad a go at me once. Know what that was for?'

'No,' said Enderby. The dwarf hopped nearer, his eyes ashine. He said, low:

'Wife and kids was out at the pictures, see. I 'ad nowt to do, not bein' much on the telly, and I'd washed up after my supper and put the kitchen straight. I'd read the paper too, see, and there wasn't much in that, all murders and suchlike and these 'ere summit conferences. Anyway, know what I'd got in my overall pocket?'

'No,' said Enderby.

'One of these big nuts,' said the dwarf. 'Don't know 'ow it got there, but there it was. Big one,' he insisted, making an illustrative ring with thumb and finger. 'A nut, you know. Not a nut you can eat, but one of these nuts you put a bolt through.' He showed, with the index-finger of his other hand, how exactly this was done. 'Do you see my meaning?' he asked.

'Yes,' said Enderby.

'Well,' said the dwarf, 'I got to lookin' at it and thinkin' about it, and then an idea come into me 'ead. Know what the idea was?'

'No,' said Enderby.

The dwarf came very close, awkward on his crutches, and seemed about to eat Enderby's ear. 'Put it in,' he said. 'Wife was out, see, and there was nowt else to do. It fitted real snug, too, you'd be surprised. Anyway, there it was, and you know what 'appened then?'

'No,' said Enderby.

'Wouldn't come out,' said the dwarf, reliving the horror in his eyes. 'There it was, stuck in, and it wouldn't come out. Right bloody fool I must 'ave looked to the cat when it come in through the window. A 'ot night, see, and the window was open. There I was, with this thing of mine stuck in this nut, and it wouldn't come out. I tries all sort of things – puttin' it under the cold water tap and gettin' a file at it, but it wasn't no good. Then the wife comes back from the pictures and she sees what I've done and she sends the kids straight upstairs. Bad enough the cat seein' it, but it wasn't right the kids should know what was goin' on. So you know what she does?'

'No,' said Enderby.

'She sends for the ambulance and they takes me to 'ospital. Not this one, though. We was livin' somewhere else at the time. Well, they tries and tries, but it's no good.

All sorts of things they tries. Know what they 'as to do at the finish?'

'No,' said Enderby.

'Send for the fire brigade. I'm not tellin' you a word of a lie, but they 'as to do that. On my God's honour, they send for the fire brigade, and you know what the fire brigade 'as to do?'

'No,' said Enderby.

'They gets one of their special saws to saw through metal and they as a 'ose-pipe playin' on it all the time. Know why that was?'

'To keep it cool,' said Enderby.

'You've got it,' said the dwarf. 'There's not many as would give the right answer like you done. To keep it cool. Anyway, they gets it off, and that's when they ask me to see this trick cyclist like what you've seen. Didn't do no good though.' He looked gloomy.

'Is that why you're back in again?' said Enderby.

'Naw,' said the working-dwarf with scorn. 'Broke my leg at work this time. Always somethin' though, int there?'

From this moment Enderby thought that, with a certain measure of help and encouragement, he might conceivably decide that it might be possible for him to want, with certain inevitable reservations, to go on living. He woke up in the middle of the night laughing at some dream-joke. The sister had to give him a sedative.

2

Flitchley, surrounded by the pink snow of apple-blossom, cuckoo-(appropriately)-echoing, green, quiet with a quiet that the clack and clock of table-tennis only emphasized the more, Flitchley was all that Dr Greenslade had said it would be. Several weeks later Enderby sat on a bird-loud terrace reading a harmless boy's book of violence ('. . . The Chink, with a sinister Oriental smile on his inscrutable yellow countenance, wrenched the knife from the back of his dead companion and threw it straight at Colonel Bill.

Bill ducked, hearing the evil weapon twang in the door. He had ducked only just in time. "Now," he said, a cold smile on his clean-cut features, "I think I've had more than enough of your treachery for one day, Mr John Chinaman." He advanced on the Chink, who now gibbered in his own outlandish language what was evidently a prayer for mercy. . .'). In the day-room was the cheerful music of the table being set for luncheon. Beyond the haha a gardener bent at work. Fellow-patients of Enderby walked the grounds or, like himself, sat at rest with sedative literature. Occasionally Enderby would lower his book to his lap, close his eyes, and say softly to himself, many times over, "My name is Enderby-Hogg, my name is Enderby-Hogg.' It was part of the process of his cure; a gently contrived change of identity. Hogg had been his mother's maiden name; soon, the Enderby silenced, it would be altogether his.

The bell rang for luncheon and, from the day-room radio, news refinedly boomed. Enderby-Hogg sat down, one of a mess of six, having first shaken hands with a Mr Barnaby. Mr Barnaby, like a dog, insisted on shaking hands with everybody at all hours of the day and sometimes, waking everybody gently up for the purpose, in the night. He had a sweet wrinkled face and, like that Enderby soon to disappear, was something of a poet. He had written verses on the Medical Superintendent beginning:

> You have certainly got it in for me and no
> Question about that, you fierce-eyed man.
> Your wife no more loves you than that black crow
> Up in the tree loves you, or that can
> Which whilom held baked beans of the brand of Heinz,
> Or that dog belonging to the lodge-keeper which so sorely
>   whines

At the same table was Mr Trill, one of the symptoms of whose derangement was an ability to name the winner of any major horse-race run in the last sixty years. He was a man of venerable appearance who, he swore, hated racing.

Enderby-Hogg now said to him, in automatic greeting, 'Thousand Guineas, 1910.' Mr Trill looked up mournfully from his soup and said, 'Winkipop, owned Astor, trained W. Waugh, ridden Lynham. Starting price five to two.' There was Mr Beecham, a master plumber who, on psychiatric instructions, spent all his day painting pictures: black snakes, red murder, his wife with three heads. Mr Shap, insurance agent, with dark glasses and a black hole for a mouth, said nothing, did nothing, but at times would scream one word: PASTE. Finally there was Mr Killick who preached, in an undertone, to the birds. He had the look of a successful butcher.

This company of six drank its soup and then was served, by two cheerful nurses of radiant complexion, with slabs of meat pie and scooped spuds. There were spoons and forks, but no knives. The meal chewed itself by pleasantly and quietly, except that at one point a dressing-gowned man at another table cried to the ceiling:

'Sink her, Number One!'

He was soothed quickly by one of the nurses, a homely Lancashire lass with a strong sense of humour. She said, 'You sink that meat pie quick, my lad. Treacle duff's coming alongside.' Enderby-Hogg laughed with the rest at this typical bit of Lancashire badinage. The treacle duff, with liberal custard, was then wheeled in, and Mr Killick, hungry after a morning preaching to the birds, had three helpings. After the meal some went back to bed, while Enderby-Hogg and others sat in the solarium. Enderby-Hogg had no money, but some obscure charitable fund invoked by the almoner supplied him with a sufficiency of cigarettes. A nurse came round with matches to light up for the smokers: no patient was allowed matches of his own, not since one Jehovah-minded G.P.I. sufferer had called Flitchley Sodom and set fire to it.

After a quiet smoke and lazy rambling chat, Enderby-Hogg went to the lavatory. The little cabinets, without doors could be looked in on from the corridor through a thick glass wall: even here there was no sense of aloneness.

After an ample healthy movement, Enderby-Hogg went to the ward he shared with eleven others, there to lie on his bed till summoned for his afternoon session with Dr Wapenshaw. He finished his boy's book ('. . . "And," grinned Colonel Bill, "despite all the dangers and hazards, it was a jolly good adventure which I'd be happy to undertake again." But, as he pulled the throttle and the mixture exploded sweet and strong, little did he think that adventure of an even more thrilling kind awaited him. That adventure, chaps, we shall learn about in our next story – the ninety-seventh! – of Colonel Bill and the faithful Spike.'). Enderby-Hogg looked forward, without undue excitement, to reading that story.

At three o'clock a smiling nurse summoned him to Dr Wapenshaw. Dr Wapenshaw said, 'Ah, hallo there, old man. Things going all right, eh? Jolly good, jolly good,' for all the world like Colonel Bill or his creator. Dr Wapenshaw was a big man whose superfluous fat proclaimed, like medals, his former Rugby football triumphs. He had large feet and a moustache and a voice like Christmas pudding. But he was a clever and original psychiatrist. 'Sit down,' he invited. 'Smoke if you want to.' Enderby-Hogg sat down, smiling shyly. He adored Dr Wapenshaw.

'Enderby-Hogg, Enderby-Hogg,' said Dr Wapenshaw, as though beginning a nursery rhyme. A thick file was open on the desk before him. 'Enderby-Hogg. Bit of a mouthful, isn't it? I think we might drop the Enderby, don't you? Keep it, of course, in the background as an optional extra if you like. How do you feel about the Hogg?'

'Oh, fine,' said Hogg. 'Perfectly all right.'

'What do you associate the name with? Pigs? Filth?' smiling. 'Gluttony?' Humorously, Dr Wapenshaw pig-snorted.

'Of course not,' said Hogg, smiling too. 'Roses. A lawn in summer. A sweet-smelling woman at the piano. A silver voice. The smoke from a Passing Cloud.'

'Excellent,' said Dr Wapenshaw. 'That will do very well indeed.' He sat back in his swivel-chair, swivelling boyishly rom side to side, looking kindly at Hogg. 'That beard's coming along all right,' he said. 'You should have a pretty good one in a couple of weeks. Oh, yes, I've made a note about glasses. We're sending you to the oculist on Thursday.'

'Thank you very much,' said Hogg.

'Don't thank me, my dear fellow,' said Dr Wapenshaw. 'After all, it's what we're here for, isn't it? To help.' Tears came into Hogg's eyes. 'Now,' said Dr Wapenshaw, 'I've explained to you already just what it is we're trying to do and why we're trying to do it. Could you recap' – he smiled – 'in your own words?'

'Enderby,' said Hogg, 'was the name of a prolonged adolescence. The characteristics of adolescence were well-developed and seemed likely to go on for ever. There was, for instance, this obsession with poetry. There was masturbation, liking to be shut up in the lavatory, rebelliousness towards religion and society.'

'Excellent,' said Dr Wapenshaw.

'The poetry was a flower of that adolescence,' said Hogg. 'It still remains good poetry, some of it, but it was a product of an adolescent character. I shall look back with some pride on Enderby's achievement. Life, however, has to be lived.'

'Of course it has,' said Dr Wapenshaw, 'and you're going to live it. What's more, you're going to enjoy living it. Now, let me tell you what's going to happen to you. In a month's time – perhaps less if you continue to make the excellent progress you're already making – we're sending you to our Agricultural Station at Snorthorpe. It's really a convalescent home, you know, where you do a little gentle work – not too much, of course: just what you feel you *can* do and nothing more – and lead a very pleasant simple social life in beautiful surroundings. Snorthorpe,' said Dr Wapenshaw, 'is a little town on a river. There are summer visitors, swans, boating, nice little pubs. You'll love it. A group of you – under supervision, of course, if you can really call it supervision – will be allowed out to pubs and dances and cinemas. In the home itself there'll be chess competitions and sing-songs. Once a week,' smiled Dr Wapenshaw, 'I myself like to come down and lead a sing-song. You'll like that, won't you?'

'Oh yes,' breathed Hogg.

'Thus,' said Dr Wapenshaw, 'you'll gradually adjust yourself to living in society. You'll even meet women, you know,' he smiled. 'Some day, you know, I look forward to your making a *real* go of marriage. Enderby made rather a mess of that, didn't he? Still, it's all over now. The annulment's going through, so they tell me, quite smoothly.'

'I can't even remember her name,' frowned Hogg.

'Don't worry about that,' said Dr Wapenshaw. 'That's Enderby's affair, isn't it? You'll remember it in your own good time. And, moreover, you'll remember it with amusement.' Hogg smiled tentatively, as in anticipation. 'Now, as far as your future generally is concerned, I don't want you to think about that at the moment. There's going to be no worry about getting a really congenial job for you – we have our own department, you know, which sees to all that, and very efficient they are. The thing for you to do at the moment is to *enjoy* being this new person we're trying to create. After all, it *is* great fun, isn't it? I'm getting no end of a kick out of it all, and I want you to share that kick with me. After all,' he smiled, 'we've grown very close, haven't we, these last few weeks? We've embarked on a real adventure together, and I'm enjoying every minute of it.'

'Oh, me too,' said Hogg eagerly. 'And I'm really most awfully grateful.'

'Well, it's really awfully nice of you to say that,' said Dr Wapenshaw. 'But you've helped no end, yourself, you know.' He smiled once more and then became genially gruffly business-like. 'I'll be seeing you,' he said, looking at his diary, 'on Friday morning. Now off you go and have your tea or whatever it is and leave me to see my next victim.' He sighed humorously. 'Work, work, work.' He shook his head. 'No end to it. Run along now,' he grinned. Hogg grinned back and ran along.

For tea they had Marmite sandwiches, fish-paste sandwiches (Mr Shap cried out PASTE with such exquisite appropriateness that everybody had to laugh), fancy cakes and a small plum cake to each mess of six. After tea Hogg walked the grounds and surprised Mr Killick whispering to some bread-guzzling starlings beyond the haha, 'Come on now, you birdies, be good and kind to each other and love God who made you all. He was a bird just like you.' Hogg returned to the sunny solarium to find Mr Barnaby triumphantly finishing another stanza of his Ode to the Medical Superintendent. He read this aloud with great feeling, having first shaken hands heartily with Hogg:

I saw you the other night out on the field
Walking with a big stick with which you struck the grass
Repeatedly, but the dumb grass would not yield
To your importunities. So it will come to pass
That that piece of china standing on your shelf
Will fall on your head and give quite a shock to your evil-
    smelling self.

For dinner there were fish and a rice pudding with sultanas embedded in it. Mr Beecham, his hands vermilion from his day's work on a large symbolical canvas, slowly picked out all the sultanas from his portion and arranged them in a simple gestalt on his bread-plate. After dinner there was television: amateur boxing which excited two patients so much that one of the nurses had to switch over to the other channel. On the other channel was a simple morality of good and evil set in the West of North America in the eighteen-sixties. It was interrupted at intervals by asthenic women demonstrating washing-machines, though some patients evidently could not see these as interpolations, taking them rather as integral to the plot. Integration was the theme: the building of a new human society under the sheriff's steadfast bright star. Hogg nodded frequently, seeing all this (conquest of new territory, death to the evil antisocial) as an allegory of his own reorientation.

3

High summer in Snorthorpe. Boats for hire by the bridge, by the bridge a hotel called the White Hart, much favoured by summer visitors. Drinkers squinting happily in moonlight on the terrace. Dogs yapping in glee, chased by children. Ducks and swans, full-fed, pampered. Willows. An old castle on a height far above the river.

A knot of men came walking, in loose formation though evidently a supervised gang, in the direction of the little town from the sunbrown fields of the Agricultural Station. They were men who looked as burnt and fit as the boating visitors, each carrying some such tool as a hoe or fork. By the bridge they halted at the cheerful command of their leader. 'All right,' he called. 'Rest for five minutes. Old Charlie here says he's got a stone in his boot.' Mr Peacock was a decent brown man, squat and upright, who treated his charges like young brothers. Old Charlie sat on the parapet and Mr Peacock helped him off with his road-dusty boot.

'Fag?' said Piggy Hogg (as he was jocularly called) to his companion. Bob Curran took one, nodding his thanks. He pulled out a cheap cylindrical lighter and struck it, the flame invisible in noon air that was all flame. Piggy Hogg bent over, sucking his fag alight.

'Won't be long for you now,' said Bob Curran.

'Won't be long,' said Piggy Hogg, taking in the long receding bank of willows. 'Next week, they reckon.' He detached a tobacco fibre from his lower lip. The lips were framed in brown beard pied with grey; his skin was tanned; he wore steel spectacles. He had something of the look of Hemingway, but there his association with literature ended. A moderately well-spoken middle-aged man evidently not used to manual work, but a good trier respected by his ward-mates, helpful as a letter-writer. Some had said that it was a waste of an educated man, putting him like they said they were going to as bar-tender in raining at a Midland hotel. But Piggy Hogg knew it was no waste.

A couple of nights back he had, after lights out, slipped on his bedroom headphones. Rejecting, with a click of the plastic dial on the wall, first the Light, then the Home, he had notched into the Third. A bored-sounding young man had been talking about Modern Poetry: '. . . Enderby, before his unaccountable disappearance . . . established as a good minor poet in the tradition . . . perhaps little to say to our generation . . . the more significant work of Jarvis, Sime and Cazalet . . .' He had listened with absolutely no interest. One was used, one was thrown away; Enderby had come out of it better than many; Hogg was looking forward to being a bar-tender. A bar-tender, moreover, who would be different from most, quite a character with his odd lines of poetry thrown out over the frothing pints. Behind the words and rhythms lay the sensations. Time for those.

'What did the old sky-pilot have to say to you?' asked Bob Curran.

'Him?' said Piggy Hoggy vaguely. 'Oh, I thought he made out quite a reasonable case for the Church of England. It's a communion of sorts. It doesn't make too many demands. He lent me some books to read, but I told him I'm not much of a reading man. If it'll give him any pleasure, I'll join.'

'I've never been much of a man for religion myself,' said Bob Curran. 'My dad was a tinker and all tinkers are atheists. We used to have a lot of fun, I remember, on Thursday evenings in the old days. You know, belly of pork and cider and somebody would give a talk about Causal Necessity and then there'd be one hell of a discussion afterwards. All in our front parlour, you know, with The Death of Nelson above the joanna.' Bob Curran was a very lean man of fifty-seven, a radio salesman recovering from schizophrenia. 'It seems to me,' he said, 'that people had more faith in those days. They *believed* more. Why, I do believe that my old man, who was nothing more than an ignorant old tinker, believed more in there not being a God than some of these religious sods today believe in there being one. It's a funny old world,' he concluded, as he always did.

'Oh, yes,' agreed Piggy Hogg, 'but it's not without interest.' After lunch there was to be a cricket match between the Home and the local St John Ambulance. Piggy Hogg had been persuaded to umpire. He had always been flustered by l.b.w. but, he had decided, when in doubt over any appeal except an obvious clean bowl or catch, always to say, 'Not out'. That night there was to be a singsong led by Dr Wapenshaw, with beer from the canteen – two bottles a man. Piggy Hogg led the winning quiz-team. He had beaten Alfred Breasley at chess.

'Right, my tigers,' called Mr Peacock. 'Old Charlie's boot's free from stones.' (Old Charlie grinned without teeth.) 'God's in his heaven, all's right with the etcetera etcetera. On our merry way. Let me see, it's Saturday, isn't it? Corned beef and mashed and beetroot and treacle tart to follow. Right, Piggy old man, stop slavering at the chops. Let's march.'

Piggy Hogg glanced up at the tiny clouds (cotton-wool stoppers from heavenly aspirin-bottles) and down at the sun-warmed boats on the shore that looked like chicken-carcasses. A swan opened an archangelic wing. Shouldering his hoe, chucking away his fag-butt, he marched.

More about Penguins

Penguinews, which appears every month, contains details of all the new books issued by Penguins as they are published. From time to time it is supplemented by *Penguins in Print*, which is a complete list of all available books published by Penguins. (There are well over four thousand of these.)

A specimen copy of *Penguinews* will be sent to you free on request, and you can become a subscriber for the price of the postage. For a year's issues (including the complete lists) please send 30p if you live in the United Kingdom, or 60p if you live elsewhere. Just write to Dept EP, Penguin Books Ltd, Harmondsworth, Middlesex, enclosing a cheque or postal order, and your name will be added to the mailing list.

Note: *Penguinews* and *Penguins in Print* are not available in the U.S.A. or Canada

Enderby Outside

Anthony Burgess

The end of *Inside Mr Enderby* saw Enderby the poet
processed into a useful citizen, brain-washed of muse.
Its sequel, *Enderby Outside*, finds Enderby as barman in a
vast new London hotel. Seemingly Killer of a cult-hero
pop-singer.

Enderby on the run, mingling with a 'package tour' to
Morocco. Enderby, pursued yet pursuing: bent on
avenging his betrayer Rawcliffe; now patron of a
beach-café in Tangier. And in the midst of it all, the muse
returns . . .

Enderby emerges triumphantly. So does Anthony Burgess:
confirming that his is truly one of the most individual
voices in English fiction today.

Not for sale in the U.S.A.

The Malayan Trilogy

Anthony Burgess

This famous trilogy wittily dissects the racial and social prejudices of post-war Malaya during the chaotic upheaval of Independence. Through a succession of splendidly colourful characters, Anthony Burgess delineates the conflict and confusion arising from the almost enforced mingling of cultures.

Time for a Tiger 'His characters are splendidly mad . . . First class' – *Observer*

The Enemy in the Blanket 'There's more meat here than in half a dozen average novels' – *Sunday Times*

Beds in the East 'Really funny . . . intriguingly well-written' – *Daily Express*

Also available

THE DOCTOR IS SICK

A CLOCKWORK ORANGE

SHAKESPEARE

Not for sale in the U.S.A.